Trey

the Walkers of Coyote Ridge, 10

Trey

THE WALKERS OF COYOTE RIDGE, 10

NICOLE EDWARDS

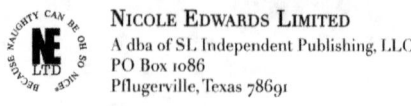

NICOLE EDWARDS LIMITED
A dba of SL Independent Publishing, LLC
PO Box 1086
Pflugerville, Texas 78691

TREY
The Walkers of Coyote Ridge, 10
NICOLE EDWARDS

COVER DETAILS:

Image: © Wander Aguiar (model: Alex C.) | wanderbookclub.com   *Design:* © Nicole Edwards Limited

INTERIOR DETAILS:

Formatting: Nicole Edwards Limited   *Editing:* Blue Otter Editing

AUDIO DETAILS:

Image: © Wander Aguiar (model: Alex C.) | wanderbookclub.com   *Narrators:* TBD

ISBN: (ebook) 978-1-64418-062-4 | (paperback) 978-1-64418-063-1 | (audio) 978-1-64418-064-8

BISAC: FICTION / LGBTQ | FICTION / Romance_General

Dedication

TO THE UNEXPECTED.

Sometimes life throws us curveballs. Some we dodge, others land right where they're intended.
Provided we expect the unexpected, there's always hope.

Dear reader,

When I set out to write the *Brantley Walker: Off the Books* series, I intended for it to be solely about Brantley and Reese. However, along the way, the other characters began speaking loudly, insisting their stories be told. And while I don't intend to write books about all of those secondary characters, Trey and Magnus have become a fan favorite. Due to an overwhelming response from readers, I promised to give you their story, and I have.

With that said, there are a couple of things to note before you read.

First, although Trey and Magnus's budding relationship started in the Brantley Walker: Off the Books series, it can be read as a standalone, meaning I've given enough backstory to bring you up to speed on where they are now without being repetitive for those who've read the series. However, if you'd like to get to know Trey and Magnus on a deeper level and see where it all began for them, you should check it out.

And secondly, this book comes with a trigger warning. At points within this book, you will read flashbacks of Ava's life that may be difficult to read. The story is ultimately about healing and persevering, but in order to get there, as is the case in real life, it requires us to open up and share pieces of ourselves that we'd sometimes prefer to keep inside. Ava suffered physical abuse at the hands of her husband, and she must reflect on that in order to move forward. I assure you, there is a happy ever after at the end, and despite the trauma Ava endured, she's strong and resilient, just as I want us all to be.

Thanks for reading!

Nicole Edwards

Prologue

Saturday, March 19, 2022

TREY WALKER STOOD OUTSIDE THE HOSPITAL ROOM door, waiting patiently in the corridor for his brother to arrive. He'd just learned the devastating news from Charlie, but before he dragged Magnus out of the room to hear it for himself, he wanted to see his brother's face to confirm that what she said was true.

God knows, if it was, it was going to be devastating.

Perhaps not so much for Magnus as it would be for Ava. Her life had been irrevocably changed in a matter of days. The effect this news would have on her was going to add insult to injury, with a bucketful of pain, heartache, and mourning to follow. Perhaps, times two. At least for Ava. She had a long, tough road ahead of her, according to her doctors.

She's alive. That's all that matters.

The little voice in his head had been repeating that every time he looked at the beaten and battered woman. It was true. She was alive. That was all that mattered, and since the prognosis was good, some of the tension had eased out of his shoulders. Mostly. Okay, that was a lie. Yeah, he was relieved that Ava was all right. Honest to God relieved, even if it meant his entire life was about to go into a tailspin.

Trey did his best not to eavesdrop on a couple of nurses talking quietly two doors down while he stared toward the end of the hall, waiting for his brother to appear. It could've been ten minutes or ten hours—time had long since stood still since they'd found Ava March beaten and broken, hovering dangerously close to death. He finally heard Brantley's voice echoing down the hallway, bouncing off the tiled floors and the false ceiling above.

He steeled himself, and the moment Brantley came into view, Trey met his younger brother's gaze, exhaling for the first time in what felt like forever. What Charlie had told him was true. Of that, he was certain.

"You have a chance to talk to Magnus yet?" Brantley asked when he was close enough to keep his voice at a normal level.

Trey shook his head. Rather than admit he'd been too chickenshit to relay the news himself, he said, "I didn't want to pull him away from her until I had to."

Brantley's expression held a wealth of sympathy. "I think it'd be best if we told him first, let him decide how he wants to relay the information to Ava."

Trey appreciated that Brantley thought he had a choice in the matter. What his brother didn't realize was that Magnus was acting like a bristly grizzly keeping his cub safe as he sat watch over Ava, ensuring no one did anything that might cause her any more pain. Trey understood the protective instinct because he felt the same overwhelming need to wrap her in cotton and tuck her away so nothing could get to her. He wasn't sure where the instinct came from, but it was there all the same.

"It won't go over well, regardless," Trey mumbled. "Bad news never does."

"You wanna grab him?" Brantley prompted, nodding toward the door.

Not really, no. He forced himself to turn toward the door, slowly opening it. His gaze shot to Ava lying in the hospital bed, looking so young, so pale and fragile after her horrific ordeal. She was hooked up to wires and tubes, stark white bandages prominent against her sallow skin, covering the damage done by the bastard Ava was married to. Trey had to admit seeing her like that pained him in a way he didn't understand. Hell, there was so much about this situation that pained him, he was surprised he could breathe without choking on his confusion and anger.

"Magnus," he said softly, not wanting to wake Ava, although the pain meds kept her sedated.

"Hmm?" Magnus's gaze lifted, those hazel eyes wary as he stared at Trey.

"Brantley and Reese are outside. They need to talk to you."

He looked over at Ava, then back to Trey. "Do I have to?"

"Yeah. You need to hear what they have to say."

Reluctantly, Magnus nodded as he slowly rose to his feet. He reached over, lightly tugged Ava's blanket higher to keep her warm before leaning down and pressing a kiss to her temple. "I'll be right back."

She didn't move, and the monitor tracking her heart rate remained steady at the side of the bed.

Taking a deep breath, Trey waited for Magnus to join him, then opened the door and let the other man precede him into the hall.

"We'll make this quick," Reese said as soon as Trey closed the door behind him. "But we figured you needed to know before someone leaked the information."

"What information?" Magnus glanced between the three of them. "Did they arrest that bastard?"

Trey squared his shoulders, preparing to let Magnus lean on him if he needed to.

"Harrison Rivers is dead, Magnus," Brantley said.

Trey appreciated the fact his brother didn't mince words.

Magnus frowned, his dark eyebrows slashing downward over tired eyes. "Dead? How?"

Trey noticed that Reese's gaze had dropped to the floor, and Trey fought the urge to look away, too.

"Ava's mother shot and killed him," Brantley relayed.

Magnus's eyes widened.

That's not the worst part, Trey thought. *Brace for it.*

Brantley plowed forward. "Then she took her own life."

When Magnus staggered back, Trey reached for him, putting an arm around his shoulders and drawing him in close.

"She's gonna be devastated," Magnus whispered, turning into Trey's arms. "She's been through enough."

That was an understatement. The only good thing about any of this was the fact that Ava had survived her husband's brutal attack and his blatant disregard when he dumped her lifeless body in a field, wrapped in a rug. The bastard had left her for dead, not even bothering to realize he hadn't stolen the life from her body completely. He couldn't fathom what that had been like for Ava. Regaining consciousness, finding herself alone. No doubt she'd been terrified, left to die in a field, having to get to safety with numerous bones shattered inside her body.

Trey held on to Magnus, letting him know without words that he was there as the anger churned in his veins. He was grateful Harrison Rivers was dead. Otherwise, there was a good chance they'd have another tragedy on their hands. One that would result in someone spending a lifetime in prison. There was no doubt in Trey's mind that Magnus was capable of killing the bastard as payback for what he'd done to Ava.

"She has," Brantley agreed, his tone somber. "I hate to be the bearer of bad news, but if it makes it easier for you, I can be the one to tell her."

Magnus shook his head, pulled himself together, and extricated himself from Trey's arms. "No. I'll do it. She needs to hear it from me."

Yes, Magnus was a better man than Trey. If it were up to him, he'd let someone else tell Ava. Then again, Trey had never been much for confrontation.

Trey looked at his brother.

Brantley nodded. "As of right now, you've officially contracted the services of Sniper 1 Security. I'm gonna talk to the hospital, let them know that we'll be stationing agents in the building to ensure no one gets up here. Give the media some time to die down."

"I can't afford it, but I'll do whatever it takes," Magnus said, his voice only slightly steadier than before.

Brantley smiled, although there wasn't any amusement in it. "We're doin' this free of charge, man."

"You don't have—"

"You're family," Brantley said firmly, his gaze briefly darting to Trey's face. "There's no other way *to* do it."

Trey appreciated everything his brother had done for Magnus over the past few days. All the work that had gone into finding Ava, rescuing her from her rescuer. He wanted to thank the woman who had safely stowed Ava away, ensuring her husband couldn't find her, but he also wanted to throttle her for putting Magnus through hell as they combed every inch of the area she'd been dumped, searching for her. It hadn't been easy, and Trey knew the hard part was yet to come despite the fact Ava was now safely recovering from her horrific injuries.

Brantley put a hand on Magnus's shoulder, squeezed. "We'll get goin', but if you need anything at all, just holler."

Something flashed on Brantley's hand, catching Trey's attention.

He reached for Brantley's arm, pulled it back. "What's this?" he asked, tapping the ring on Brantley's finger.

Brantley pulled his hand away, but not before Trey noticed the blush on his brother's face. Had the man ever blushed before?

Trey looked at Reese. "Did you...?" His gaze shot to Brantley. "Are y'all...?"

"He did, and we are," Brantley said firmly, clearly closing the door on the conversation by adding, "And that's all we're gonna say about it." Brantley narrowed his gaze. "And don't you dare tell Mom and Dad."

His brother was getting married. Despite the somber moment, Trey was thrilled for him but decided to refrain from celebrating. That would have to wait until later.

With a quick wave, Brantley turned and strolled back the way he came, Reese right next to him.

"How do I tell her about her mom?" Magnus asked, looking up at Trey.

Trey honestly didn't know. He knew so very little about Ava March as it was, having only met the woman once.

"I'll be right there with you," he assured Magnus, wanting the man to know that regardless of what the future brought, he had no intention of drifting too far away.

He had a feeling his life was about to take a very different turn than anything he could've anticipated, but Trey knew what he felt for Magnus was real. Real enough that he had already committed—at least to himself—for the long haul.

Little did he know, but that *different turn* was going to alter everything he'd once thought about himself.

THURSDAY, MARCH 31, 2022

Magnus sat at Ava's bedside, watching over her as she slept. She'd been awake more today than yesterday, which was significant progress considering she'd been kept sedated for nearly the entire first week she was in this bed. The doctors were easing up on the pain medication now that her surgeries were completed. With time, she would be as good as new, they had assured him.

What exactly did that mean? As good as new? What constituted new? The woman had been beaten and left for dead by a man who had vowed to love, honor, and cherish her for the rest of her life. How the hell did someone get past that? Much less reach a place in their mind when they were *as good as new*. Sure, maybe the scars would fade over time, but would the memories ever fade? Doubtful. Magnus knew from experience what tragedy felt like.

As it did any time he thought about his parents and his sister, his chest tightened, and his sinuses heated. Thirteen years was a long time, and during that period, his heart had mended some, but there were still cracks that would always remain, ones that he'd stopped trying to heal because it was useless. At times, the memories would make those cracks grow, then he'd face life as he knew it now, and the pain would slowly dissipate until the next time he thought about it.

Try as he might, he couldn't bring himself back to the present, his thoughts drifting to that fateful day thirteen years ago.

"Magnus, there's someone on the phone for you."

Magnus looked up from his spot on Mrs. Teton's couch, where he'd been playing video games with his best friend, Brian, since Magnus got to their house last night. They'd dozed here and there, alternating between that and playing the video game they'd been waiting a million years for. At least it felt like it had been that long.

"Did your girlfriend find you?" Brian chided, punching Magnus in the leg when he stood up.

"Quit it, asshole." Magnus laughed, shoving his shoulder as he hopped over him to get to the phone sitting on the highboy in the Tetons' game room. *"Yeah? Hello?"*

"Magnus, you need to come home, son."

"Edgar?" Magnus chuckled. *"Tell my dad I'm not workin' today. He said I—"*

"Magnus, come home," Edgar reiterated, his voice strained. *"There's been an accident."*

A cold chill washed over him, the phone clutched tightly in his hand. *"What's wrong?"*

"I'll tell you when you get here, son."

Magnus wanted to tell him not to call him son because he damn sure wasn't. The old man worked for Magnus's dad, but he wasn't family. He didn't speak the words aloud because his throat felt tight. Edgar would only call if it were important.

"Fine," Magnus said. *"I'll be home in a minute."*

He hung up the phone and marched over to the couch. He dropped down so he could pull on his shoes.

"You gotta go, dude?" Brian asked, sparing him the briefest of glances as he continued to play the game.

"Edgar said somethin' happened," Magnus admitted.

"Prob'ly just one of those dogs got sick or somethin'," Brian muttered.

Magnus knew it wasn't that. His dad wouldn't have Edgar call him because one of the dogs at the kennel was sick. He would've just called the vet like he did every other time.

With a huff, Magnus got to his feet, grabbed his coat off the back of the couch. *"I'll call ya later, dude."*

"Cool," Brian muttered absently.

Magnus heard Mrs. Teton calling out a goodbye as he headed for the front door. He stepped out onto the porch and stared up at the sky. It was gloomy today, and the wind was colder than it had been yesterday. There was a hint of smoke in the air. Probably someone had their fireplace going. Winter had finally arrived after dragging out summer for far too long.

He grabbed his bike and walked it to the gravel driveway that would take him to the main road leading back to his house. They lived in the sticks, so there weren't a lot of houses, only fields and cows because that's what you got in a small town. And their town was so small they didn't even have a stoplight in downtown.

Frustrated that Edgar had made him leave, Magnus let his temper warm him as he left his best friend's house and rode the two miles to his. He passed the warn and weathered sign that signaled Storme Kennels was up ahead. He didn't understand how his dad could be so proud of that sign and then let it get all run-down and shit. If Magnus owned the kennel, he would make sure the sign was shiny all the time. Let people know he cared about what he did. Instead, his dad put all the money into taking care of the dogs he had, running himself ragged just to keep up instead of trying to bring in more business.

It wasn't all bad, though. Magnus made money working for his dad, helping out. At first, he'd hated it. But he'd been six when his dad first told him to go scoop dog poop. Worst job ever. But after a while, it was just something he did, and now his dad let him do more. He kinda liked it, but he wouldn't tell his dad that. No way was he gonna let his dad think he'd one day take over the kennels. He had bigger plans. Ones that involved going to college and getting a degree. In what, he didn't know yet, but by God, he wouldn't be scooping crap for the rest of his life.

Magnus reached the end of his driveway and stopped for a minute. He pulled the collar of his coat up around his ears to block out the wind. He should've grabbed his gloves and hat before he left yesterday.

The smoke smell was thicker here. He looked around, trying to find the plumes drifting up into the sky, but there weren't any. The ranch down the road probably burned brush last night. They did it all the time, and it stunk up the air for days.

He hopped off his bike and walked it up the driveway. He ran through a dozen conversations he intended to have with his dad about what it meant to be a teenager. They'd told him he could stay at Brian's. Nobody said nothing about having to come home early. Didn't he know that defeated the purpose of hanging out?

God, why couldn't they just accept that he didn't want to work at the kennels every day? He had better things to do. No, he didn't mind the work, but only because there was money, but still. He preferred to hang out with his friends on the weekends. He and Brian were gonna go to Chelsea Upling's house today. Her mom was working, and her dad didn't live there anymore, so she said they could come over and hang out for a while. Magnus wouldn't get to make out with her on the couch if he had to stay home and work at the stupid kennels.

He reached the bend in the driveway, the last point before the house would come into view. If he knew his dad, he was waiting on the front porch for him to appear. He always did that. Shouting at him to get a move on and get his butt to the kennels to help out. Magnus stopped walking. What would they do if he didn't come home right now? It's not like his mom or dad were gonna go to Brian's and drag him outta there. He could just go back, pretend Edgar never called. No one would even know.

Magnus sighed. He'd come all this way already, and his hands were so cold they were numb. He might as well face the music, get the chores done, and then he could go back and—

Magnus turned the corner, and his house came into view. He stopped walking, his heart leaping into his throat. Fire trucks and police cars dotted the landscape, blocking the view of the house. He dropped his bike and took off running, choking on the fear and anxiety that flooded his bloodstream.

He reached the house, his vision blurred by tears as the worst-case scenario hit him. They'd lost the house and everything in it. Did his parents even think to grab his model car collection?

"Magnus! Stop!"

He heard Edgar's voice, but it barely registered as he ran full out toward the house. He was almost there when strong arms banded around him, effectively stopping him by swinging him around.

"I gotta get my cars!" he shouted.

"Magnus. Son! Stop!"

"I'm not your son! Let me go!"

"You can't go in there. They won't let you."

"My dad'll make them," he countered hotly, struggling to release his grip.

Magnus stared blankly at the foot of Ava's bed. That had been the day his entire world had shattered. Edgar hadn't held him back so he couldn't get to his stupid cars. He'd held him back so he could break the devastating news that his parents and his sister had died in the fire that destroyed half of their house.

His gaze strayed to Ava, and for a brief moment, he saw the little girl who'd lived next door. The cute little blond girl who was always doing cartwheels in the front yard, a huge smile on her face. The one who had been there for him every day after that for as long as she could. She'd suffered a loss that day, too. Magnus's sister had been Ava's best friend. They were thick as thieves, inseparable. Until that one fateful night when the cold temperatures forced his father to break out one of the old space heaters.

He wanted to think that if Ava could make it through that, she could make it through this. Magnus had lost all the family he had that day, so he understood what Ava was going through. Her mother had been her only family, and now she was gone.

Magnus recalled the devastating look on Edgar's face when the old man had relayed that information. It had nearly broken him because they'd all been like family to Edgar. How in the hell was he going to break the news to Ava that her mother was gone forever?

Two weeks later...

"You're goin' home today," Magnus announced when he strolled through the hospital room door.

Ava wasn't sure why he sounded happy. Didn't he realize she couldn't go home?

She glanced over at him, grateful for his presence even if she couldn't spare a smile. Her mind was muddled. She couldn't recall much of the conversations that had taken place over the past few weeks. She remembered the police coming to talk to her, but she wasn't sure what they'd asked, much less what she'd told them. She recalled Magnus mentioning something about her mom when Ava insisted they bring Renee to the hospital. She probably should've paid more attention, but the truth was, she'd let the drugs lull her, gave her an excuse not to care about anyone or anything for a little while.

Now she was right back where she started, only with more scars and very little hair. And it was time to go home.

Even the thought caused tears to fill behind her eyes.

Ava did not want to get within a hundred miles of her bastard husband. She knew if she did, she would end up in the same situation. Only next time, he wasn't going to be so careless. He wouldn't just leave her for dead; he'd bury her in the ground to ensure she stayed dead.

If only she'd followed her heart all those years ago. Maybe if she had, she'd be married to Magnus, helping him run Camp K-9. They might even have a kid or two by now. But no, she'd gone and done something stupid, desperate for love from anyone who would graciously offer it. Then that bastard had come along and snowed her with his sweet talk and kind smile. A monster in human form, that was what Harrison Rivers was.

"What's wrong, little one?" Magnus asked, his tone both soothing and teasing.

Magnus had called her that for as long as she could remember. Since they were kids and Ava and Tabby were pelting him with questions about everything. She knew he'd been picking on her at first because that's what boys did, and since she'd always been the smallest kid around, everyone had picked on her. Despite Magnus's teasing back then, he'd been the brightest light in Ava's young heart. She'd been so in love with him that she'd even vowed to one day be Mrs. Magnus Storme.

Of course, those had been the musings of a little girl. She hadn't been old enough to know what love really was when his mere presence made her heart flutter for the first time. Despite her crush and the events that had changed both their lives, Magnus had always been there for her. Always remained her friend, a strong shoulder to lean on when she had no one else.

Ava was so eternally thankful he'd been with her these past weeks as she started the long road to recovery that the doctors had laid out for her, but she knew that time was coming to an end.

"Nothing," she lied easily, forcing a smile. "I'm just ready to get outta here."

"I'm sure you are." He stepped around to the side of the bed, his muscular body filling the space and making her feel safer than she had in longer than she could remember.

His expression sobered as he placed his hand over hers. Ava's gaze snapped down, staring at his sun-kissed skin as it covered her much paler one. Oh how she'd wanted this man to touch her for so long. Back before she'd made the biggest mistake of her life and married a monster. Now it was too late. She'd made her bed, which meant she had to lie in it.

She let her gaze skim over him briefly as she exhaled. His beautiful hazel eyes churned with emotion, something she'd seen quite often over the years. Magnus wasn't one of those men who shielded everyone from what he was thinking. He was the guy who told you how it was and didn't feel bad about it. The longer she stared, the more she saw, and she knew he was going to break the bad news that she had to go back to Harrison. She was still so tired, something the doctors assured her would pass. The more she healed, the better she would feel, but she had to be patient.

"I don't wanna go home," she whispered, hating that tears were forming in her eyes. Not that she wanted to stay here either, but she didn't know where else to go. She needed to figure out where her mom was. If she knew Harrison, he'd put her in a hospital somewhere, locked her away to rot. That was what he always threatened to do. When he wasn't threatening to slit her throat, that was.

Magnus didn't remove his hand from hers even as he reached for the chair he'd sat in for days on end, dragging it closer to the bed.

When he took a seat, she met his gaze again and saw something familiar in them. They held the same remorse and grief she'd seen once before. Back when his parents and sister had died in the fire.

Her heart pinched in her chest as realization dawned. Bits and pieces of those forgotten conversations came back to her. Tears formed on her lashes. She tried to hold them back because she'd cried far too many this past month. "He killed her, didn't he?"

It was the only explanation for why her mother hadn't come to see her. She'd figured Harrison hadn't let her, but Ava knew that was wishful thinking.

Magnus's fingers curled tightly around her hand. "No, little one."

"But she's dead." She knew that like she knew her own name. She could see it in his eyes.

He nodded, his head barely tilting with the movement.

"When? How?"

She watched as his jaw clenched and his throat worked on a swallow.

"Tell me," she insisted, her head too heavy to lift off the pillow.

"The night we found you," he said, his voice rougher than usual. "Your mom ... she killed Harrison and then..."

"Took her own life," Ava whispered, her chest squeezing.

Magnus nodded.

Ava stared at him as the news sank in. She wouldn't lie and say she wasn't grateful Harrison was dead. She felt nothing for him anymore. After what he'd done to her, the bastard deserved to be rotting in the ground. She only hoped he'd suffered beforehand.

"Ava? Talk to me."

She wanted to be angry that Magnus hadn't told her, but she was too numb to do that. It wasn't his fault anyway. Her mother had been trying to end her life for so long it was inevitable that it happened.

"How'd she kill him?" Ava rasped, tears clogging her throat.

"Ava," he crooned, his thumb brushing over the top of her hand.

"Tell me, Magnus."

His gaze briefly shifted toward the door. He looked like he was trying to compose himself. When he met her gaze again, she saw the same conviction she'd seen in the young boy who'd lost his mom, dad, and sister in one devastating night.

"She killed him with his own gun."

"How?" She wanted to know the details. She wanted to know how that monster's life had ended. It was only fair since he'd attempted to take hers.

Magnus took a deep breath. "She shot him in the back of the head while he was sleepin'."

Ava sucked in a heavy breath and turned her gaze away. "How did she get the gun?"

"They don't know. It was a revolver. They found three bullets in her bedroom, and there was one left in the gun."

Which meant she had intended to do what she did—one bullet in Harrison, one in herself. If Ava knew her mother, she'd kept the other three hidden away so that if Harrison found the gun, she could steal it back and be able to do what she'd intended to do all along. Only Ava knew that killing Harrison hadn't been part of Renee's plan. She'd only intended to end her own suffering.

A sob escaped. She closed her eyes and let the tears fall.

"Ava … we'll get through this together. I'll be with you every step of the way."

She knew he meant that. Magnus didn't make promises he couldn't keep. Certainly not to her.

Ava managed a nod, more tears falling.

"God, baby, I'm so sorry."

She swallowed the lump in her throat. She didn't bother to tell him they weren't so much tears of sadness or loss. They were from relief.

For the first time since she'd met Harrison Rivers seven long, painful years ago, Ava felt like a weight had been lifted off her shoulders.

No more abuse.

No more lying to people about the bruises and scars she carried.

No more having to lie next to the devil every night.

And her mother, despite all the pain and misery they'd suffered together because of her illness, had given that to her. She'd ultimately saved her.

Accepting that, Ava let the tears fall.

Chapter One

Three months later…
Friday, July 8, 2022

"SEE YOU IN THE MORNIN', GIA," TREY called out as he headed toward the main office in the Camp K-9 building. The trek didn't feel that long despite the size of the entire campus. The large metal buildings had been pieced together over time, growing as their clientele had.

"It's your turn to bring breakfast," she said with a smile in her voice.

"Round Rock Donuts?" he offered, knowing it would make her happy.

"I'll love you forever, Trey Walker."

At least someone will, he thought to himself, hating the morose turn his subconscious had taken these past four months. At the same time, he didn't know how to change it. These days, he was going through the motions, grateful that Ava was back on her feet and things were getting back to normal. Didn't matter that normal had taken on an entirely different meaning than before.

In an effort to help things along, Trey had been filling in at Camp K-9, helping out while Magnus dedicated his waking hours to taking care of Ava. During that time, Trey had come to enjoy what he was doing. Working with dogs, learning the ins and outs of the kennel, as well as observing the training sessions that took place gave him a sense of peace he wasn't sure he'd ever known before. It was a far cry from the stress of working against the clock in search of missing people, which he'd done as a member of the Off the Books Task Force for the year prior to Ava's disappearance. While it had pained him to do so, he'd made the difficult decision to quit the task force, and he felt significantly better for it despite having left his brother and the team in the lurch. While he suffered some guilt, Trey figured if he hadn't quit when he had, his mental state would've been significantly worse than it was now.

And wouldn't that just be fucking sad?

Trey ignored the inner voice that had been speaking up far too often these days.

While he enjoyed his temporary work, Trey knew he would have to move on sooner or later. He couldn't continue to ride the coattails of Magnus's new life simply because he didn't want to walk away. His relationship with Magnus, which had been new and exciting, had turned into something else entirely. They'd reverted to the way it had started when sex was merely a means to an end, a distraction, if you will. Trey wanted more, and at one point, they'd been on the cusp of a breakthrough.

Right up until Ava's disappearance.

Since then, Trey and Magnus had both retreated emotionally, giving each other space until the rift had formed on its own. Trey still wanted more, but he damn sure didn't intend to ask for it, and since Magnus wasn't broaching the subject, he figured the only option he had was to take a permanent step back. Hence the reason he'd been putting more distance between them in recent weeks. The expiration date was nearing, and as soon as he could get up the nerve to walk away permanently, his time with Magnus would be nothing more than a fond memory.

Trey

Grabbing his phone from his pocket, Trey shot a quick text to Magnus, letting him know he was leaving for the day and that he'd be back first thing in the morning. It was a chickenshit thing to do, but saving face wasn't high on his priority list these days.

Before he could get out the door, his phone chimed with a response.

Come by the house before you leave.

Trey opened the door and stepped out into the gravel lot, his gaze darting over to Magnus's house.

It would've been in his best interest to get in his truck and drive away, pretending he hadn't seen Magnus's request. If he went to that house … if he went inside…

Trey exhaled heavily, his cock thickening just from the mere thought of getting a few minutes alone with Magnus. Those instances were few and far between these days, and the absence of the intimacy they'd once shared was weighing on him heavily. Sure, it was Trey's fault, but the longer he let himself feel something for Magnus, the worse it would be when they reached the inevitable end. Which he feared was coming much faster than he'd anticipated.

While neither of them had officially put a name to this thing between them, there was no denying a relationship had formed despite Trey's adamance that they keep things casual. That was his fault, too. He was the one who'd claimed Magnus as his boyfriend back when they'd been searching for Ava. It had been a knee-jerk reaction, one he wished he could regret if for no other reason than it would make things so much easier.

For months, Trey had tried to pretend things were normal, that there wasn't an enormous obstacle establishing a permanent residence between him and Magnus at this very moment. That obstacle had a name: Ava March. There was no doubt in his mind that Magnus was in love with the beautiful wisp of a woman who'd come a long way during her recovery. Physically, she was healed, but emotionally, she had a long road ahead of her.

Of course, Trey had always feared it would come to this. Being with a man who was admittedly bisexual hadn't been the smartest move he'd ever made, but Trey wasn't really known for his intelligent actions. He let his heart lead, even when he fought the damn thing tooth and nail.

The back door of Magnus's house opened, and the man appeared, effectively derailing Trey's thoughts. His breath lodged in his chest when he saw Magnus standing there, his broad, muscular torso bare, accentuated by a pair of athletic shorts riding low on his lean hips. With his dark hair tousled and his jaw unshaven, he looked like Trey's darkest fantasy. As many men were prone to do, Magnus had spent the better part of the last four months focused on working out as a way of shoving aside the emotional turmoil. Because of that, he'd honed an already superb physique, turning it into a masterpiece. One Trey craved like all the other vices he'd come to yearn for over the years. And like an affinity for alcohol, Trey knew this particular addiction was only going to end badly.

With a crook of his finger, Magnus motioned him over.

Trey knew he shouldn't.

He really, *really* shouldn't.

But he would because … fuck.

Resigned to his fate—he'd been a glutton for punishment his entire life—Trey headed that way, tucking his phone in the back pocket of his jeans as he sauntered closer, meeting Magnus's gaze. He held his stare as he stepped up onto the deck. As he approached the door, Magnus moved back, giving him room to come inside.

Go home, man. Don't make this any harder than it has to be.

A mirthless laugh rumbled in his chest as he wondered whether or not his brain was talking about his dick or his heart. It could be either because Trey wanted this man with a passion that no longer made sense.

He took another step forward, although he was mentally shouting at his legs to go in the opposite direction.

Another step, then another, and he was walking into the house.

No turning back now.

Once inside, Trey closed the door behind him.

"She's asleep," Magnus whispered, referring to Ava. Gesturing toward the living room, he added, "In there."

Trey resisted the urge to look in on her. He couldn't quite pinpoint the reason he'd become so fond of Ava March, but he couldn't deny the fact he cared about her well-being. Fine, that was an understatement. Trey genuinely liked her. Probably had something to do with her upbeat attitude, the way she put one foot in front of the other despite the trauma she'd endured. Ava wasn't living in the past, dwelling on what had happened. She was relying on her strength and her resolve to move forward, and he admired that about her.

Ever since they'd found her, Trey had been watching her from afar as she healed. With every passing day and every ounce of strength she regained after her harrowing ordeal, he admired her a little more. She was strong and smart, sweet and kind. She could've easily become bitter and resentful after what she'd been through. Because she wasn't, Trey had come to know her on a friendly level, and he liked the woman. More than he should, considering Trey knew, when it came down to a decision, the man he loved would choose her over him.

"Trey," Magnus whispered, moving toward him.

Swallowing hard, Trey held Magnus's stare. He could see the heat churning in those hazel eyes, the desperate gleam that told him what he wanted.

Magnus's face was leaner, his jaw more prominent even with the scruffy beginnings of a beard he was working on. The man was so handsome it sometimes hurt to look at him. At twenty-six, Magnus was in the prime of his life, his health and strength like a beacon that called to Trey in the night. He wanted just a little taste of that, even if it wouldn't last. Trey had started to feel young himself there for a while, and that was all thanks to Magnus.

The next thing he knew, Magnus had him pressed up against the door. The heat of his body seared him as their lips collided. With a heavy inhale, Trey succumbed to the kiss, licking his way into Magnus's mouth. He didn't aim for gentle, but he was making an effort to be quiet, swallowing the moans that threatened to rip up his throat.

In all his life, Trey had never been with a man who unhinged him the way Magnus Storme did. From the beginning, Trey had known he was merely setting himself up for failure, but he'd done his best to keep his distance from the then twenty-four-year-old who managed to make Trey feel ten years younger than he was, which only helped to ease the twelve-year age gap by a bit. Although Trey had an aversion to their age difference, he had still developed an addiction to the man early on, craving every touch, every taste. And for a year and a half, Trey had been giving in to his baser urges the same as he was now.

He couldn't explain this overwhelming, deep-seated desperation that consumed him whenever he was with Magnus. There was an ache inside him that refused to be sated, regardless of how hard Trey tried to do just that. Each time they were together, Trey wanted him more, until he could hardly breathe for how badly he ached.

Without hesitation, Trey shoved his hand into Magnus's shorts, gripping the steel-hard flesh beneath. His other hand clutched Magnus's neck, keeping their mouths fused while he stroked the velvet-smooth length of Magnus's cock. Thick and hard, the smooth flesh moved easily beneath his palm, earning a few growls from Magnus. Oh, what he wouldn't give to flip him around and drive into his hot, tight ass. It had been too long since they'd had sex, but they hadn't yet figured out how to hold off on this part.

When Magnus jerked his mouth free, Trey was panting. More so when Magnus pressed his mouth to his ear. He could feel the warmth of his breath, but it was the words that nearly undid him.

"I need you, Trey," Magnus whispered, his voice so soft it could've been Trey's imagination. "I need to feel you inside me. Filling me. Stretching me. *Fucking* me."

A raspy groan escaped him despite his best efforts.

Magnus's hips pumped as Trey continued to stroke him. He managed to slow things down, tightening his grip and taking back the control Magnus was working to strip from him.

Magnus shoved his shorts down his hips, freeing his cock and giving Trey more access.

It wouldn't be nearly enough, but for now, he was going to settle for getting this man off. Once he did that, he'd go home, take a shower, and let his hand and his imagination sate him enough so that, hopefully, he could sleep tonight.

AVA CURLED UP SILENTLY ON THE COUCH, feigning sleep. It was a skill she'd honed many years ago, starting first when she was dealing with her mother. Then it had become second nature after she'd married a monster. It didn't get by her that two of the most influential people in her life had refused to give her any breathing room.

These days, she did it for a similar reason, but not because she felt suffocated. While Magnus hovered like a mama bear protecting her cub—a fact she reminded him of constantly—Ava didn't purposely avoid him for her benefit. It was more for his. She appreciated everything he'd done and all he was continuing to do, but she hated that she'd become such a burden on him.

The man she considered her best friend and one of the only people she trusted implicitly had become her caretaker. Magnus spent every waking hour, and even some when he should be sleeping, ensuring she was fed, hydrated, and comfortable. She wasn't sure how he had any time to simply be, thanks to all his efforts to look after her. Worse than that, she didn't need a flashing neon sign to notice that her presence had done some serious damage to his love life.

At this very moment, she could hear Magnus in the kitchen with Trey. They were speaking in hushed tones, so she couldn't make out what they were saying, but it sounded like every other conversation they'd had as of late. Kinda friendly but with a hint of desperate undertones. She related it to her relationship with ice cream. There were those moments when you craved it so much, but you knew by giving in, you'd be required to do some extra walking to burn it off, so it was easier to resist. But the longer you did, the more intense that craving became, until you snapped and gobbled down an entire pint.

Yep. That was Magnus and Trey. One was the pint of Ben & Jerry's, the other the spoon. Both were necessary to satisfy that craving, and at some point, they would make contact.

Like they were doing right this minute.

Through slitted eyes, she watched the open doorway, waiting for one of them to appear. She didn't care which of them stepped into view, because they were both delicious to look at. Magnus and his ridiculously hot body, all those muscles covered by sun-bronzed skin. She appreciated the fact he liked to walk around the house without a shirt on ... because eye candy, anyone?

Then there was Trey ... oh what she could say about Trey Walker. Six feet, three inches of lean, succulent man. There was so much about him that she found hot, but mostly it had to do with the hair and the beard. Something about the long hair set her girly parts aflame. While on the outside he looked like a bad boy, deep down, she knew he had the heart of a kitten.

They were both yummy.

Doubly yummy when she could catch a glimpse of them making out when they didn't think she could see them. Those instances were the highlight of her day. Seeing two fine-ass men lip-locked and groaning ... she needed a fan.

Hence the reason she found herself feigning sleep so often. It helped that she no longer whiled away hours in a daze, numbed out by pain medication that worked wonders on her physical pain but did nothing for her mental anguish.

Of course, Magnus was still convinced her broken bones were never going to heal, that she would forever be walking around with a limp due to the multiple fractures she'd sustained to her tibia and fibula in her right leg, plus the shattered ankle the doctors had surgically repaired. Or she'd never carry her purse again because her clavicle had been fractured and they'd surgically repaired it with screws. Or she'd never write a love note to anyone since her wrist and elbow had been busted.

But the fact was, she was healed—her shoes, purse, and those future love notes had nothing to worry about. Her stamina had returned, and the pain had diminished. Her bones had knitted back together thanks to the magic of surgery and modern medicine. She could walk, talk, think, and probably even drive if Magnus would stop hovering long enough for her to steal his keys. Her hair was even growing out, a cute little pixie cut she was starting to like.

And fine, she still limped when she didn't consciously think about walking. And there were twinges in her shoulder from time to time. Usually, only when she lifted her arm over her head, which she rarely did. And once in a while, there'd be an ache in her wrist or a pain in her shin. She wasn't without the scars as reminders, but for the most part, she was as close to one hundred percent as she was going to get. Considering what she'd been through, Ava preferred the term *healed*.

More importantly, from a mental perspective, she wanted to be normal again.

The problem was Magnus wasn't ready for her to be healed. Ava was sure he needed a reason to hover, and insisting that she wasn't one hundred percent was his way of keeping her on this couch. She knew if Magnus had his way, she'd be on bed rest—or couch rest as was the case now—for the foreseeable future.

So not happening.

Although Magnus babied her like she was still broken and battered, she couldn't keep going on like this. One of these days, she expected to wake up to find her mind was also on the mend. When that day came, she would have to leave, have to go back to the life she'd abandoned and stop pretending it hadn't happened. She wasn't ready for that yet, which was the only reason she continued to humor Magnus, allowing him to dote on her.

Ava thought for sure he would stop when the doctor had released her from his care, signing off on her physical progress even though he'd left her with a parting suggestion that she seek therapy to deal with the mental damage she'd incurred from the ordeal. She'd promised him she would, because somewhere deep down, she knew it was necessary, but the day she accepted that, it would mean she was ready to move on to the next phase of her life. Whatever that might be.

Right now, it was easier to pretend this was her new life, and Magnus and Trey were part of it.

It was selfish on her part, but she wasn't ready to let them go. She wasn't prepared to spend her life alone, to start over, to figure out what the next steps were.

"Trey … oh, fuck … let me touch you."

Ava's body flashed hot, but she pretended the air conditioner was broken and that she wasn't having a thermonuclear reaction to him and Trey getting down and dirty in the kitchen. There was something extremely hot about those two sexy men doing wicked things to one another. And, boy, did they. She'd witnessed one particular moment when Magnus had been on his knees in front of Trey…

Ava had to fan herself, letting her head flop back on the pillow as the memory took hold. She'd never seen two men together before that, never even fantasized about it. Now that she'd secretly watched Magnus sucking Trey's cock—a major violation of the friend code, she was sure—Ava was hoping to catch another glimpse.

Not for the first time, she imagined what it would be like to have a front-row seat to the action. She liked the idea because it allowed her to recognize the fact that she wasn't completely broken. Her libido still had hot embers glowing, although she wasn't quite ready to have sex with anyone, even if she tingled in private places when she fantasized about Magnus and Trey bringing her into the fray. This was so much easier. Living vicariously through them, sating some of those urges by being a voyeur to their lust.

Of course, she would be remiss if she didn't admit that spending her spare time thinking about Magnus and Trey was merely a diversion tactic. It was far more interesting than thinking about what had actually happened to her. It was bad enough that she relived that horrific night whenever she closed her eyes, trapped in a vicious never-ending nightmare. But it hadn't been a nightmare, she'd lived through the entire thing, and for some reason, her subconscious wanted to relive the horror over and over again by assaulting her in her dreams.

The sad thing was, she wasn't the only injured party here. She got the feeling Magnus blamed himself for what she'd been through, although he certainly wasn't at fault. He hadn't played a part in it at all, yet when he looked at her, she could see how much it hurt him to remember what she'd looked like the day they'd found her at Gloria Steiner's house. The kind woman had taken her in and done her best to patch Ava up, promising not to let her husband find her.

That had been four months ago, exactly sixteen weeks, and as far as Ava was concerned, the past was behind her. So Magnus could continue to look at her with pained sympathy etched on his handsome face, but she had no intentions of being that battered, broken girl ever again.

While she woke up screaming night after night, she wasn't willing to play the victim. At the same time, she recognized she was still bottling things up, which wasn't a good thing. She figured if she followed the doctor's suggestion that she see a therapist to help her work through the ordeal, she would've made significant strides by now. It was the only way she'd truly heal.

She knew that. She did. She was a lot of things, but an idiot she was not. Therapy was in her future, but right now, it was easier to pretend she was whole and would one day find that happily ever after she'd been dreaming of all her life.

One day.

A low growl sounded from the kitchen, followed by Trey's throaty mumble.

Ava wondered whether Magnus would consider her healed if he knew just how hot listening to them made her.

MAGNUS WAS HANGING ON BY A THREAD. His body was strung so tight, it was a wonder he didn't snap clean in two any second.

It didn't help that Trey's hand was curled around his cock, stroking him slowly, firmly.

"Let me touch you," Magnus repeated, attempting to rip at the button on Trey's jeans.

Trey's response was an adamant shake of his head.

One of these days, Magnus was going to lose his shit. Trey was pushing him toward it, in fact. He could only handle this for so long before he shattered into a million pieces. And he wasn't talking about the smooth, self-satisfied way Trey jacked him off, either. He was all too aware of what Trey was doing. The way he was putting distance between them—emotionally, at least—taking metaphorical steps back each day. Pretty soon, they would no longer share these moments either, and Magnus wasn't prepared for that to happen.

He pulled back so he could look into the steel-blue eyes that haunted his dreams and made him want things he'd never imagined himself wanting. They glittered with promise as Trey took a step forward, forcing Magnus back. But it wasn't the promise of a future. Trey's mind was clearly in the moment, and his one and only vow was to get Magnus off. If only Magnus could settle for that, they'd be fine. They could continue … just … like … this.

The next thing he knew, Trey was easing down to one knee.

"Oh, fuck me," Magnus muttered as he watched Trey's mouth open and those perfect lips on that perfect face wrap soundly around the engorged head of his cock.

He was a goner.

Magnus lost all preconceptions of resisting, giving himself over to the sheer pleasure of the heated suction that stole his breath and made his head spin. He kept his eyes locked on Trey's handsome face as he worked him with his lips and tongue. The light scrape of Trey's beard across his inner thigh as Trey dragged his wicked tongue along his shaft, the sweet bump of his throat when he took Magnus to the root. It was too much.

"I'm gonna come," he warned, no longer caring that his groans and moans might wake Ava, who was sleeping in the next room. At the moment, the only thing he could focus on was the pleasure obliterating him.

Trey's eyes darkened with hunger and glittered with challenge as he drew on him once more, taking Magnus's cock as deep as he could.

Widening his stance, Magnus thrust his hands into Trey's hair and held his head. He took over from there, fucking Trey's face, chasing that elusive release that would mean another sweet surrender. He tightened his hold on Trey's head and saw the flash of surprise in the man's eyes as he took control of the situation, driving himself right to that precarious edge. He rode the fine line between pure bliss and erotic ecstasy for several seconds before he drove deep into Trey's throat and let himself go.

He managed to remain upright on shaky legs, stumbling back, the world coming into sharp focus. He was panting, his chest heaving from exertion as he grabbed hold of the countertop to keep himself vertical. As he came back down to earth, Trey got to his feet, adjusting his jeans.

Oh what Magnus wouldn't give to take care of that man right now. He'd been trying for weeks, but Trey was holding himself back. For the life of him, Magnus didn't know why, wasn't sure what it meant for the two of them. The one thing he was certain of was the fact that pushing Trey Walker to do anything he didn't want to do was a surefire way of setting fire to whatever remnants of their original relationship that still remained.

That was the only reason he wasn't throwing the man to the ground and having his wicked way with him right now. Well, that and the fact Trey was the dominant one in their relationship, a fact Magnus had come to enjoy immensely.

"I'll be back in the mornin'," Trey said gruffly, his back ramrod straight as he took a hesitant step forward.

Magnus stood tall, gripping Trey's hips when he eliminated the distance between them. "You could stay the night."

Trey gave him the same answer he'd given every single time Magnus had said the very same thing: a subtle shake of his head.

Then Trey leaned in and pressed his lips to Magnus's mouth. The kiss was gentle and sweet. It felt more like a goodbye than a promise, but Magnus was pretending the same way Trey was. As long as he didn't acknowledge the fact Trey was adding distance, it wouldn't be real.

The question was: how long could this go on before Magnus was nothing more than a shadow in Trey's memory?

Chapter Two

AVA HUFFED. IT WAS TIME TO PUT her foot down. Not literally because she was comfortable where she was on the couch, but in her mind, she was squaring off with Magnus, her hands on her hips, staring him down as she said, "It's time for you to go back to work."

No response.

Of course not. Why in the world would Magnus make this easy on her?

Ava had been talking to him for the better part of ten minutes, but it appeared he wasn't listening. What she wanted to do was shove Magnus right out the door. She might even find amusement in the task if he would stumble down the stairs and fall face-first into the dirt. She could laugh while he dusted himself off and then acknowledge, finally, that she was strong enough to take back the reins of her life.

Fine. If she shoved him, she doubted he would move an inch, much less down four steps, but the idea was amusing. She was stronger, sure, but she was no match for Magnus Storme. A shove from her might make him sway. Maybe. Okay, doubtful. But still.

He'd done this to her. He'd put her in this snarky mood with his grumbling and grousing, the way he stomped through the house with that dark cloud hovering over his head.

"Did you hear me?" she prodded when he made another pass through the living room. He'd been pacing one giant circle for the past five minutes, making his way through the kitchen, the breakfast nook, back to the living room, down the little hallway, and into the kitchen once more. Rinse and repeat.

Of course, he didn't respond because he was grumpy, and when Magnus was grumpy, he didn't listen with his ears.

Dadgum men.

When he returned to the living room, she started again, raising her voice to be heard over the heavy fall of his footsteps.

"Go!"

Stomp-stomp-stomp. (More stomping since it was a good distance.)

"To!"

Stomp-stomp-stomp. (And more stomping.)

"Work!" She screamed the last word at the top of her lungs and effectively got Magnus's attention. He came to an abrupt stop, his eyebrows slamming down over his pretty hazel eyes as he glared daggers in her direction.

"What?"

"Oh, don't pretend you didn't hear me," she snapped. "I said you need to go back to work. Do something with yourself, Magnus. No one likes a whiny man. Doesn't matter how hot you are."

He stared at her for a painfully long moment before a smile pulled at his lips. Those were pretty, too, just like his eyes. She wouldn't say everything about him was pretty, but he wasn't hard to look at, that was for sure. But he was far too masculine to be pretty with all those muscles, especially the enormous ones in his shoulders and arms. And his chest ... and those abs ... and—

Yep, she needed a fan again.

"You think I'm hot."

Ava noticed it wasn't a question. She snorted. "Get over yourself."

Magnus's grin widened as she'd hoped it would.

"Seriously, Magnus," she said, erasing all teasing and snark from her tone. "You really should get back to work. I know Gia and Billy would be grateful for the help. As would Trey. They've been workin' their butts off these last few months so you could play nursemaid." She held up her hand before he could interrupt. "Don't get me wrong, I appreciate it more than you'll ever know, but I'm fine now. I'm all healed up. I can go to the bathroom by myself and everything."

God, she remembered the first time he had helped her to the bathroom after her surgery. If she hadn't been in significant pain and hopped up on painkillers, she would've been mortified. The memory was bad enough.

"The doctor said—"

"Magnus," she drawled like she was talking to a three-year-old, easing her feet out from under her and standing tall. "The doctor said I'm completely fine. See?" She wiggled her arms, then her legs. "I've got use of all my limbs. I can bend over and touch my toes." Which she did to prove she could. "I could probably even do a cartwheel." She decided against that for the time being, what with the furniture and all.

"Who's gonna make your lunch?"

Oh, now he was grasping, that was obvious. "I think I'm quite capable of ordering from DoorDash the same way you do every single day."

She'd been meaning to talk to him about that. Ava didn't care for fast food, but she hadn't complained because she knew Magnus had no business in a kitchen. Toaster waffles were about the only thing he was capable of making without burning the house down.

That thought obliterated her good mood. With the wind out of her sails, she eased back down to the sofa. It wasn't that she'd forgotten what had happened to his parents and sister, but sometimes it wasn't the first thing she thought about. It had been years since their lives were stolen by the smoke and the flames that had destroyed a good portion of this house. She was merely glad she'd had the good sense not to speak the words aloud.

"Please," she said softly, staring up at him. "Please go back to work. I think it'll be good for both of us." When he looked like he was going to argue, she tacked on, "I'll even go with you. I have no problem—"

"Ava, we've talked about this."

"—scooping poop. That or I can go work at the camp, and you can stay here and watch mindless television all day long. Take your pick."

She'd purposely ignored him because she hated that he was holding that ultimatum over her head. Magnus had told her she was welcome to work at the camp as soon as she started therapy. He'd even promised her a full-time paying job.

Which meant she was the one standing in her own way.

Magnus dropped his head dramatically and stomped toward her. He took a seat on the couch, close enough that she could feel his warmth and strength, smell the fresh woodsy scent of his body wash. Because she welcomed his nearness, Ava leaned into him, and when his arm went around her shoulders, pulling her against him, she lost her train of thought.

She'd been friends with Magnus for so long she wasn't sure how to exist without him in her life. She'd grown up next door to him, been best friends with his sister. And even after the fire, after Tabitha died, and after Ava's mother had packed them up and moved them out of Embers Ridge, Ava had kept in touch with him. He was a reminder of the good years of her life, and he was the only person in her life who had never asked or demanded anything from her.

Without thinking, Ava turned toward him, resting her head against his shoulder and placing her hand flat on his chest. She could feel his heartbeat, strong and steady, just like the man she'd had a crush on since she was a little girl, too young to know better. She wished she could say she'd gotten past the crush, but it would be a lie. However, their friendship was something she'd grown to need more than anything, which was why she knew nothing could ever develop from that crush.

It didn't mean she didn't long for these moments when Magnus made her feel safe and loved. He was the one person in her life who had never let her down, never used her for his own gain. For that, she would always be in love with him, even if she would never admit it aloud.

MAGNUS STARED AT THE WALL AND CHERISHED these few minutes with Ava.

The way she snuggled up to him, the trust she offered, had a calming effect on him. This wasn't the first time he'd noticed. Ever since that fateful day when Ava showed up on his doorstep, grinning wide and boasting about how she'd graduated from high school, he'd seen her in a different light. She'd gone from being his little sister's best friend to a stunningly beautiful woman in the blink of an eye.

That was six years ago. So much had happened since then. Ava had gotten married to a bastard of the highest order. Said bastard had tried to kill her and frame Magnus for the murder. Ava's mother had then killed Harrison and taken her own life to protect her daughter. And while Ava was suffering at that bastard's hands, Magnus had gone and fallen in love with Trey, knowing full well that he would not be complete without Ava. He couldn't explain why, but he'd always had this steadfast desire to find a man and a woman to love for all of eternity. It was how he envisioned his life.

He hadn't actually pictured it coming to fruition until recently. There'd been a few times over the past four months when Magnus had fantasized about Ava and Trey being the two people who would complete him. But that's all it was. A fantasy. Because while he was lusting after Ava, she saw him as her friend. And Trey ... well, where should Magnus begin? Trey was still licking old wounds, that much was obvious, so even the idea of being with one person was too much for him. Hence the reason they'd been doing the whole friends-with-benefits thing since the beginning.

Of course, there was the fact that Trey was gay. The man didn't have a sexual attraction to women. Never had.

Add those things up and they came up to one resolute conclusion: Magnus wouldn't be able to live out the rest of his life with Trey and Ava, no matter how much he wished he could.

Not that he'd made any efforts to test the waters.

While Magnus harbored this deep-seated lust for Ava, he had never acted on it. Had never intended to, either. But then Harrison Rivers had beaten her nearly to death and left her for dead. From the moment he'd learned Ava had disappeared, his feelings for her changed. Or maybe they hadn't changed so much as they'd come to light. Her disappearance had made him realize how much he loved her. He'd stopped at nothing to find her, and with the help of the Off the Books Task Force and Trey, they'd found her. That incident had changed him and made him see that life was short and that nothing should be taken for granted because it could be ripped away within a moment's notice.

That was why he'd been trying to live out a PG version of his fantasy. He tried to tell himself it was enough just to have Ava here while he was clinging to the last frayed threads of his relationship with Trey. It wasn't ideal, but it sure as shit beat the alternative.

"Magnus?"

He tilted his head down, his chin resting on the top of Ava's head. He loved how her hair always smelled like strawberries. It was her shampoo. He'd learned that when he found the bottle in his shower. "Hmm?"

"You really should go back to work. It's okay to start slow."

He smiled. "That's your way of tellin' me I'm gettin' on your nerves."

She giggled softly. "Just a little bit."

Magnus didn't fault her for her honesty. The truth was, he'd been getting on his own nerves as of late. He was ready to get back to work, but he'd been using Ava as an excuse. As long as he was tending to her, he didn't have to face Trey. He knew the moment he returned, Trey was going to walk away. It was only a matter of time.

But Ava was right. He couldn't keep putting it off.

Magnus slid his hand down her arm, over soft, smooth skin, and stopped when his hand covered her much smaller one over his heart.

He remained like that for a moment, pretending this was a lover's embrace, that he was comforting Ava and she was comforting him. He wanted nothing more than to move past this friendship and jump feet first into something more with her. However, Ava had lived through hell and come out the other side. She had healed on the outside, but he knew the damage to the inside was still a bloody, gaping wound that would continue to fester until she sought treatment for it, too.

"I'll go back to work under one condition."

She tilted her head back to peer up at his face. He glanced down, forcing his eyes to remain on hers and not lingering on her soft lips. He'd never kissed her, but he'd wanted to so many times.

"What condition's that?"

"You call Dr. Briggs and see if you can get an appointment."

Ava huffed, but she didn't pull away.

"Even if you make it for a month from now, you need to take that step."

"Okay."

He held her stare. "Promise?"

Ava tapped his chin. "I said I'd do it. Don't push the issue."

Magnus smiled, then leaned down and kissed her nose. "Fair enough."

"HEY, TREY. WOULD YOU MIND DOING EVENING meds?"

Trey poked his head out of the small laundry room as Gia strolled past. "No problem. You headin' out?"

"Not for another hour, but I need to go through the SAR training schedule for next week."

"I'll get it done," he assured her and went back to folding the towels they used to clean up spills and messes.

"Thank you!"

"Yep," he muttered to himself even as he smiled.

He found it amusing how these mundane tasks made him feel useful in a way he'd never felt at his previous jobs. Having been a security guard at various hotels for most of his adult life, he'd never had to care much for anyone but himself. Here he had four-legged canines to keep him company all day, and they gave him purpose, even if it was cleaning up after them.

Once the towels were folded, he carried them to the storage closet and placed them neatly on the shelves. With that task out of the way, he turned to go to the medical supply closet, only to come up short when he saw Magnus blocking his path.

"Everything okay?" Trey asked, surprised to see Magnus in the building. The man hadn't left Ava's side in months.

"Ava kicked me out."

He couldn't help it; he laughed. Trey had been expecting her to drop the hammer down sooner rather than later. Although she'd been a good sport about Magnus waiting on her hand and foot, he'd sensed the woman was hoping for a little more breathing room.

"What can I help with?" Magnus offered.

Realizing he was staring at Magnus as though seeing him for the first time, Trey looked away. "Ask Gia. I've gotta get the meds; then I'm headin' out."

Unfortunately, he had to walk toward Magnus to get where he was going, and the man didn't make it easy on him, refusing to move out of the way. Trey had to brush against him as he slipped past, but he forced himself to do it, pretending not to notice the way his body hardened from that simple touch.

He really was fucked up when it came to Magnus. Didn't matter how many talks he'd given himself over the last few months, Trey was still hanging on to something that was no longer there.

Just as he stepped past Magnus, the man grabbed hold of his wrist.

Trey stopped, staring down at Magnus's fingers clutching him. He slowly lifted his gaze until he was staring into the hazel eyes that haunted him whenever he closed his eyes.

"We need to talk."

"About?"

Magnus's expression morphed into the one that said, *What do you think?*

"Ah. Now that you're back, I'm not needed here anymore? I knew it was comin'. No hard feelin's. I'll stick around for another week while you get up to speed."

Magnus's grip tightened. "That's not it, and you know it. I don't want you to quit."

Yeah, well. Trey didn't necessarily want to quit, either. He loved this job, but it had never been his to have. He was merely filling in, and they both knew it was a temporary gig. They had more than enough staff to handle everything without him, and since Magnus could work circles around him, Trey figured it would be best for everyone.

"Another week," he repeated, slowly disengaging his arm from Magnus's hand. "Gia's workin' on the SAR trainin'. You might need to weigh in on that."

When he turned away, Trey heard Magnus's frustrated sigh. It loosened something in his chest because it meant Magnus had given up. At least for the moment. He knew that if Magnus pursued him, if he pressed the issue, Trey wouldn't be able to resist him.

Magnus Storme was his Achilles' heel. And right now, Trey couldn't afford a weakness. Giving in to Magnus was all he wanted, but it wasn't in his best interest. One of these days, Magnus would act on his affection for Ava, and Trey would be forced to step away because sharing the man he loved with anyone felt wrong on so many levels. It was better to do that now.

Rip the Band-Aid off, as they say.

Chapter Three

TREY WAS THE FIRST TO ARRIVE AT Camp K-9 on Monday morning, relieving Gia after her overnight shift. He'd had his first weekend off in a long time, and it'd given him time to catch up on some rest. He'd hoped it would bring more perspective, but since he'd forced himself not to think about Magnus—a task that was far more difficult than it sounded—he hadn't dedicated much time to figuring his shit out.

But here he was, counting down the days until it was time to move on. T minus five.

"Have a good day," he told Gia with a smile.

"Mm-hmm."

Oh, yeah. Magnus's right-hand woman was still pissed.

Ever since Trey had told Camp K-9's head trainer that he would only be working for another week, she'd been giving him the cold shoulder. She should've been happy that things were returning to normal because it meant she would have Magnus back. While Trey had learned quite a bit during his stint here, he knew he was a drag on the daily grind. He couldn't do things quite as efficiently as the others who'd been here for years, despite his best efforts. He didn't trust himself on overnight shifts because it meant he'd be alone in the event of an emergency. Trey was a lot of things, but being good in a crisis wasn't one of them. And because he was lacking, Gia and Billy were forced to alternate shifts more often since Magnus wasn't on the schedule. At some point, Trey figured he would've been on par with them, but that was something he no longer had to worry about.

"Good mornin', guys," Trey greeted the dogs in their cages as he flipped on the overhead lights. "Sleep well?"

A few excited barks sounded, and he pretended they were answering him. Of course, those barks were drowned out by the ear-piercing yip from Franklin, the little chihuahua in residence since last Wednesday. Franklin was harmless, but he was annoying as fuck. Not that Trey would tell him that. He wasn't cruel, after all.

"All right. How about we get some fresh air before we have breakfast?"

He went through the motions of releasing them all from their cushy doggy jails so they could go out into the play yard and do their business. As he was unlatching the last cage, Aurora, Magnus's five-year-old black lab, came strutting in.

"Hey, girl," he greeted, twisting his upper body to give her a scratch on the head when she nudged his arm. "Night shift go okay? No mishaps?"

She stared up at him, her tongue lolling out of her mouth.

"What's up? You look happy this mornin'." The more he talked, the more her tail whipped back and forth. "Have a good weekend now that your dad's back?"

He could swear she was smiling. Trey remembered a time he would smile when he thought about Magnus, too. These days, thoughts of Magnus merely induced an ache in his chest that was the equivalent of being suffocated.

Thankfully, there were things to do, which meant he could shift his focus for a little while.

For the next half hour, he weaved his way between the dogs as they sniffed and played in the yard. He scooped shit when it was necessary and gave head scratches when they were requested. He even jogged around to get the dogs to follow. A little morning exercise as the sun was coming up, the birds awakening in the dense trees that lined the property. It was going to be a scorcher of a day, but at least the humidity was down.

"We've gotta get some chow before the day starts and your friends arrive," he told them as he herded them back inside.

They had less than an hour before the daycare pups would begin showing up. Used to be, dogs would lounge around the house and wait for their owners to return from work. These days, owners didn't want their pooches cooped up alone for ten hours a day, so they brought them to places like this where they could play all day and get the attention they needed.

"Be good for me, yeah?" he muttered to his furry friends. This task worked better with more than one person since it required him to put them back in their cages, but Trey didn't mind. Gia usually helped, but he understood she was angry with him. That was her way. Before the end of the week, she would be high-fiving him and begging him to stay. Maybe.

Rather than bitch about herding the dogs, Trey coaxed them with sweet talk, something he'd gotten reasonably good at. Franklin was the only one who gave him trouble, but Trey persevered in the end. Then it was a matter of preparing their food. He didn't trust himself to remember all the special instructions, so he relied on the list Gia produced daily. Camp K-9 didn't merely board dogs; they catered to their every whim. Owners were offered a selection of packages from the basic all the way up to the Grand Poobah that offered plush accommodations and a variety of special treatments for the four-legged friend, including overnight companions, extra walks, and even special treats. Basically, they would do anything the owner requested, provided they would pay for it.

However, they didn't have any divas in residence at the moment, so Trey merely had to pay attention to the different diets of the dogs. Once the food and water were delivered, he stepped back and gave them a moment to devour their breakfast.

He was still standing there minutes later when he heard the door open, the bells overhead jingling to signal an arrival. He knew who it was, so he didn't bother to rush to the front to greet him. If Magnus had something to say, he could come find him.

The rest of the day went much like the morning. Trey did the chores as they were due and helped the others with the dogs. Six part-time employees filled the gaps throughout the week, helping the three full-time employees—Magnus, Gia, and Billy—as needed. Trey was an addition they hadn't budgeted for, which meant he wasn't needed now that Magnus was back. And because of that, he felt as though he was beginning to get in the way since Magnus had resumed his role, as though he'd never missed a day.

By the time three o'clock rolled around, Trey had gotten in the way one too many times for his own peace of mind, so he decided to head out. He wanted nothing more than to tell Billy Daniels, Gia's counterpart, that he was heading out early, but he couldn't bring himself to do it. It felt like a chickenshit thing to do to Magnus, and because he'd never been one to slack off before, facing the music was his only option.

"Hey, Billy. You seen Magnus?"

Billy didn't look up from the computer screen in front of him as he said, "In his office."

"Thanks."

Trey marched down the long hallway to the small room everyone referred to as Magnus's office. It probably should've been a storage room due to the fact it was only six feet by six feet, with barely enough room for the cheap desk and chair Magnus used when he was forced to deal with the *shitty parts of the job*, as Magnus liked to refer to paying the bills. Without a window to provide light and only a single bulb in the ceiling, it felt more like a punishment than a solution to their space problem.

He stopped at the door and put his hand on the jamb, his gaze settling on Magnus sitting at the desk. Sarge was snoozing in the corner, curled up on the small dog bed Trey had snuck in here a few months ago.

Trey didn't want to admire Magnus, but it came naturally. He'd tried to fight his insane attraction to this man from the first day he saw him at Brantley's house, back when Reese had signed Tesha up for training. At the time, Magnus was doing on-site training for those who needed it, visiting Brantley and Reese a couple of days a week. Trey had failed then just like he failed now because, try as he might, he would never tire of looking at this man. Every time he did was like the first time, filling him with exhilaration and lust. He couldn't explain it because he'd never had this reaction to another man before, although he'd been attracted to plenty. Not even his ex-husband had tripped his trigger the way Magnus could. Trey admired Magnus's youth and strength, his exuberance and determination. There were times Trey felt as though if he were with him long enough, maybe he could harness some of it for himself.

Unfortunately, he would never know.

Trey cleared his throat to get Magnus's attention. "I'm gonna head out."

Magnus glanced up at the round plastic clock on the wall. "Early, huh?"

"Unless you need me to do somethin' else."

Magnus turned in his chair to face Trey directly. For a few heartbeats, their eyes met and held, not a word spoken. Trey felt the heat of Magnus's gaze all the way to his soul.

Times like this were when he hated how things had turned out for them. He often reflected on everything he'd done that had brought him to the moment he met Magnus, wondering if he could've done something different along the way. If only he'd never agreed to work with Brantley, Trey wouldn't have met Magnus. And if he hadn't met Magnus, Trey never would've fallen in love with the man.

But *if only* never got him anywhere because he *had* gone to work for Brantley, and he *had* met Magnus, and he *had* fallen in love with the man. Now it was up to him to move on, to get past this so Magnus could find the happily ever after he yearned for. The one he deserved.

MAGNUS COULDN'T LOOK AWAY FROM TREY AS he filled the doorway of his office. He looked good. He'd been growing out his hair for quite a while now, and the dark silky strands were past his shoulders, but he kept it pulled back with a leather strap when he was working. The style accented his widow's peak and emphasized his steel-blue eyes. Magnus preferred his hair down because it was sexy with the beard he'd been growing out. It made him look like a modern-day outlaw. However, Magnus's favorite thing about Trey's hair was when he had the chance to run his fingers through it while Trey was sucking his cock.

He immediately shook off the thought. The last thing he needed right now was a hard-on, although it was inevitable whenever he was around Trey. He'd never had such a visceral reaction to anyone. Not like this. His attraction to Trey wasn't merely because of how good he looked. From the beginning, he'd felt a connection to the man, and it had grown stronger over the past year and a half. So strong, Magnus knew that if it were ever severed, he would never be the same.

Since he had a lot of experience with not spooking scared animals, Magnus got to his feet slowly. He could see the way Trey's muscles flexed and bunched. He was gearing up to retreat, but Magnus couldn't let him. Not until they talked about this. Magnus needed to know where they stood and how they could get back to where they'd been four months ago.

"I'll see you tomorrow," Trey said, dropping his hand from the doorjamb.

Magnus grabbed his arm and pulled, bringing him in close.

Trey's blue-gray eyes locked onto his, his mouth forming a hard line.

"We need to talk," Magnus told him, and it felt like the hundredth time he'd said it over the past few months.

"No, we don't."

"Why not? Something's clearly bothering you. I deserve to know what it is so I can fix it."

Trey huffed. "You can't fix it."

"Sure I can."

Trey shook his head, his tone firm when he said, "No, you can't."

Magnus couldn't contain his frustration. "Why the fuck not?"

Trey's eyes narrowed, his words coming out in a gravel-rough rasp. "Because it's who you are."

Magnus staggered back from the harshness of the words. "What does that mean?"

"Jesus, Magnus. Don't play dumb. It's beneath you."

He glared at Trey, refusing to respond. Yes, he knew what the fucking problem was, but damn it, he wanted Trey to admit it. It was the only way they could address it and find a resolution.

Trey sighed, then slid his hand over his hair. "It means you want Ava," he said, his tone cooler than before, "and you deserve to be happy."

"I want *you*, Trey," he declared. "I've always wanted you."

"Well, to have me, you can't have both."

Magnus thrust a hand in his hair and turned away. There wasn't room to pace, so he took a single step away from Trey. "That's why you've been retreating? Because you think I want Ava?"

"Are you tellin' me you don't?"

Magnus met his eyes. He knew what the correct answer was, but he also knew that would be a lie. And he couldn't lie to Trey. He wouldn't. "That's not what I'm sayin'."

"Exactly." Trey exhaled heavily. "I'm headin' out. I'll be back in the mornin'."

Magnus grabbed him again, this time in the hallway outside the office. He jerked him back, then pushed him up against the wall. "Just because I want her doesn't mean I can have her, Trey."

Trey swallowed, and Magnus was sure he saw something flash in his eyes. Hurt? Resentment?

"And I can't be your second choice, Magnus. Maybe you don't get Ava in the end, but you've told me from the beginning that you want both. I'm just not built that way."

"That was before I..." Magnus choked back the words. He couldn't tell Trey he'd fallen in love with him. It would send the man running before the last syllable was out of his mouth. "Before I met you."

Trey leaned his head forward, bringing their mouths close together. "Tell yourself whatever you need to, but we both know nothin's changed."

That wasn't true. Everything had changed. However, Trey was right. Magnus hadn't changed in that regard. In fact, with Ava and Trey here, he'd never felt more complete. And while he thought he could find happiness with only one of them, he still wouldn't be whole.

Funny how that had never been a problem for him before. He'd dated plenty of men and women over the years, never looking for anything serious. Until Trey, monogamy had been a word deleted from his vocabulary. Now, it had become his way of life, and he wasn't sure he could go back to his old tomcat ways.

"What can I do?" Magnus whispered, taking advantage of Trey's proximity. "I'll do anything, Trey."

"Anything?"

Magnus nodded.

"Then step back so I can leave."

Magnus swallowed past the tightness in his throat. He forced himself back a step, allowing Trey the space he needed to leave. And when the man turned and walked away without so much as a single glance back, Magnus felt the last thread snap. This thing they had was over, and there wasn't a damn thing Magnus could do to salvage it.

And if that weren't enough, the fucking ache in his chest would be a steady reminder.

"DID YOU CALL DR. BRIGGS?"

Ava peered up from her iPad as Magnus appeared in the doorway between the living room and the kitchen. "Not yet. But I will."

"Goddammit, Ava!" He spun on his heel and marched back through the kitchen, then down the hall.

She flinched when she heard his bedroom door slam shut.

Ava might not be the smartest woman in the world, but it didn't take one of those to figure out that Magnus's frustration wasn't because she hadn't called the psychiatrist yet. If she had to guess, Trey had done or said something. It seemed Magnus was operating on a hair trigger these days, counting down until something happened. Since she'd witnessed the two men drifting apart over these past four months, she figured they'd either cut ties completely or were dangerously close. She sincerely hoped not because she'd seen the two of them together. What they had was special, and it was real. They brought out the best in the other.

Setting her iPad aside, she leaned back against the cushion and closed her eyes. She wished she could go back in time and do things differently, because if she had, she wouldn't have come between them. And though she knew it was nothing she did or said, her mere presence had presented a roadblock for some reason.

She was pretty sure Trey liked her. In a friendly way, of course. They laughed and talked, and there'd been those few times back at the beginning of her recovery when he would sit with her through the night, watching over her so Magnus could get some sleep. Once or twice she would watch him through slitted eyes, listening to the sound of him breathing, wondering how anyone could be that still and be awake. And she'd made a point to thank him for his help and kindness throughout. Truth was, she liked Trey. And fine, there was a good chance she'd developed a crush on him, too. But that was all it was. A silly crush conjured up by a lonely woman forced to sit around until her wounds were completely healed while two ridiculously hot men tried to punish the other with orgasms.

So why is your ass still on the couch?

Oh, how that voice irritated her. She'd been fighting the damn thing for the past week, ever since she accepted that she should not be confined to the house anymore. What she wanted to do was help Magnus and Trey with Camp K-9.

She used to love working at Storme Kennels when Magnus's father ran them before Magnus changed the name. They weren't quite what they were today, but the work was relatively the same. It had expanded, a few upgrades were made, and a little more pampering went into it nowadays, but that seemed fair since dogs were people, too. Or so Magnus always said. But for Ava to make a contribution, she would have to start counseling. Magnus had made it a stipulation. And since she couldn't muster the courage to make the appointment, she was forced to sit here and wallow in it.

Only she didn't have to sit here.

Getting to her feet no longer took any effort. She could probably use some exercise to strengthen her unused muscles, but aside from that, she felt good. More so as she neared Magnus's bedroom door. She lifted her hand to knock but stopped herself. If she gave him the option of permitting her to come in, he would tell her no. Magnus liked to sulk in silence, and he did so in his bedroom.

So, she did the only thing she could. She turned the knob and walked in like his bedroom was her own.

Since he'd moved everything from the guest bedroom—which he'd been using as a game room—into here in order to give her a room of her own, space was in short supply. The room was relatively large for a house this old, but that was because he'd remodeled in recent years, changing the original floor plan. The fire had demolished most of this side of the house, which had been two rooms—his parents' and his sister's. It had originally been repaired—back when Edgar had become Magnus's legal guardian—but it had been rebuilt exactly as it previously was. When he'd remodeled, Magnus combined the two rooms and added a master bathroom, turning a three-bedroom, one-bath house into a two-bedroom, two-bath. She didn't know the first thing about resale value like they talked about on the home improvement shows she'd watched when nothing else was on, but it worked nicely as a bachelor pad.

His bedroom was the ultimate in masculine design. His king-size bed with the oversized walnut headboard was on the right side of the room, neatly positioned between two windows, with matching, single-drawer nightstands on each side. The bed was always made, the navy-blue comforter perfectly straight, and the pillows staged like they do in furniture stores. Directly beside the door was a large armoire, which usually stood sentry on its own. Now a gaming desk with all his equipment was tucked behind it, mostly hidden from view when you walked in.

Ava expected to find him sitting in his chair, controller or keyboard in his hands, but Magnus wasn't at his desk.

She headed toward the bathroom. The door was open, and the shower was running. She knew she should give him privacy, but there was a little ornery voice in her head telling her he'd violated hers so many times these past four months it would serve him right if she walked right in.

So she did.

And she stopped short when she saw him in the shower. Her brain instantly snapped an image of his masculine beauty so she'd have something to reflect on later. Magnus had one hand planted on the wall, his head hanging down, his other hand wrapped around his cock. His *enormous* cock. Holy crap. That thing had to be like ten inches long.

Ava stared brazenly as he took his time stroking up and down his thick shaft, the water sluicing over all those glorious muscles covered by golden skin. She'd never seen anything quite as intriguing as this man in the shower pleasuring himself.

Every so often, a grunt or groan would echo off the tiled walls, but he never lifted his head, and he never stopped stroking. Ava knew it was wrong to watch, but she couldn't look away. If she moved even an inch, he would likely see her, and he would stop what he was doing. That felt like a crime in the making because … holy crap, the man was beautiful.

You should move.

Yes, yes, she probably should. But she didn't.

And she still didn't.

Magnus's fist worked up and down, his pace gradually quickening, as did the rise and fall of his chest. She could hear the rough rasp of his breaths, even over the white noise of the shower.

Ava welcomed the warmth that pooled between her thighs and the twinge in her core, although she ignored both. She couldn't remember a time she'd ever been turned on like this. Maybe back at the very beginning of her marriage when Harrison had treated her with a modicum of respect. That didn't last long, though, and they'd only been married a few weeks when sex became a chore she despised. And when she'd stopped wanting it altogether, Harrison took it upon himself to use her body without her consent, insisting that since she was his wife, it was her duty.

Because of him, Ava had grown to hate sex. She figured she always would—that she would never want another man's hands on her, never want to feel a cock inside her. Only she knew that wasn't true because she'd always been attracted to Magnus. She knew being with him would be how it was meant to be. Which was probably why seeing Magnus like this triggered something. It made her want, made her ache.

"Oh, fuck," Magnus rasped, jerking himself harder now. "Please … I need…"

Ava ignored the way her insides trembled and her clit pulsed as she watched him pleasure himself. She wondered who he was thinking about as he pumped his hips, driving his cock into his fist. Was he thinking about Trey? Did he imagine Trey on his knees, his enormous cock sliding into his mouth? Ava could almost see the image in her mind. She probably would've if there weren't a small selfish part of her that wondered if he was thinking about her. On her knees, her fingers curled around the base while she tried to take him deep in her throat.

She swallowed the whimper that erotic fantasy induced.

There were times she'd wanted Magnus to kiss her. Mostly that was back before what had happened, but there'd been a couple of times since. She saw how he looked at her, and sometimes she was convinced that he wanted her the same way she'd wanted him all those years ago when her teenage heart set its sights on him.

"Ah, Jesus … Trey…"

Well, that answered her question.

"Fuck … suck me while Ava sucks you."

Trey

This time she couldn't stop the sharp inhale that filled her lungs, her surprise so potent she nearly fell to the floor. Magnus was thinking about both of them.

"Jesus fuck!" Magnus threw his head back as his cock pulsed in his fist, streams of cum splashing against the tile. He looked so beautiful like that, every muscle in his body tense, a masterpiece of planes and angles.

His head tilted back down, his arm tensing as he continued to prop himself on the wall.

She was about to turn around and leave when he said her name.

Ava didn't reply, willing herself to be invisible.

Magnus didn't lift his head, didn't look her way. "Ava, you should leave now."

"I should," she agreed, whispering the words as she turned and fled.

Chapter Four

TREY OPENED THE BACK DOOR OF MAGNUS'S house to the sound of feet pounding on the floor. A second later, a door slammed.

"Hello?"

No one answered, so he stepped inside and closed the door behind him. He felt like shit for how he'd left things with Magnus, and while he was still convinced this was the best thing for them, he couldn't just walk away. It wasn't in his nature. At the very least, he wanted to part on relatively good terms. It was the only way he could move on. Some probably thought of it as closure. More like facing your demons head on.

Trey peeked into the living room, but it was empty. Ava's iPad sat on one cushion, tossed aside as though she'd been in a hurry. He peered down the hall that led to the bedrooms. The only open door was the one to the small bathroom. He headed down the hall, stopping in front of Ava's bedroom. He put his ear near the door but heard nothing coming from inside. He moved on to Magnus's door. Trey was about to lean in and listen when he heard Magnus's voice approaching rapidly.

"Ava! We need to talk about this!"

The door swung open, and Magnus slammed right into Trey, knocking him back a step.

"Oh, shit." Magnus huffed deeply. "You scared the shit out of me, Trey. What are you doing here?"

The bigger question was: what were Magnus and Ava doing? Since Magnus was wearing a towel around his hips and his hair was dripping wet, the logical assumption was that he'd been in the shower. Had Ava been with him? And when the fuck had they started doing that shit?

"You know what?" Trey said firmly. "Never mind. Clearly, I've come at a bad time."

"Wait, goddammit," Magnus barked, grabbing for Trey's arm.

Trey stopped moving but didn't turn to look back at Magnus. He couldn't. Thinking about him and Ava…

"It's not what you think," Magnus stated.

A mirthless laugh escaped. "And what exactly do I think?"

Magnus exhaled heavily, releasing him to go back into his bedroom. Trey should've used that as an excuse to leave, but his damn feet weren't on the same page, because he turned around and followed Magnus into the room.

"Fuck," he bit out, turning around when he realized Magnus had dropped the fucking towel in order to pull on a pair of shorts.

"You've seen me naked plenty," Magnus snapped. "Get over yourself, Trey."

There were times, like now, when Trey was reminded of Magnus's age. Although he was an adult, the fact that Magnus was twelve years younger and not at the same level of maturity was glaringly obvious.

"You know what? Go fuck yourself, Magnus. I'm done."

Trey spun on his heel and marched out of the room. He made it two feet before he changed his mind and turned around. He'd come this far; he needed to finish it. God knows he wasn't eager to do it a second time.

He let his emotions get the best of him as he grabbed Magnus by the throat and backed him up against the wall. He made sure not to hurt him, but he was damn sure going to remind Magnus of how this worked between them. Trey wasn't the one who bowed to Magnus, it was the other fucking way around.

Magnus's eyes were wide, and his Adam's apple bobbed against Trey's palm as he swallowed.

Something in that surprised look hit Trey square in the chest. Before he knew what he was doing, he slammed his mouth down on Magnus's and kissed him so hard they'd both be bruised afterward.

"Oh, fuck, yes," Magnus groaned as Trey dragged him to the bed, shoving him down as he crawled over him, never letting his lips get too far away.

Trey kissed him harder, inhaling every breath, tasting every moan. He wanted Magnus so fucking much he ached from the need. It consumed every minute of his day, overwhelming his dreams. He was losing his goddamn mind because he knew they couldn't keep going like this. But he'd known that from the beginning. When he'd learned that Magnus was bisexual, Trey understood that there was an expiration date on their relationship.

Might as well go out with a bang.

"Take off my shirt," Trey growled, biting Magnus's lower lip.

Trey lifted his arms so Magnus could drag the cotton off of him.

"Unbutton my jeans."

While Magnus did that, Trey toed off his boots, letting them fall to the floor beside the bed. When his jeans were down to his thighs, he climbed off the bed and stripped them off, kicking them away.

"Shorts off now."

Trey jerked open the drawer in the nightstand and grabbed the lubricant he knew Magnus had stashed there. He watched Magnus watching him as he generously greased his throbbing dick. When he was satisfied, he put one knee on the bed and instructed Magnus to pull his knees to his chest.

Ah, Jesus.

Trey never seemed to be prepared for the sight of Magnus waiting for him like that. On display and submissive, his hard cock, his heavy balls, and that goddamn inviting puckered hole had a way of breaking down the last of his resistance.

Without preamble, Trey crawled forward and guided his cock into Magnus's tight hole. He wasn't gentle, wasn't even sure he could be if he were in his right mind. Which he damn sure wasn't. Trey was coming apart at the seams knowing that this was the last time they were going to be together. Regardless of what he wanted, he knew he could never be what Magnus needed. And for that reason alone, he had to end things.

This was it for them.

Trey clung to that as he fucked Magnus, driving in as deep as he could, retreating, and slamming in again. He drilled him into the mattress, planting his hands on the back of Magnus's thighs and pressing his full weight down, pinning him there, forcing him to take every punishing thrust.

The entire time, he could feel Magnus's hands as they gripped his legs, hear his soft grunts and choked whispers for more. Magnus was holding on, giving himself over to Trey the only way he could. It nearly unraveled Trey completely, but he shoved it down. He would deal with the aftermath later. Right now, the only thing he cared about was coming inside this man. He wanted Magnus to remember this for the rest of his life. When he was living a grand life with a man and a woman who could willingly share him between them, Trey hoped Magnus would still think of *this*.

"Trey ... oh, fuck..."

Trey's lungs worked overtime as sweat trickled down his spine. He continued to thrust until his hips were sore, but even then, he didn't stop. He shifted so Magnus's legs were draped over his shoulders, changing the angle of penetration until Magnus was panting as hard as he was, begging him to make him come.

"Goddamn you," Trey growled as he drove into him once, twice... On the third time, he slammed in deep and roared his release, hoping the sound rattled the walls.

It wasn't until he was spent that Trey realized Ava was in the next room over. He hadn't thought about her for a single second while he was fucking Magnus. Hadn't considered that he might be doing something that he shouldn't be doing. If Magnus and Ava had started a relationship, Trey had no designs on the man anymore.

"Fuck," he snapped, sitting up and dropping his feet over the edge of the bed.

"Don't go," Magnus pleaded.

Trey glared at him, hating himself more in that moment than he had in a long damn time.

It was definitely over.

AVA COULD HEAR THEM.

The sounds coming from Magnus's bedroom could only be one thing. They were fucking.

She knew it was wrong to be turned on by them, wishing she could see how beautiful they were when they were in the throes of passion. She wanted that more than anything, but she remained where she was. As their grunts and groans grew louder, her hand drifted into her shorts. She teased her clit, touching herself for the first time in so long her clit was so sensitive it was nearly painful.

Somehow she managed to push through until she found just the right rhythm to match the squeak of the bedsprings in the other room. In her fantasy, Trey had Magnus bent over, and he was impaling him from behind, driving into him, his hands gripping his hips, holding him still while he pleasured them both. She closed her eyes, and the image shifted a little, showing her lying with Magnus's shoulders between her thighs, his tongue sliding over her clit.

She whimpered and moaned, not caring because she knew they couldn't hear her over the ruckus they were making. She wanted to come. No, she *needed* to come. Each day the pressure continued to build, and she knew one day she would explode from it.

Unfortunately, relief didn't come, no matter how much she rubbed herself. She couldn't orgasm from her hand. Hell, she wasn't sure she could orgasm at all. She'd learned to fake it like a porn star, though. It was the only way to get Harrison off her in the beginning. Then it had simply become a means to an end. He had never cared whether she orgasmed or not, but she soon learned that if he thought she did, it would tip him over the edge, and she could be done with him.

Her hand stilled when she heard Trey's garbled shout. He was coming, and she was envious. Not only that he could, but also because she wished she was in that room with them.

Ava shook her head and stared at the ceiling. It was definitely time to make that therapy appointment.

AFTER TREY LEFT, MAGNUS TOOK ANOTHER SHOWER. This one was quick and cold, doing little to cool him off. He was still reeling from Trey, his body throbbing with the need to come, something he hadn't done because Trey hadn't been focused on Magnus at that point. He'd had one goal in mind, and he'd succeeded.

If Magnus had thought for one second that they might be able to get back to where they were, that moment had sealed it for him. Trey was likely the most generous lover Magnus had ever had, but today he'd been too far gone to care.

It didn't matter that Magnus had come shortly before in the shower while he let his fantasy of Ava and Trey play in his mind. That felt like eons ago. He'd needed Trey. He still did.

Once he was done, he pulled on a pair of shorts and left his bedroom. He peeked out the back window, checking to see if Trey's truck was still there. It wasn't. He'd known it wouldn't be, but a guy could fucking hope, couldn't he?

Magnus went to the living room, intending to ask Ava if she wanted something for dinner, but she wasn't there. Her door was shut, but it was always shut, didn't matter if she was in there or not.

They needed to talk about what she had witnessed earlier. He hadn't realized she was in his bathroom until it was too late and he'd whispered her name and Trey's seconds before he exploded. He wanted to explain to her that he would never do anything she didn't want. That it was only a fantasy. The last thing Magnus wanted was for her to be scared of him. She'd spent years with a man who took what he wanted because he thought he was due. Magnus would never hurt her like that. Regardless of how much of a temptation she was.

He stopped outside her door and tapped lightly. If she were awake, maybe she would acknowledge him.

When she didn't answer, he sighed and returned to the kitchen. He made himself a sandwich, scarfed it down standing up, and then grabbed a bottle of water before heading to the living room. He turned on the television and got settled in the spot Ava had occupied for the past four months. He could smell her on the cushions. Her sweet strawberry scent seemed to be everywhere in the house these days. He hadn't realized how much that unique scent soothed him.

Magnus tried to relax, flipping through channels until he found a rerun of NCIS. At the very least, he could find satisfaction in looking at Mark Harmon. There was something insanely sexy about the older man. He watched for a few minutes, and when his eyes became too heavy to keep open, he closed them and drifted off.

Sometime later, he jolted awake, jumping to his feet when Ava's terrified scream pierced the air.

His mind had become accustomed to the sound of her nightmares, instantly shattering the dregs of sleep. He hurried down the hallway to her bedroom and opened the door. She was on the twin bed, thrashing around as she screamed and pleaded with the monster who plagued her dreams.

"Ava. Wake up, Ava," he said, brushing her arm lightly. He'd learned not to startle her awake because it only made it worse. He continued to call her name until she settled, her eyes finally opening as she looked around.

"You're safe," he assured her, sitting on the edge of her bed, ensuring he wasn't touching her. "It was just a nightmare."

"I know," she whispered, her voice hoarse. "I'm sorry I woke you."

"Don't be sorry."

He wanted to hold her, but he refrained. Magnus was careful with Ava, never wanting to make her feel as though he was pushing himself on her. He always waited until she instigated it before he would put his arms around her.

"Can I get you anything? Water? Milk?"

"No, thank you."

"Do you want me to go?"

Her face was in shadow, only a hint of light coming into the room from the hallway, so he couldn't see her eyes clearly.

"Would you stay with me? In the living room?"

"Of course." Magnus got to his feet and headed for the door, waiting for her to follow.

He let her pass, then pulled her door closed and followed.

As they had many times over the months, Magnus got situated on the couch, lying down with his back against the rear cushions, leaving enough room for her to lie in front of him. When she settled, and he was spooned around her, his arm beneath her head, the other draped over her narrow waist, he pulled her back against him, offering his warmth. It wasn't much, and he knew it wouldn't eradicate the demons that haunted her, but it usually brought her some peace. Enough that she could sleep for a few hours.

Although he wanted to bring up what she'd witnessed earlier, Magnus held back. He figured when she was ready to discuss it, she would bring it up. Until then, he would settle for knowing she was safe in his arms.

Chapter Five

Wednesday, July 20, 2022

WANT TO GRAB A BEER AFTER WORK? Figured we could catch up.

Trey responded to the text from Brantley with: *Fuck yes. But you're buying.*

When do I not? See you there around six.

Trey shot his brother a confirmation, then headed up to the front office. Covering the front was usually Billy's job on Wednesdays since they were Gia's day off, but he had called out sick this morning. Magnus had asked Trey to cover since he was leading one of the SAR training classes. Trey didn't mind because it required more effort to stay awake than anything else. It did give him time to spend with Sarge and Aurora. Magnus had taken Adira with him to the training site, leaving the other two Labrador retrievers behind.

"Lazy bums," he greeted with a smile when he found them camped out on their beds in the corner.

Sarge lifted his head, his tongue lolling out of his mouth as soon as he noticed him. Trey's grin grew wider. He hadn't paid much attention to how attached he'd gotten to the dogs. He was going to miss seeing their smiling faces every day.

Maybe he should consider getting a dog of his own.

No sooner did the thought process than he shrugged it off. He had no idea what he'd be doing after Friday, so the last thing he needed was someone depending on him. Hell, he hadn't even made an effort to find another job and wasn't looking forward to the task. Thankfully, he had enough in savings to last him a while. Probably six months if he was frugal. Not that he intended to sit on his ass that long, but he didn't want to jump into anything too quickly. He figured he'd take some time to focus on the important things. If he was lucky, once he did that, he'd see whatever path he was supposed to follow. And if not, there was always security work he could fall back on.

He caught movement out the window and leaned over, watching as Ava stepped out of Magnus's house, taking the path toward the Camp K-9 office.

Shit.

Trey considered making a break for it but held his ground. The least he deserved was to endure a scolding if she wanted to bring up what had happened on Monday night. He hated himself for not thinking that one through before he let his emotions get the best of him. Fucking Magnus so ruthlessly hadn't been on his agenda, but like plenty of other times, his need for the man had won out. But it was done, and there was nothing he could do to change it.

"Hey," Ava greeted as she opened the door, a smile on her pretty face, her brilliant blue eyes practically glowing.

She looked good. Really good, actually. Her blonde hair was slowly growing in, and it was now long enough she could style it with whatever product made it look naturally tousled and cute. He remembered she called it a pixie cut or some shit. With the little diamond studs in her ears, she looked closer to eighteen than twenty-five, which she would turn in a couple of weeks. She was wearing a black tank top that hugged her breasts and midsection and showed off her shoulders and arms. A pair of tiny white shorts made her legs look tanner than they were and lovingly showcased her ass, while a pair of white tennis shoes was just begging to get scuffed with dirt.

No doubt about it, she was a beautiful woman. Even a gay man could admit that. And while Trey didn't usually admire a woman past her natural beauty, this wasn't the first time he found his gaze lingering longer than normal. He couldn't explain it, but there was something about Ava that drew him toward her.

He forced a smile. "If you're lookin' for Magnus, he's off-site."

Her brilliant blue eyes sparkled as she peered up at him. "Actually, I was looking for you."

Trey swallowed, his smile faltering. "Well, you found me."

"I did." She came around the counter to join him, pulling up the second stool and taking a seat with only a foot or so between them.

Trey glanced over when she rested her arms on the countertop. Her fingers tapped against the linoleum countertop, drumming rhythmically.

"What's on your mind?" he prompted when the silence began to choke him.

"I'm working."

He chuckled, and his mood lightened. "Oh, really? This your new job?"

"I'm hoping so." She stared over at him. "After all, I did call Dr. Briggs. I've got my first appointment on Tuesday."

"Good girl," he said, praising her for making that leap. "I'm proud of you."

Her eyes twinkled as her smile grew wider, revealing pearly-white teeth, and he realized what he'd said. From the very first time he met Ava—here in this very office, sporting a black eye and a split lip after she'd managed to escape the clutches of her abusive husband—Trey had felt protective of her. That had grown tenfold during the course of her recovery, and the more time he spent with her, watching her come into her own once again, the more he found he not only wanted to protect her but he genuinely liked her. Trey wasn't sure what he felt for her could ever be considered a physical attraction, but he certainly didn't see her as a sister.

"I was hoping you would drive me."

"I ... uh..." He swallowed past the lump in his throat and averted his gaze. "I won't be workin' here then."

"I know."

His head snapped over, eyes meeting hers.

"Magnus told me you quit. He also told me you don't have a job lined up. Figured you'd have some free time."

What could he say to that? She'd pegged him accurately, which meant if he declined, she'd probably take it personally.

"Yeah, I can drive you."

"Maybe we could grab lunch before or after."

He swallowed again, and he was sure it was loud enough for Ava to hear. "Maybe," he muttered, glancing out the window.

Ava's hand settled on his forearm, drawing his attention. He stared at it for a moment, curious why his cock twitched. Her fingers looked ridiculously small against his arm, accentuating the significant difference in their sizes. At six feet three inches, Trey wasn't a small man by any stretch of the imagination. Ava had to be a solid foot shorter and probably one hundred pounds lighter. He couldn't imagine she weighed one hundred pounds soaking wet.

Since when do you catalog a woman's physical attributes?

That was a damn good question. One he did not have an answer for. Sure, he found her cute in a little-girl kinda way—Okay, that was a total fucking lie. Trey did not see a little girl when he looked at Ava. He saw a strong, beautiful woman. There was nothing childlike about her, and he figured that had something to do with the life she'd lived, the hell she'd survived.

However, he did *see* her. Enough that he was questioning why there was a tightness in his groin. He knew it damn sure wasn't because he was repulsed by her touch, because he certainly didn't have the urge to extricate his arm. So what the fuck was it?

"I'm glad you came by the other night. Magnus was in a mood. I think he needed to see you."

Trey's gaze darted out the window. He had nothing to say to that. What Magnus needed was no longer Trey's concern. He couldn't let it be. This woman was the reason he needed to move on. He saw the way Magnus looked at her, knew he cared for her more than a friend would. With Trey out of the picture, they would have a real shot at seeing if something might happen between them. And once they figured that out, they could find another man who would complete the triad Magnus longed for.

And the thought of either of them with another man…? That doesn't make your gut churn?

Thankfully, the door swung open, effectively silencing the stupid little voice. Magnus walked in, his eyes immediately focused on Ava's hand resting on Trey's arm.

The only reason he didn't pull away was so he didn't make it awkward. It was nothing. She'd been thanking him for Magnus's sake.

"What're you doin' here?" Magnus asked Ava, a smile forming as he stepped closer.

"I work here now," she chirped.

"Is that right?"

"Yup. My first appointment is next Tuesday. Trey said he'd take me."

Trey felt the heat of Magnus's gaze, but he refused to meet his eyes. Instead, he pushed to his feet and stepped back. Ava's hand fell away from his arm, the absence of her touch more disappointing than he'd expected.

"I've got shit to do," Trey said, refusing to look at either of them.

He really didn't have anything to do, but he'd damn sure find something. He just hoped he could find something that would distract him from whatever that moment was he'd just shared with Ava.

At six o'clock, Trey was already perched on a barstool at Moonshiners. He had his first of many beers in front of him, listening to the mundane chatter taking place around him. He'd said his pleasantries to those he knew, but the small bar was mostly empty at this time of evening. Especially on a Wednesday.

The faces were familiar because they were residents of Coyote Ridge, the town built on land that originally belonged to Trey's family. His uncle Curtis had parsed it out years ago and changed the name of the town to honor his wife, Lorrie. Generations of Walkers had grown up here, many of whom were still around, making up a good portion of the population of fewer than three thousand people as of the last census count. The real estate was relatively cheap, which was why there were rarely any homes for sale or lease. Those that were up for grabs were usually reserved for friends or family looking to secure the future of their children.

But the best part about it was the inclusiveness of the town. People greeted you when you walked down Main Street, they ventured out when the town council did one of its many festivals, and they asked about you when you were away for a while because they cared enough to worry. It was the one place Trey considered home, and he couldn't imagine living anywhere else.

He appreciated that he could come into this bar and be greeted by people he knew. He could carry on a conversation with the bar's owner, Mack, and get the juicy gossip since Mack was married to the sheriff, Jeff, who happened to be one of his cousin's father-in-law. Or he could chat it up with Rafe Sharpe, who shared the bartending duties with Mack. Rafe wasn't directly related to Trey but rather a branch off of the extended family tree. He could also talk to Bailey Weber, one of the waitresses. Her mother owned the bakery down the road, and Bailey filled in there from time to time. And if they weren't up for conversation, there were a wealth of others who would venture in on occasion.

Fortunately for Trey, no one had come in yet, because he was the one not up for idle chitchat tonight. He was looking forward to catching up with Brantley since he hadn't seen his brother in a while. Trey had spent some time with his other brothers, Cal and Griffin, as well as his three sisters a couple of weekends back when the family got together for a barbecue, but Brantley had been working a case, so he'd been MIA.

As though he'd conjured the man from thin air, the door opened, and Brantley sauntered in. He was wearing a chest-hugging black T-shirt, a pair of black tactical pants, and black combat boots. It was his outfit of choice, something he'd obviously gotten used to during his time as a Navy SEAL. Trey knew Brantley's best friend, JJ, had been working on getting him to change his wardrobe since his return to Coyote Ridge, but apparently, she hadn't set fire to all the clothes in his closet yet.

"Where's Reese?" Trey prompted, referring to Brantley's fiancé and partner on the Off the Books Task Force, a team of people who'd once worked as a specialized task force for the governor's office. Since then, they'd shifted into the private sector and now took orders from Sniper 1 Security.

"He'll be along in a bit. He was gonna stop by and talk to Atticus."

Trey grinned against the lip of his beer bottle. "How's that little shit doin'?"

Trey'd had the pleasure of meeting Atticus James—no relation to Brantley's Girl Friday, Jessica James—the newest member of the task force. From what Brantley had told him, they'd encountered the former bounty hunter on a case they worked on in Dallas back in May. After the kid had come through on a stunt they instigated to fool a local wannabe mobster, Brantley offered Atticus a job, and he accepted.

"Still a little shit," Brantley said with a gruff chuckle as he signaled Mack for a beer.

Trey waited until Mack delivered the beer, then got to his feet and headed for an empty table at the back. He had no desire to discuss anything remotely personal while sitting at the bar. There was a good chance there'd be attentive ears lingering nearby, and the last thing he wanted was his personal shit aired in the *Coyote Ridge Gazette*.

"How're things over at Camp K-9?" Brantley asked as he eased into the booth across from Trey, scooting so that his back was to the wall and his legs were extended on the wooden bench.

"As good as can be expected."

"And Ava? How's she doin'?"

"Doctor released her." Trey smiled. "She's got her first appointment with Piper next week."

"Yeah?" Brantley chuckled. "I still find it amusin' that she moved her practice here. The girl who used to threaten to punch Cal in the junk is a psychiatrist."

That she was. Piper Briggs was also one of their many cousins. The second oldest of their aunt Maryanne's six children had moved down to Austin after she graduated from medical school. She'd initially intended to become a cardio-thoracic surgeon, but with an unexpected pregnancy and the ensuing fall-out with the baby daddy, she'd shifted her priorities and become a psychiatrist. According to Piper, concessions had to be made, and spending time with her son was the only thing she cared about.

"How's JJ? She and Baz get moved into their house?"

"Oh, yeah. All set up and countin' down the days until the baby comes."

Trey could feel Brantley's eyes on him and knew his brother was humoring him by answering the random questions. It was what he did. Taking a long pull on his beer, Trey pretended not to notice.

"All right, spill it," Brantley finally said, his voice low and gruff. "What's goin' on with you? Don't think I missed how you glossed over how things are at Camp K-9. Or that you haven't brought up Magnus once since we sat down."

"I quit."

"What?"

"Technically, I didn't quit because I didn't officially work there."

"Magnus didn't pay you?"

"Well, yeah."

"Then you worked there."

Trey huffed. "Fine. I worked there. And I quit. Friday's my last day now that Magnus is back."

Brantley leaned back and lifted his bottle to his lips, but he didn't take a drink. Instead, he said, "But I thought you liked workin' there."

"I did. But it was only meant to be temporary while Magnus was takin' care of Ava."

"Did *he* say that?"

"Not in those words." Trey took a long pull on his beer. "It doesn't matter. It's time for me to do somethin' else anyway."

"Like what?"

Trey leaned back. "Don't know yet. I've got time to figure it out."

Brantley's eyebrow rose slowly.

"No," Trey said quickly, shaking his head to emphasize. "I don't wanna come back to the task force."

"You know I'd take you back in a heartbeat."

"I know. And I appreciate that, but I'm not suited for the stress of that job."

"Not many people are."

No, they weren't. But Brantley was. Hell, he made it look easy, and Trey admired him for it.

"You could always go work with Griffin at the bank," Brantley suggested.

Trey snorted. Not in a million years would he work for his stodgy nerd of a brother. "Yeah, that ain't happenin'."

Brantley nodded as though considering. "Probably wise. Not sure I'd trust you around other people's money either."

"Fuck off," he said without heat.

"Leif and Lance got their security system install business goin'. You could always work for them."

"Pass."

"Travis and them have the resort."

Trey snorted again. "Not my cup of tea."

"Kaden and Keegan have the whole ranchin' thing down."

"Too much work."

"True that." Brantley took a drink. "What about—"

"No, I'm not gonna work with Ethan and Beau. I'm not mechanically inclined." Trey huffed a laugh. "I appreciate you bringin' up all the family members who might need help, but I've got it covered."

"Fine." Brantley grinned and nodded his beer bottle toward Bailey. "You could always waitress. I hear Mack's gonna be hirin'."

"Bailey goin' somewhere?"

"Rex and Jack are lookin' to hire someone to manage the B and B. She applied for the job. I'm sure once she goes for the interview, they'll hire her on the spot." Brantley peered over at him. "You'd look mighty good carryin' around that tray full of beers with that little apron around your waist."

Trey flipped his brother off. He had no desire to be a waiter or wear a fucking apron.

Brantley turned, and his expression shifted to serious. "You know, there is one thing you might consider."

"If you're gonna—"

"You could always open a dog boarding place here in Coyote Ridge. There ain't one of those yet."

Trey exhaled heavily. "Between you and me, I've considered it. But I don't have the qualifications or the know-how that Magnus does. Plus, I wouldn't want him thinkin' I was tryin' to steal his business."

"Embers Ridge is half an hour from here and the opposite direction of Austin. I guarantee you don't see anyone drivin' way the hell out there to have their dog attend day camp."

"Maybe not, but still no."

"What did Magnus say about you quittin'?"

Trey downed the rest of his beer and set the empty bottle on the table. "I didn't give him a chance to say anything. We're done."

Brantley's dark eyebrows lowered. "What do you mean y'all are done?"

"I ended it." Trey signaled for Bailey to bring two more beers.

"Why? What happened?"

"He's in love with Ava."

"Did he say that?"

Trey stared at his brother. Magnus didn't have to say it. Trey could tell.

"For fuck's sake, Trey."

"What? You and I both know it never woulda worked out with him. I'm too fuckin' old for him, for one thing. And another, he's bisexual."

"So fuckin' what?"

"He wants…" Trey swallowed and glanced down at the table. "He wants what Travis had with Gage and Kylie."

"Oh."

Yeah. *Oh.* "I don't swing that way."

Brantley's eyebrows slammed down. "Meanin' you're gay? Or meanin' you can't bear the thought of sharin' him with a woman?"

"Hell if I know." When he'd first learned that Magnus wanted a man and a woman, he never could've imagined sharing him with anyone else. Then Ava came around, and he worried about it a little less. When he thought about the two of them together, he never considered it sharing because Trey had a piece of her, too. Not sexually, of course. But he did have her friendship. So in a sense, it worked.

However, intimacy would become a thing at some point, and Trey damn sure wasn't cut out for that shit.

His gaze lowered to his arm, and he swore he could still feel the coolness of her fingers against his skin. He shook off the thought, looking up at the same time Bailey approached to deliver another round. Trey thanked her before she sauntered off.

As soon as she was out of earshot, Brantley spoke, his voice lowered. "I'm gonna tell you somethin', and I want you to listen to me closely."

Trey met his brother's eyes, held his stare.

"When Reese got shot and nearly fuckin' died, I thought my world had ended. And when I found out he'd been out with his ex-girlfriend *when* he got shot, I knew it had."

"And you left him," Trey reminded him.

"You're right. I did. And I hated every fuckin' second without him. I felt empty. I hated myself for walkin' away, but he'd made a choice. Or I thought he had, anyway." His voice lowered a little more. "When he came back, I was pissed, but I knew I loved him and didn't want to spend my life without him. If you care about Magnus like that, you need to take a damn hard look at what you want before you give him up."

"Nice to know you've got my back," Trey bit out.

"I've always got your back. No matter what. You tell me Magnus needs his ass kicked, I'll call up Travis and them, and we'll line up with our fuckin' boots laced tight. You tell me Ava's makin' a move on your man, I'll sic JJ on her. But if you wanna tuck your tail between your legs before you know what's what … that's on you, Trey."

This conversation certainly didn't go the way Trey had expected, but he had to admit—at least to himself—Brantley had a fucking point.

The shithead.

Chapter Six

Friday, July 22, 2022

MAGNUS KNEW TREY WAS COMING BEFORE HE stepped foot in the main office. For the better part of the day, Trey had been hanging out in the play yard with the dogs. And when he wasn't there, he was hanging out with Sarge and Aurora, taking them for walks, feeding them lunch, sneaking them treats when he thought Magnus wasn't looking. The guy spent more time lounging than he did working. Not that Magnus gave a shit. Trey had more than pulled his weight, stepping in at a time when Magnus would've let the entire place go to shit because he hadn't cared about anything but Ava.

Trey had cared enough not to let that happen. He'd been there throughout, learning the ropes, filling in when someone called in, and coming in early to relieve Billy and Gia from the night shift. According to Gia, Trey continued to apologize for dragging them down, but she didn't understand why. She'd told Magnus that he certainly didn't give himself enough credit. Magnus knew that to be true because that was the way Trey was. With everything. For the past four months, he hadn't missed a single day.

And come tomorrow, Trey would no longer be coming in. He was quitting.

If Magnus knew a way to keep him, both at the camp and in his life, he would be doing it now. Only he was at a loss because he didn't know why everything had gone to shit in the first place. One minute Trey was introducing himself as Magnus's boyfriend, the next, he was fucking him goodbye. Oh, yeah. Magnus had no doubt in his mind that the other night had been Trey's way of saying thanks for the good time but sayonara, asshole.

"I gave the evenin' meds," Trey drawled when he stepped into the office.

Magnus waited for Trey to look at him, but he didn't.

He knew now would be the time for him to throw himself on Trey's mercy and beg him to reconsider. If he didn't want to work here, so fucking what? Magnus didn't care one way or the other. Just as long as Trey didn't walk out of his life for good.

He just couldn't bring himself to grovel at Trey's feet. For one, when Trey Walker made up his mind about something, nothing short of a miracle was going to change it. And yes, Magnus was well aware that Trey quitting this job was a euphemism for their relationship. It allowed him to say goodbye without actually owning up to ending things.

Whatever.

For four months, with every step forward that Ava made, Trey had taken one step back. Although he didn't want to admit it, Magnus knew Trey had been on his way out from the very beginning.

Trey still wasn't looking at him when he said, "Anything else before I go?"

"No."

"Well ... later."

Magnus watched Trey walk out the door and right out of his life.

Two hours later, after he had spent more time than was necessary cleaning the kennels, Magnus forced himself to go to the house. He hadn't seen Ava in a few hours, and he figured she would be getting hungry by now. For the past couple of weeks, she'd been waiting for him to eat, and he'd enjoyed their time together.

Trey

Problem was, Magnus wasn't hungry. His stomach was twisted in knots. Or maybe that was coming from his chest. He didn't fucking know, and he damn sure didn't want to psychoanalyze it. He knew the reason, but there wasn't a damn thing he could do about it.

He started for the living room but stopped when he didn't see Ava sitting on the couch. Her blanket was draped over the quilt rack she'd insisted he buy. He headed down the hall, wondering if she was in the shower. The bathroom door was open, but no one was inside. He stepped across the hall and leaned toward Ava's door, listening for any sounds from inside. He figured if she was awake, he could check on her, but he didn't want to wake her if she was taking a nap.

He heard nothing from inside, so he moved to his bedroom. He needed a shower to clear his head. After that—

Magnus came up short when he opened his bedroom door and found Ava in his bed. Her eyes were closed, her back arched as she worked her hand inside her shorts. She was gasping and moaning softly, but rather than pleasure, it sounded like she was in pain.

Back up! Retreat!

Those were damn good instructions, but Magnus ignored his inner angel. The devil sawing that fiddle of gold on his shoulder was louder. He remained where he was, admiring her as she writhed and moaned, clearly desperate for release. His cock thickened in his shorts, tenting the loose fabric. If Ava were to look over, there would be no way he could hide what seeing her did to him.

He swallowed, releasing the doorknob. When he did, the damn thing sprung back, making a sound that had Ava jerking her hand out of her shorts, her eyes flashing open and slamming into him.

"Oh my God. Magnus. I'm... I know what this looks— I'm sorry."

He frowned, confused why she was gushing apologies. Rather than leave her with a bit of dignity, Magnus took a step forward. Then another and another until he was standing at the side of his bed.

She started to climb off on the other side, but he stopped her with a softly spoken, "Don't go."

Ava dropped back down to his pillow, her eyes imploring him, a plea in her gaze. He wasn't sure what she wanted him to do—let her leave or make her stay—but he knew he couldn't let her run and hide from him. If he did, they'd never get past the awkwardness of the moment.

Magnus put a knee on the bed and then crawled up beside her. He kept space between them, not moving against her the way he wanted to.

"I thought you were goin' out tonight," she muttered, clearing her throat.

"Nope." He let his eyes roam over every inch of her beautiful face. "Do you do this often? Masturbate in my bed when I go out?"

The color in her cheeks rose until they were nearly as pink as her perfect lips. "No. I've never. I promise."

"I'm not upset." He added a smile to reinforce his words. "Just curious. Why my bed?"

She shrugged and jerked her gaze away, staring up at the ceiling. She exhaled on a huff. "I wanted to come."

Magnus chuckled. "Clearly."

Her head turned, her eyes slamming into his face. "Don't laugh at me."

He schooled his expression.

She huffed again. "There's something you don't know about me."

"Then tell me," he urged.

"I've never..." Her sigh was less dramatic this time. "I've never had an orgasm before."

He masked his shock but barely. "Never?"

She shook her head and stared up at the ceiling. "Not by myself or with..."

He was grateful she didn't say his name. The bastard didn't deserve to be in a single one of Ava's memories, and he hoped like hell one day she could exorcise him from her dreams.

"I've tried ... in my room, I mean. Recently." She swallowed, her throat tightening with the movement. "But I still couldn't. Not even..."

"Not even what?" he prompted when she went silent.

Her voice was merely a whisper when she said, "Not even when you and Trey were in here fucking."

Magnus smiled. "You tried to get yourself off while you listened to us?"

"I didn't mean to," she said quickly. "It was after I saw you in the shower and…" She shrugged. "Doesn't matter. I think I'm broken."

"And you were in here *why*?" he asked again.

"Because I thought if I could smell you on your pillow…"

Jesus. Fucking. Christ.

Magnus had never heard anything quite so erotic in his life. The fact that this woman wanted to use him to get off… he didn't give a fuck if she merely liked the way he smelled.

"You're not broken, Ava."

"How do you know?" she blurted, looking his way again. "Maybe I am."

"I could prove it to you right now if you'd like me to."

Her eyes went saucer-wide, and there was a slight tremble in her softly spoken, "What?"

Magnus didn't move. He didn't shift even an inch as he held her gaze. "I could make you come. With my fingers or my mouth," he clarified.

Her eyebrows slammed down.

"I'm not talkin' about sex, Ava. I'm not expectin' anything from you. But I'll gladly make you come if you want me to. Just say the word."

AVA COULD NOT BELIEVE THEY WERE HAVING this conversation.

Hell, she couldn't believe she hadn't launched out of the bed and run out of the house screaming.

She'd never been more mortified than she was when she realized Magnus had caught her in his bed. The only reason she was still here was because … well, because he was Magnus. He was her friend, her confidant. He'd helped her through the most painful times of her life—losing Tabitha in the fire and Harrison's attempt to kill her. Sure, she liked to think that she'd helped him through some rough times, too. Like after his parents and his sister died. Ava had been there for him the same way he was there for her. She had held his hand at the funeral because he was the only person who truly understood the magnitude of her loss, although his was infinitely worse. She'd only been a kid at the time, but so had he.

They'd been friends through the years, and though she was gone for a few when she moved out of Embers Ridge, Ava came back as soon as she was old enough to drive. She'd visited a few times when she could borrow the car, helping out with the kennels just to spend some extra time with him. Then she'd come straight here after graduation because she'd wanted to see the smile on his face when she told him.

Ava had never expected anything more from Magnus, and she knew the same was true in reverse. They'd been friends, nothing more. Magnus had always been her one true anchor in the storm. He was the only person in the world she trusted implicitly. She knew he would never hurt her. He would never ask for anything she wasn't willing to give.

And here he was, offering to give her an orgasm. Her *first* orgasm. It was both humiliating and intensely arousing to think about.

Just say the word.

Because she couldn't find her voice, Ava did the only thing she could think of. She accepted his offer.

He made her feel bold, and she wanted to exert some of that courage she'd been working to build, so she moved slowly, sliding her thumbs into the waistband of her shorts and pushing them down, along with her panties.

She watched Magnus's face the entire time, saw the moment his attention shifted to see what she was doing. She also witnessed the gleam in his eyes, the way he drew his bottom lip in with his teeth. He wanted her, and while a few months ago that might've scared her, it didn't now. It actually made her feel good, powerful. In control for the first time in her life.

"Take them all the way off," Magnus whispered, his eyes meeting hers once again.

She held his stare, shoving her shorts down until she could kick them away. The amount of time it took felt like years, not seconds.

"Either take off your shirt or raise it over your tits."

She felt a gush of warmth between her thighs at his gruff command. Ava pulled the formfitting tank top over her breasts, but she didn't take it off. She wasn't wearing a bra because the straps on the tank top were too narrow, and it had one of those built-in bra things. Not that she needed a bra at all. Her tits were small enough that she could get by without one.

"Pull your feet up, knees toward the ceiling."

Ava wasn't sure what he was getting her to do, but she followed his direction.

"Now, drop your knees outward."

She slowly spread her knees apart, her left knee bumping his thigh as she did. The position put her most private parts on display, but it was the cool air caressing her sensitive flesh that made her gasp. The whisper of air over every inch of her made her tingle and had her nipples pebbling tightly. Had that been his intention? For her to experience the sensation? If it had, it worked, because she could feel the exquisite chill across her skin, and it heightened the arousal.

Magnus propped himself up on his elbow, resting his head on his hand. He didn't move closer, didn't reach for her, but now he had a better view of her intimate places.

"Now I want you to lightly tease your pussy with one finger."

She swallowed a moan. For whatever reason, hearing him say pussy turned her on. She'd always been prim; even Harrison had expected her to be. But deep down, she'd wondered about the opposite side of that coin. What it would be like for a man to whisper dirty, raunchy things while he did them to her. A man who wouldn't use her body against her but wanted to arouse and incite in equal measure.

Ava focused her eyes on Magnus's corded neck as she did what he asked. She grazed her labia with her fingertip, circling her outer lips and enjoying the sensation. She continued to do that, gradually moving closer to her slick inner folds. When she did, she gasped from the sensation but didn't stop teasing herself. She dragged her finger over her entrance, then higher toward her clit. She teased the nub briefly before sliding her finger back down and dipping the very tip inside herself.

"Are you wet?"

"A little," she admitted.

She wasn't sure when she'd started watching Magnus's face again, but Ava was entranced by the way his eyes followed the trail of her finger.

"Keep touchin' yourself," he drawled. "And I want you to imagine it's my finger, not yours."

She took a slow breath in as she closed her eyes and tried to envision him touching her. Although she was all too aware that her touch wouldn't be nearly as pleasurable as his, it worked. She could feel the slickness on her finger as she thought about Magnus's big finger teasing over her flesh.

"Now show me what you do to get yourself off," he instructed.

Ava turned her face toward the ceiling, keeping her eyes closed, as she began rubbing her clit, focusing all her attention on the sensitive nub. It felt good at first, but, like always, it soon felt more like a chore than sensual gratification.

"Ava."

The way he said her name made her clit throb. She opened her eyes and peered over at him, her hand stilling.

His eyes were hooded and hot. "Let me do it for you."

She nodded, her hand falling to her side.

"Whatever you do, don't close your eyes. I want you to watch every single thing I do. And if you want me to stop, tell me to stop."

She nodded again, propping her head up on his pillow as Magnus shifted closer.

He was fully dressed, but she could feel the warmth of his body beneath his clothes along her side. He wasn't pressing up against her, but he was close enough she could smell that woodsy scent she loved so much and hear his deep, even breaths.

Ava dragged in a deep breath when his work-roughened fingertip caressed her hip. He reversed the move, using two fingers, a light whisper along her skin. And once more, sliding his knuckles along her thigh. He continued to touch her, gently, slowly, until her breaths were ragged and her pussy was clenching with need. But she didn't say a word, didn't look him in the eye as he brought her body roaring to life.

She watched his sun-kissed hand move between her legs, his fingertips dragging over her flesh in a touch so light she could've imagined it. He circled her mound, teasing along the inside of her thigh where it met her hip. Because she was watching, she noticed how her hips flexed as she tried to get closer to his touch. If Magnus noticed, he didn't say a word. He simply continued to caress her until she was nearly panting.

When Magnus's finger glided along her slit, she heard his sharp inhale.

"You're so wet," he whispered, his tone almost reverent.

"It's because of you," she admitted.

His gaze briefly shifted to her face. He met her eyes, but then they lingered on her lips for another second before he peered down between her legs again.

Magnus did what she'd done earlier, coating her clit with her slick juices before gliding his finger down to her entrance. When he dipped the tip inside, she gasped.

"Hurt?"

"No," she exclaimed on a ragged exhale. "It feels good. So good."

She heard the change in his breathing as he began to finger her, gently pushing his finger inside, pulling it out. He did that for a minute, maybe two, before moving his finger to her clit. He applied the perfect amount of friction to have tingles erupting in her womb. It didn't take much before she was soaring toward that ragged cliff, clutching it because she didn't want to go over yet.

Magnus must've known because his finger returned to her entrance. This time he fucked her deeper, a little faster. Ava rocked against his hand, loving how he filled her. She'd never felt anything this good in her life.

"You like me fingerin' you."

It wasn't a question, but she nodded anyway.

"Let me show you somethin' else you'll like."

Ava wanted anything and everything he was willing to give her, but she kept that to herself as he pushed up onto his knees and positioned himself at the bottom of the bed, his shoulders between her legs. She stared down at his face as he breathed against her sex. She whimpered softly.

Magnus pushed two fingers inside her, causing her back to arch from the pleasure that obliterated her. Her pussy clamped onto the intrusion as she waited for the delicious friction. He held his fingers still for a moment, and she felt the brush of his tongue along her cleft. He licked higher, lightly grazing her clit, then more insistently. As he drew her clit between his lips, he began moving his fingers again. He didn't stop this time, fingering her while he flicked his tongue over her clit.

Ava gripped the comforter tightly as she bucked her hips toward his wonderful mouth. She began moaning in earnest as a steady tingling ignited in her core. It grew stronger and stronger as he fucked his fingers into her and suckled her clit. Warmth spread through her entire body, then the tingling followed until it branched out through her extremities. Her whole body was taut, her muscles locked as the sensation tore through her, wave after delicious wave. She thought it would never end, wished that it wouldn't, but eventually, it passed completely through her, and she was left panting and smiling.

Magnus pressed a kiss to the inside of her thigh, then returned to his spot on the bed where he'd originally started. He didn't touch her, but he was smiling as he watched her face.

"You are so beautiful when you come."

Ava smiled back at him. For the first time in a really long time, she felt beautiful. And she knew he was the reason.

Chapter Seven

BY THE TIME TUESDAY ROLLED AROUND, TREY was going stir-crazy. He'd spent the entire weekend tending to his house, cleaning out closets, throwing shit away. Not that he had a lot of stuff to begin with, but he did have a lot of junk he no longer needed. He figured there was no time like the present to make a fresh start.

And when he ran out of closets to declutter, he moved onto the kitchen cabinets, then into the garage. He got sidetracked in there, tinkering with tools. On Sunday, he mowed the lawn, and on Monday, he sat around and wondered what the fuck he was going to do with the rest of his life. Although he needed the brief reprieve, this wasn't something he could sustain.

So, he was thankful that he'd agreed to drive Ava to her therapy session. It gave him something to do.

On his way out of town, he stopped at the bakery for a cup of coffee and a chocolate croissant. He sipped the coffee on the way to Embers Ridge, wondering why he'd thought he needed the caffeine. He was jittery enough as it was, but he had no fucking idea why. It wasn't like he was the one who would be spilling his guts to a stranger.

When he arrived at Camp K-9, he noticed Magnus's SUV was gone. He was both grateful and disappointed by that. It meant he wouldn't have to (*or get to*) see him, something that he was conflicted about, obviously.

Ava came out of the house with a smile on her face, hurrying around to the passenger side of the truck. Today she wore a pair of denim shorts and a black and white checkered shirt with puffy sleeves and tapered over her belly. On her feet were a pair of black western boots. The mere sight of them flipped a switch inside him. For some damn reason, that was the sexiest fucking thing he'd ever seen a woman wear.

"You're in a good mood," he noted when she climbed in and put on her seat belt.

"Do you realize I haven't been away from this house for nearly five months? Of course I'm happy."

Trey smiled because her excitement was infectious. "Well then, I guess you don't need this," he said as he passed the paper-wrapped croissant to her. He was hoping that would be enough to keep her from wanting to have lunch. Trey didn't relish the idea of spending an hour alone with Ava. He wasn't sure his heart could handle spending time with a woman who was so close to Magnus, regardless of whether Trey considered her a friend.

Ava slowly unwrapped it, and her grin widened. "Did you know these are my favorite?"

He chuckled but didn't answer as he put the truck in Drive and pulled down the driveway back to the dirt road. He did know those were her favorite because she'd mentioned it during one of their conversations. He also knew she loved strawberry soda. When she'd revealed that tidbit, he'd told her she was probably the only person in the world who did.

Trey had listened when Ava spoke because he'd wanted to know more about the woman who meant so much to Magnus. And part of the reason he knew he had to end things was that, during those conversations, he realized that Magnus's love for Ava wasn't one-sided. She loved Magnus, too. Trey was pretty sure she always had.

"Well, if you don't mind, I'd like to save it until after the session. I figure I'll either need it for comfort or celebration. But thank you. That was very sweet."

Like she had the other day, Ava rested her hand on his arm. He cut his gaze to the console where her fingers rested, and he swallowed hard, turning his attention back to the road.

"Am I supposed to be nervous about this?" Ava asked once they'd reached the main highway leading back to Coyote Ridge.

"About therapy?"

"Yeah. Have you ever been?"

"A few times," he admitted.

"For a traumatic incident?"

Trey glanced her way briefly. "For couple's counseling. Before my divorce."

"Oh. I didn't know you'd been married."

"Long time ago."

When she didn't say anything, he offered some advice. "If you're puttin' in the effort to go, give it everything while you're there. Believe it or not, talkin' helps."

"Does it?" She sounded skeptical. "Is that the route you and Magnus plan to take?"

Trey's jaw clamped shut, a surge of anger darkening his mood. She had no right to confront him about his history with Magnus.

"I'm sorry," she said, although she didn't sound sincere. "It's just I know he's suffering right now."

"Is he?" Trey snapped. "He's got you to confide in, after all. It's what he's wanted all along."

Ava shifted in her seat, turning to face him, her voice softening when she asked, "What are you talking about?"

"Magnus loves you, Ava. Only a fool couldn't see it."

"Well, I guess I'm a fool then," she bit out. "I thought he was my friend."

Trey started to snap back at her but stopped himself. The last person he wanted to talk to about Magnus was the woman who'd stolen him away.

His thoughts came to a screeching halt. He hadn't even realized he'd laid any blame at her feet. After all, it was his decision to end things. He knew Magnus would've continued on like they were right up until Trey found himself in a threesome somehow.

"Trey, I'm sorry," she said sincerely, gently touching his arm. "It's not my place to talk about your personal business. It's just ... I care about both of you, and Magnus isn't happy, and I don't think you are either. Back when I first came to Magnus's, y'all were ... doing things all the time. But as I got better, it's like y'all drifted apart."

"Doin' things?" He had no idea what that even meant.

"Sexual stuff ... you know, like ... blow jobs and shit," she stammered.

Trey's jaw tensed again, and he swore his temperature skyrocketed.

"I didn't mean to invade your privacy, but y'all did a lot of *things* in the kitchen. I could only pretend to be asleep for so long. I promise, I never saw anything." She turned to look out the window. "Well, that's mostly true. There was the one time when Magnus was sucking your..." She waved it off. "And I did see Magnus in the shower the other day. He was ... you know. I didn't mean to watch, but I couldn't look away. Then when he said your name..."

What? For fuck's sake, don't stop now!

"Anyway, that *was* an invasion of privacy. I ran out of his room so fast ... and then you showed up a little while later, and I heard y'all through the walls."

So that's what had happened when Magnus came out of his room wearing only a towel. He'd been jacking off in the shower, thinking about him? And Ava had watched?

Jesus Christ.

"If it's any consolation, I thought it was hot."

He wanted to ask, *Which one? Magnus suckin' my dick or Magnus jackin' off?*, but managed to keep his lips clamped together.

Okay, now his cheeks were turning a ridiculous shade because this woman was talking about sex.

So why's your dick hard if you don't like it?

Trey ignored the stupid-ass voice. His dick was hard, but that was a natural reaction. It had absolutely nothing to do with this sweet young woman talking about Magnus blowing him or how she'd listened to them fucking.

Fuck.

"You don't like talking about this much, do you?"

"You think?" he muttered, keeping his eyes locked on the exit to Coyote Ridge.

Ava giggled softly. "You're adorable, you know that?"

He knew no such thing.

Twenty minutes later, after that fun—albeit slightly embarrassing—conversation with Trey, Ava was seated in the waiting area of Dr. Piper Briggs's small medical office as she came strolling down the hallway, peering at a chart in her hand.

When she looked up, she smiled softly. "It's nice to meet you, Ava. I'm Dr. Briggs."

Ava studied the woman who stepped into the reception area to get her. Neither of them made an attempt at a handshake. Ava would have, but her palms were too sweaty, so she settled for discreetly sliding them along her hips.

She had to admit Dr. Briggs was not at all what she expected to see. She'd been envisioning an older woman. One with gray hair and glasses, wearing a bright orange smock and Crocs on her feet. She had no idea where she'd come up with that ridiculous idea, but this woman was nothing like that.

Dr. Briggs was tall and nicely curved, and in those four-inch heels, she likely topped out close to six feet, if not more. Her hair was short, cut in a dramatic angled bob around her face that had her hair brushing her shoulders, but it was very short in the back. The style and the color made her gray eyes pop. Or maybe that was because of the black, rectangular-framed glasses she had on. She reminded Piper of a librarian. The kind men fantasize about.

"Come on back to my office," Dr. Briggs said.

Ava took a deep breath and stood up, following the doctor down a short hallway and into a large office.

Well, she assumed it was an office because there was a four-legged white desk on the far side of the room, beside it, a two-drawer filing cabinet. Both were tucked into the corner in front of a large picture window that looked out onto a courtyard decorated with rose bushes. The desk was clear of clutter, holding a small decorative lamp, a pen in one of those fancy holders that doubled as a picture frame, a laptop computer, and a thin vase with a single rose in it. The walls were painted a soothing taupe with crown molding at the ceiling and a narrow railing halfway down the wall that circled the entire room. It felt more like a conversational room in someone's house than a therapist's office. The rest of the space was a seating area. Two cream-colored leather couches faced each other on a large gray and cream rug. A coffee table in the middle held a single box of tissues, as did the side tables at each end of the couches. Two additional chairs were positioned near the ends of the sofas, facing each other.

"Are you expecting me to cry?" Ava asked.

Dr. Briggs glanced at her and smiled. "It is certainly not my intention to make you cry."

Ava could've told her she wouldn't, but even she knew that would be a lie. Any time she even thought about what had happened, tears pooled in her eyes.

"Please have a seat, Ava. Anywhere you'd like."

"Should I lie down?"

"If you'd like, but it's not required," she answered, her tone slightly amused and going a long way to putting Ava at ease. In fact, her entire demeanor put Ava at ease.

Ava chose to sit on one of the sofas, tucking herself in near the end. She made herself small, something she'd gotten used to doing over the years. As a kid, she did it in the hopes of not inciting her mother's mood. And after she'd married Harrison, she did it hoping she would become invisible.

Once Ava was situated, Dr. Briggs took a seat on the opposite sofa directly across from her. She crossed her legs at the knee and placed her hands in her lap. The entire time she watched Ava, smiling as she did.

"It's all right if you relax, Ava," Dr. Briggs urged. "We're only going to talk."

Ava nodded because that seemed to be the desired response.

"I'd like you to tell me why you came to see me today, Ava."

Ava wondered why the doctor repeated her name so often. Was it to make it personal? Or so she didn't forget her patient's name? And now she was purposely trying to stall, which seemed the opposite of her reason for being here. Trey's words whispered through her mind: *If you're puttin' in the effort to go, give it everything while you're there. Believe it or not, talkin' helps.*

Taking a deep breath, she decided to take his advice. "When I was released from the hospital, my doctor suggested I seek therapy to deal with the ... trauma."

Dr. Briggs had a notebook sitting on her lap. Ava could see there were some things written on it, but the woman didn't look down at it once. "And the trauma you endured ... is that something you'd like to discuss with me?"

"I thought that was the point."

Dr. Briggs smiled. "The point of therapy is to improve the quality of life. Our objective in these sessions is to discuss you and whatever issues you might have so we can address them and get you to a point where you can cope. With that said, I truly believe talking about what happened would be beneficial, but that's entirely up to you."

"Okay."

"Have you ever talked to anyone about what happened to you?"

"No." Ava hadn't even told the doctors because they had already been informed. At least to the point they knew she'd been beaten and left for dead in a field, which was enough for them to address her physical ailments.

"Why don't we make this an easy session?"

Ava snorted. "Easy?"

"Yes," Dr. Briggs said, her eyes kind. "Start by telling me about you. Your family, your friends, where you live."

"I'm twenty-four years old, and up until five months ago, I was married, living with my mother and my ... Harrison."

"He was your husband?"

Ava nodded.

"Why do you not want to refer to him as such?"

"Because I hate him," she admitted, hearing the fury in her tone.

"Very well."

Ava cleared her throat when Dr. Briggs watched her as though expecting her to continue.

"Anyway. Now I'm a widow, and I haven't gone back to my house because I can't stand the thought of going inside."

"How did you meet Harrison?"

"At school."

Dr. Briggs's eyes narrow slightly. "College?"

Ava shook her head. "No. High school. I was seventeen, just starting my senior year. It was a school function." She paused briefly, debating on how much she wanted to reveal. She sighed, letting Trey's words play in her head before continuing. "Career day, I think. There were a lot of people there to discuss our future and potential career opportunities."

"And he was there?"

Ava nodded. "He was."

"What was his job?"

"He was a state senator."

"And he was discussing careers in politics?"

"Honestly, I don't know. I wasn't paying much attention to any of them. It was my senior year. I was more worried about what my friends were doing after school that day than what I would be doing years from then." She chuckled softly, recalling how ridiculous she'd thought career day was. "I didn't meet Harrison at the presentation, but I remember seeing him. He smiled at me, and my friends said something about how hot he was. They were joking about how he was my chance to hook up with an older guy. Since I hadn't actually *hooked up*"—she used air quotes for emphasis—"with anyone at the time, I laughed it off."

Dr. Briggs continued to watch her, so Ava continued.

"I worked at a grocery store part-time after school and on weekends. I was trying to help my mother out. She worked—mostly odd jobs like cleaning houses or billing for small independent clients—but they never lasted long. She usually got fired after a few weeks. Her … uh … mental state didn't allow her to be prompt or consistent."

Dr. Briggs acknowledged her with a nod but didn't ask another question, so Ava continued.

"After my stepdad bailed, we moved into a one-bedroom apartment. It was the only thing we could afford and barely that." Realizing she'd gotten off track, she shifted back to Harrison. "A few days after the career thing, Harrison came through my line at the grocery store."

"Did he live in the area?"

"No." Ava glanced down at her hands because she knew which direction Dr. Briggs was headed, and she was right. "He was stalking me."

Dr. Briggs nodded. "And this is something you came to realize at the time? Or later?"

"Much later. In the beginning, I was flattered." Ava recalled how he'd flirted with her that day and how it had made her feel. She'd been walking on a cloud from his obvious appreciation. "Here was this sophisticated, wealthy older man who liked me. He took me on dates to fancy restaurants, gave me wine, bought me nice clothes and other gifts, told me he loved me. I fell hard and fast for him because it felt real to me."

"It wasn't real?"

Ava lifted her gaze to the doctor. "None of it was real. Harrison Rivers was a wolf in sheep's clothing, and I was the idiot who fell for his lies."

"First of all, I don't think you're an idiot, Ava. I think you were a young girl who got caught up in the romance. He did all the right things, said all the right things. Why *wouldn't* you take him at face value? After all, as you said, he was an older man, a state senator. Someone you were supposed to be able to trust."

Ava nodded her head as the tears dripped onto her cheeks. She couldn't stop them. "Whenever I think about how we met, I feel sick," she admitted. "I was so stupid. So naive. If only I'd been smart enough to see through his bullshit, none of this would've ever happened."

"None of what, Ava?"

"Everything." Ava grabbed two tissues, wiped her nose, and then clutched them in her hand.

"You mentioned your mother lived with you? Are you two close?"

Ava sobbed as she thought about her mom. Although Renee March had been sick for so long and Ava had been stressed from taking care of her, she missed her so much.

"My dad left when I was little. Then my mom met my stepfather. She seemed happy with him—at first—so I tried to be nice. He wasn't so bad, but I don't think he wanted kids. I got good grades, stayed outta trouble. He would go out a lot, so I kept her company. Eventually, he got tired of the long drive to work, so he moved us out of the house I'd grown up in. I had to change schools and move away from my friends.

"My mom pretended to like living in the city, but I could tell she didn't. I took care of her, made sure she took her medication and went to regular appointments. She was diagnosed with bipolar disorder. She'd be sullen or angry for days, and then suddenly, she'd be so excited she couldn't contain herself. She'd insist we go shopping and spend money we didn't have, or she'd call up old friends she hadn't talked to in years." Ava met Dr. Briggs's gaze. "I won't lie; I liked my mother during those … episodes, but I'd read up on the disease, so I knew it wasn't right.

"But the bad times outweighed the good. She tried to kill herself many times, starting when I was a little kid. My stepdad didn't last long. She would get mean when she was depressed. They fought all the time. Finally, he left. Said he wasn't cut out for family life. My mom fell into a deep depression. It lasted about a month, then one day, I came home to find everything in the apartment smashed to pieces. She'd graduated to anger. I tricked her into seeing a counselor. I told her it was for me. It helped a little. She was just coming around when I met Harrison."

"What happened to your mother, Ava?"

Ava looked up and met the doctor's kind eyes. "She killed herself. But not until *after* she killed the man who tried to kill me."

Dr. Briggs's expression remained unchanged. "Harrison Rivers?"

Ava wiped her nose. "Yes. I was lying in a hospital at the time, so I don't know what led up to that, but I figure she had stopped taking her medication. She told me she hated it, told me that Harrison was trying to kill her."

"Do you think he was?"

"No." Ava shook her head in emphasis. "Killing her would've removed his leverage over me. But he did have her medication changed to something that kept her out of it most of the time. Harrison didn't like my mother because she was an obstacle he couldn't eliminate. I refused to marry him unless my mother could live with us. He agreed but a week after we got married, he had her put in a hospital. Three months that time. She seemed better each time she came home, but then he would drug her again. He used her against me. Whenever I did something he didn't approve of, he would send her away. Always threatened to have her committed forever."

"What sort of things didn't he approve of?"

Ava smiled, but it lacked any humor. "It would be easier to tell you what he *did* approve. Nothing was good enough for Harrison. How I ate, how I spoke, what I wore. He didn't like that I slept on my stomach or the shampoo I used. He didn't want me talking to anyone because it would take time away from him. I wasn't allowed to go shopping unless he went with me, and he was too busy for that."

"He was controlling."

"He was a monster," Ava retorted, a violent rage coursing through her veins as she thought about him. "He told me what to do, where to sit, what to watch on TV. As soon as I graduated, he alienated me from all my friends. I got fired from my job at the grocery store because he stalked me all the time. One time he confronted a male customer in the parking lot. Accused him of flirting with me."

"How did you come to learn this? Were you there?"

"No, my manager told me. The customer came in later that week to complain."

"And what did your manager do?"

"He talked to me about it. Said he couldn't have his customers being accosted by my friends. That was the first time, though. When we were dating. It only got worse. Until finally, I got fired. Harrison was happy. That's what he wanted." She sniffled. "He wanted me all to himself even though the only thing I was good for was sex. And he controlled that too."

"Did he force himself on you, Ava?"

She shrugged. "Can it even be considered force? I was his wife. It was my job to do that for him."

"Ava, look at me."

Her chin trembled, but she managed to look at Dr. Briggs.

"No one has that right." Her eyes narrowed, her gaze laser focused on Ava's. "No one."

Ava nodded; once again, she didn't know how she was supposed to respond.

"If you hear nothing else I say today, Ava, I want you to hear that."

"But I let him."

"Did you?"

"Well, yeah, because if I didn't…" Ava hated thinking about what he'd done to her the first time she refused him.

"Look at me, Ava. What would happen if you didn't?"

"He would hit me, and then he would force me anyway. It was easier just to lie there."

"That's what's known as self-preservation, Ava. It doesn't mean you consented."

Ava nodded.

"I'm going to repeat myself: no one has that right, Ava. If it isn't consensual on both sides, it's rape."

Ava took in a deep, cleansing breath. She didn't know why hearing that relieved some of the tension, but it did. She'd always hated herself for giving in to Harrison, hated how he would blame her afterward. He would tell her she sucked in bed or that she was frigid and cold. He would slap her when he demanded oral sex because she would gag when he shoved his cock in her mouth. She hated the taste of him.

"Thank you, Dr. Briggs," Ava whispered, wiping her nose again.

"For what?"

"For saying that. I think I needed to hear it."

"And I want you to remember it."

Ava nodded, forcing a smile.

"Well, our hour is up, but I sincerely hope you'll be back to see me. I think we had a good session today, Ava."

Ava wasn't sure she'd say it was good, but she did feel marginally better.

Trey

"I think so, too," she said as she got to her feet and grabbed a couple more tissues to go.

Chapter Eight

TREY HAD BEEN SITTING IN HIS TRUCK, listening to the radio, when the door to Piper's office opened. Since her practice was in one of the few houses near downtown that had been converted into businesses, there wasn't much to look at, so when that door opened and Ava appeared, he sat up straight.

And a second later, when he saw her tear-ravaged face, he opened his door and got out, hurrying around to meet her in front of the truck.

"Hey," he greeted softly. "You okay?"

She wiped her nose with a tissue and peered up at him. It was then he noticed her eyes were clear, and there was a slight smile on her face. The tears were gone; only the light trails remained. Before he knew what he was doing, he was wiping one away with his thumb.

The moment he touched her, he felt something move through him. Trey couldn't explain it, didn't know if he wanted to. Her hand curled around his briefly, holding his fingers to her face, and he was positive he had stopped breathing. Maybe she did, too, because a few seconds later, Ava took a deep breath and released him. Trey let his hand drop, but that didn't eliminate the sensation that lingered inside him.

What the ever-lovin' fuck was that?

Thankfully, those words remained firmly planted in his head, not tumbling out of his mouth.

When Ava didn't say anything, Trey guided her to the passenger side and opened the door. He waited for her to get inside, but she turned to face him first.

He frowned, studying her face. "What's wrong?"

"Would you...?" She swallowed. "Would you hug me for a second?"

"Gladly," he said as he pulled her into him.

Trey was surprised by how well she fit in the circle of his arms. The top of her head didn't quite reach his chin, but he didn't mind. Her arms curved around his waist as she pressed her cheek to his chest and held on tight. Trey didn't move, didn't speak. He would gladly stand there for as long as she needed him to. Or until his legs gave out. Whichever came first.

Luckily, his legs weren't weak when she finally pulled back.

She smiled up at him and touched his beard-covered jaw with her cool fingers. "Thank you."

"Not sure I did anything, but you're welcome."

She laughed softly, then climbed into the passenger seat and gifted him with another smile.

Feeling strangely shaken by her, Trey closed the door and walked around to the driver's side. He got in, put on his seat belt, tried to get his chaotic thoughts in some semblance of order. He fumbled with the radio, anything to stall for a moment.

When he'd calmed down enough to focus, he put the truck in reverse and glanced over at Ava. "Do you need to stop anywhere before we head back?"

"I think I'm good for now. But I might take you up on that next time."

"So there's gonna be a next time?"

"I made an appointment for Thursday. Same time. Would you mind taking me?"

Trey peered over at her. "I wouldn't mind at all, but Ava, I think you should ask Magnus."

She frowned. "Why?"

"Because he's very protective of you, and I know he's worried."

"And how do you know this?"

Trey huffed a laugh. "Well, it could be the five text messages he's sent me in the past hour." He nodded in her direction. "You might wanna text him to tell him we're headin' that way."

She pulled out her phone, and Trey focused on the road.

The trip back didn't feel as long. Probably since there were no more conversations about sex. Trey had spent the better part of her hour with Piper thinking about what Ava had said. Not because he wanted to relive it but because he couldn't *stop* thinking about it. For the life of him, he couldn't figure out what was so intriguing about that conversation.

More importantly, he couldn't figure out why he couldn't stop thinking about *her.*

AS SOON AS MAGNUS RECEIVED THE NOTIFICATION that someone had come onto the property, a security measure he'd put in place to watch for clients, he headed from the main office and out into the parking lot. He'd been anticipating Ava's return, and he wanted to be there when she got back.

He could admit he was a little disappointed that Ava hadn't asked him to take her, but Magnus had kept that to himself. When she said she asked Trey, there'd been a warring sense of hope and anguish. The latter because she hadn't wanted him to be there, and the former because it meant that Magnus would be seeing Trey again. And maybe because it was a sign Trey and Ava were establishing a friendship.

Admittedly, Magnus had chickened out right before Trey was supposed to arrive and made an excuse to leave the property. Ava hadn't asked any questions, and it was a good thing because he couldn't have come up with a reason if she had.

Trey's truck appeared around a turn in the driveway. Seeing it made Magnus's chest tighten, but he ignored it. This wasn't about him or his feelings for Trey. This was about Ava and how she'd fared after her first session. She'd texted him to let him know they were on their way back, but she hadn't given any details about how it went.

Trey pulled the truck close to the house and got out. Seeing him had Magnus hesitating, watching as Trey came around to open Ava's door for her. He admired them both for a second before his feet got with the program. He made it a few steps but paused again when he saw Ava turning toward Trey, smiling up at him as she placed her hand on his cheek and leaned in, pressing her lips to his.

If he hadn't been standing still, he would've stumbled over his own two feet because what was likely meant to be a friendly peck … *wasn't.*

He noticed the way Trey's back tensed as his hand moved. Because the door was blocking his view, Magnus couldn't see what he was doing, but he imagined Trey had put his hand on her. Maybe her back or her leg. Then Trey's head tilted to the left while Ava's went opposite, and they leaned into each other.

Magnus pinched his arm and winced.

So this wasn't a dream? His ultimate fantasy was coming true? No. Couldn't be. Could it?

What the hell had happened during that session?

The kiss didn't last long, and when Ava pulled back, she stared up at Trey in surprise. Then her gaze darted toward him, and Magnus saw when she realized he was standing there.

Before he could ask her how the session went, she hopped out of the truck and raced inside without a backward glance. Trey was slower to move, closing the door as he stared at the back door of Magnus's house.

"What the hell was that?" Magnus asked, the words coming out harsher than he intended.

Trey turned to look at him, his eyes narrowed slightly. "I have no fuckin' idea."

"Did you kiss her? Or did she kiss you?"

"Yes?" Trey answered, staring blankly at him.

Magnus wasn't sure what he was supposed to say. Yes, he'd fantasized about this happening, but that was before Trey had dumped his ass. *Now* Trey wanted to explore his straight side with his … with Ava? No fucking way.

He wanted to lay into Trey to tell him to get the fuck off his property, but he was too pissed to form the words. Instead, he spun around and marched up the stairs and into the house, slamming the door behind him.

"Ava!"

"I'm right here," she said softly, her voice coming from his right.

Magnus looked over to see her leaning against the kitchen counter, a glass of water in her hand. The sun was shining perfectly through the picture window, highlighting her smooth skin and the gold in her hair. Just seeing her settled him.

"If you're gonna grill Trey over that kiss, you can save it. It was my fault, not his."

"I don't give a fuck whose fault it was," he snapped, then realized he actually did care. "What do you mean it was your fault?"

"I couldn't help myself." Her eyes lowered to the floor. "I can't even explain why I did it. I mean, of all the men in the world, you're the one I want to kiss, but then Trey was there, and I—"

"You want to kiss me?" Magnus interrupted, taking a step closer.

Ava peered up at him, her eyes widening. Was that fear? Or curiosity? He couldn't tell, but he didn't move any closer, not wanting to crowd her.

"Magnus, I've wanted to kiss you since I was ten years old," she said softly, holding his gaze as a smile pulled at her mouth.

"So why didn't you?"

Ava shrugged. "Because it would've been weird. You were too cool for me. Or you thought so, anyway. You would've yelled gross and called me names." She laughed. "Plus, Tabby hated when I told her how cute you were."

Magnus couldn't help but smile at that. He believed it.

"And I'd been telling her that since I was seven, and you used to call me a brat."

"You were a brat." He took a step closer. "A real pain in my ass."

Ava set her glass on the counter. "And what about now?"

Magnus closed the distance completely, holding her stare as he did. He kept his arms at his sides until Ava's settled on his hips. The moment she touched him, he cupped the side of her face and tilted her head back.

"You're still a brat, Ava," he whispered, sliding his hand to the back of her head, cradling it gently as he leaned down and fused his mouth to hers.

The world might've stopped spinning for those few moments as Ava's soft lips parted under his. When he licked into her mouth, and she met his tongue with hers, he had to lock his knees. A simple, sweet kiss from this woman made his cock harden behind his zipper. That had never happened before. Then again, the other women he'd kissed hadn't been Ava. His sweet, sweet Ava.

He could've kissed her for hours, but Magnus suspected her unusual behavior had something to do with her therapy session. Now was not the time to do something she might regret later, so he pulled back and stared down at her. He caught movement out of the corner of his eye and glanced out the window. Trey was still standing there, staring into the window. He looked ... well, Magnus wasn't sure how to describe it.

But then Trey dropped his head and shook it as he marched around to the driver's side of his truck. He got in and peeled out of the gravel drive a second later.

Ava's attention had shifted to the window, and the expression on her face was nothing short of horror.

"Oh, my God." She peered up at Magnus. "What did I do?" She put her hands on her cheeks and sidestepped him. "I can't believe I just did that."

Magnus couldn't quite understand why she was horrified. "What's wrong?"

"I kissed Trey, and then I kissed you."

"And?"

Ava spun around and put her hands on her hips. "Magnus Storme, don't be an idiot."

His mouth fell open, but he didn't know what to say. So Trey had seen them kissing. So fucking what? Magnus had watched *them*. It seemed only fair.

"Trey's gonna think I'm playing games," she said quickly.

"Are you?" He didn't mean to ask it like that, but it came out sounding as though he blamed her.

"Of course not." She frowned. "The last thing I want is to come between you." She waved her arm dramatically. "I already did that because I've overstayed my welcome. Y'all were happy before I came along."

Magnus snorted. "We were a lot of things, but I wouldn't go that far."

Ava's eyes narrowed. "But y'all were together."

Magnus shrugged. "Kinda."

"What does that mean?"

He turned and paced into the living room. "It was only supposed to be sex. That's what Trey wanted."

"Like a one-night stand?"

Magnus nodded, and a mirthless laugh escaped. "A series of them. Over a year and a half."

Ava laughed, a loud sound that made Magnus grin. "And *why* on earth would y'all let it go on that long?"

Magnus turned and met her gaze, his expression sobering. "Because I fell in love with him, and the thought of not seein' him… I wanted whatever he was willin' to give me."

Ava's smile fell, and her eyes softened. "And I screwed it up."

Shaking his head, Magnus moved toward her. He ignored his rule about touching her first as he put his hand on her hip and drew her toward him. "No, Ava, you didn't. Trey's had one foot out the door since the beginning. We weren't in alignment on what we wanted."

"Because you're bisexual?"

He shook his head. "Because I've always imagined bein' with a man and a woman to be happy."

"Isn't that the same thing?"

He smiled, loving her innocence. "No. Bisexual is when you're attracted to more than one gender. It doesn't mean you can't find happiness with one person."

Her forehead creased.

"You could fall in love with one person of any gender and be happy."

Understanding dawned on her face. "But you want to be with a man and a woman."

"It's not so much I want it, but I feel I need it."

"But you've never fallen in love with a woman."

Magnus held her stare, then decided it was time to tell her the truth. "Ava, I've been in love with a woman for a long, long time."

"Who?"

He canted his head, raising an eyebrow. He figured he could turn this into twenty questions until she figured it out for herself, but this conversation felt far too important for that. So he said, "You, Ava. I'm in love with you."

Her eyes moved over his face, but he could tell she was skeptical. Since he hadn't intended to push this issue, he pulled back and stepped away from her.

"I think I need some air."

He wasn't surprised that she didn't try to stop him.

RATHER THAN CHASE AFTER MAGNUS, AVA DECIDED to let him be. The conversation they'd just breached was far too important for them to hash out after her first therapy session. As it was, she felt raw and untethered. If she admitted to Magnus that she was in love with him, too, he'd think it was a result of her emotional turmoil.

She was certain of one thing: he would come back.

However, the same couldn't be said for Trey, so she grabbed her phone and pulled up his name on the text app. He'd given her his number a long time ago in the event she needed him while he was working. The message thread was lengthy because when she got bored, she would text him inane things with the sole intention of making him smile. And believe it or not, sometimes he would do the same.

Based on what she'd done, she wasn't sure she'd ever get another text message from Trey, period, but she sure as shit was going to try.

Knowing it was a long shot, she went with: *Would it be possible for you to come back? I really think we need to talk about that kiss.*

She eased onto the edge of the couch and stared at her phone like that might make him respond faster. It didn't help, but fifteen minutes later, she did get a message.

Trey: *Nothing to talk about.*

Ava: *Please don't be like that.*

Trey: *Be like what? You kissed me. I kissed you back. No big deal.*

Ava: *It's a big deal to me.*

Trey: *Doubtful since a minute later, you were kissing Magnus. I've got nothing left, Ava. Let it go.*

Ava stared at her phone in horror as she read the message several times. It was true. She had kissed Trey and then Magnus, but in her defense, she'd wanted to kiss them both. She hadn't done it to get Magnus to kiss her. She'd kissed Trey because she couldn't help herself. It wasn't until the drive to the therapist that she realized how much she missed him. He'd only been gone for a few days, but when she'd seen him every single day for months on end, it felt like an eternity. And then, when she'd watched him blush as she boldly talked about a subject that had her belly twisting with anxiety, she'd been smitten. Trey Walker was not like other men. He was kind and sensitive, and his heart was so much bigger than his ego. How could she not fall in love with that?

Her head jerked up, and she stared at the wall. What now? In love with him?

Could she really be?

Because if that was the case, that meant she was in love with two men. Magnus *and* Trey.

Oh, boy. This probably wasn't going to go over well with Trey *or* Magnus. Or her therapist, because God, Ava was going to have to talk this out with someone, and since Trey didn't want to talk and Magnus didn't want to talk...

She sighed and flung herself back on the couch. Maybe this was some sort of medical-related Stockholm syndrome. Instead of falling in love with her captor, she'd fallen in love with her saviors. Was there another term for that? More importantly, what was she going to do now? Tell them? She didn't see that getting her very far.

"It could be worse," she muttered to herself. "You could be waking up wrapped in a rug out in a field."

Ava giggled hysterically as she briefly wondered whether she was insane. No way was she joking about that horrific event. It was way too soon for that.

Right?

An hour later, after she'd started a load of laundry, emptied the few dishes from the dishwasher, and had a brief text conversation with Gloria Steiner, the woman who had taken her in and protected her until Magnus and Trey found her, Magnus returned. Ava had no idea where he'd gone, nor did she ask. He no longer looked like he wanted to crawl in a hole, so she considered that a good thing. But the words that came out of his mouth certainly didn't make her feel better.

"I really didn't mean to lay that on you like that."

"What? That you're in love with me?" she teased, hoping to get a smile from him.

It didn't work.

"I swear to you, I won't—"

"I love you, too, Magnus. I always have. I figured you knew that already."

His mouth remained open as though his words were stuck on his tongue, and he didn't know whether to spit them out or swallow them. Ava waited patiently, wanting him to say *something*.

This time when he didn't speak, it was so much better, because Magnus moved toward her, cupped her cheek, and pressed his mouth to hers. It was soft and sweet, and she relished the warmth of his body, wrapping her arms around him because she wasn't ready for him to stop.

"What do you say we sit on this conversation for a day," she suggested when he pulled back and stared down at her. "We can talk about it more tomorrow."

He nodded. "You want me to order somethin' for dinner?"

"I was thinking more along the lines of I would make a grilled chicken salad."

As she'd expected, Magnus grumbled, but it did put him in a better mood.

Chapter Nine

Thursday, July 28, 2022

"IT IS VERY GOOD TO SEE YOU again, Ava," Dr. Briggs greeted when she came out to the reception area to call Ava back to her office. "How have you been since we talked on Tuesday?"

Ava noticed that Dr. Briggs was more at ease with her today. Not quite so stoically professional.

"Pretty good," she admitted as they stepped into her office. "I started working full-time, so I feel like I'm making a contribution to society again."

Dr. Briggs paused at the seating area and gestured for Ava to pick a spot. "Where do you work?"

Ava went to the same spot she'd sat in the last time. "Camp K-9. It's in Embers Ridge. It's a doggy daycare. They also board dogs and train search and rescue dogs and their owners."

"I know the place," Dr. Briggs said with a smile. "My cousin's married to one of the owners of Dead Heat Ranch, which is not too far from there. I've seen the Camp K-9 sign. Do you like it there?"

Ava smiled, and it was genuine. "I love it. I've wanted to work there since I was a kid. My best friend's dad owned it. Back then, it was Storme Kennels."

"It changed ownership?"

Ava shook her head. "Magnus changed the name when he expanded."

"Who's Magnus?"

"He's Tabby's older brother."

"And Tabby would be?"

"His younger sister?" Ava teased.

Dr. Briggs caught on to her game and smiled.

Ava decided to elaborate. "My mom and I lived next door to the Stormes when I was a kid. Before my stepdad made us move. Anyway, Tabitha was my best friend growing up. We did everything together. We were in the same class. My mom was friends with her mom. They would drink coffee together and talk a lot. My mom was happier then." She smiled at the memory. "I would hang out at Tabby's house a lot because my mom didn't like a lot of kids in our house. Or that's what she said." Ava's smile fell away.

"Are you still friends with Tabby?"

Ava shook her head. "Tabby and her parents died when a space heater caught on fire. Magnus was at a friend's house that night. That's why he's still alive."

"How old were you when this happened?"

"Eleven." Ava swallowed the lump in her throat. "I still miss her. I think about her all the time."

"She's a fond memory. That's natural," Dr. Briggs noted. "How long did you live there after that?"

"Not long. A couple of years, I guess. I got to go back to visit a couple of times when I could talk my mom into taking me."

"Visit who?"

"Magnus."

"You remained friends with Tabitha's brother?"

Ava nodded, another smile creeping up. "I kinda had a crush on him when I was little. I had this dream that one day we'd get married and live there and run the kennels together. He's always been there for me, even after Tabby died. He's a couple of years older than me, but that didn't matter to him. He still befriended me, checked in on me. When Harrison would ... when I needed to get away from Harrison, I would go see Magnus because he's always felt like my safe place."

Ava looked at Dr. Briggs. "Magnus is the one who found me. He's the one who put together a search party to look for me."

"He sounds like a good friend."

"He's more than that," she mused. "He stayed with me at the hospital and took me to his house once I was released. He's taken care of me. Got me to and from doctors' appointments, made sure I took my medicine, fed me soup, and bought me ice cream when I asked for it." She laughed. "He's been like a mother hen this whole time. I don't know where I'd be without him."

"He cares for you," Dr. Briggs acknowledged.

"He's in love with me," she admitted. "He told me so."

Dr. Briggs didn't say a word, merely continued to watch her.

"He's a good man," she tacked on quickly. "He doesn't hold me back. He takes care of me. He let me have a job, and the only thing he asked in return was that I see a therapist. He wouldn't let me work until I made an appointment."

"Why do you feel the need to defend Magnus to me?"

"Because I know what you're thinking."

"And what would that be?"

"That he's taking advantage of me. That he's using me." Ava huffed. "He's not. I can't even get him to kiss me."

"Do you want him to kiss you?"

"More than anything. Especially after he *did* kiss me. But it was only one time. Since then, he's kept his distance."

She decided to leave off what had happened when he found her in his bed. Since they hadn't discussed it since then, she was under the impression that Magnus had chalked it up to a one-time thing. Truth was, Ava had been thinking about it endlessly ever since, and she was constantly wishing for a repeat.

Ava sighed. "I kinda think he only kissed me because he saw me kiss Trey."

"And who is Trey?"

"A friend."

"And do you have romantic feelings toward Trey?"

"Yes, but…"

"But what, Ava?"

She exhaled slowly. "Magnus isn't only in love with me."

"He's in a relationship with someone else?"

"He was," Ava clarified. "They broke up. Things were tense for a while but now…" She looked down at her hands, wringing them in her lap. "I'm the reason they broke up."

"Because he's in love with you?"

"Because he's in love with both of us, but Trey … that's the man he loves … can't accept that Magnus is bisexual."

Dr. Briggs was silent for a moment. She looked like she was trying to piece it together, so Ava waited.

"Okay, help me understand. Magnus is in a relationship with Trey? But they recently broke up, and you kissed Trey?"

"It sounds bad when you put it that way, but yes."

"When you say Trey can't accept that Magnus is bisexual, what do you mean by that?"

"Trey is gay, so he's never been with a woman before."

"But you kissed him?" Dr. Briggs's eyebrows dipped low. "I'm not sure I follow."

"Magnus wants to be with a man *and* a woman. He says that's the only way he'll be truly happy."

"You're avoiding the question, Ava. You're going down a different path. But do you believe Magnus when he tells you that?"

"He's stood by that for as long as I can remember. We've talked about it before. At first, I didn't understand, but then it made sense to me."

"When did it make sense to you?"

Ava remained silent for a minute. She knew how to answer that question but wasn't sure if she should.

"Ava?"

She looked up. "It made sense to me when I realized I'd fallen in love with both of them."

"So you're in love with Trey and Magnus? Have you spent a lot of time with Trey?"

"He's been taking care of me, too. He's been helping out at Camp K-9 so Magnus could stay with me. But he would watch over me at night sometimes so Magnus could sleep. We've talked. A lot. He drove me here. The other day, I mean." She looked up to see Dr. Briggs watching her closely. "It's not weird," she defended. "To be with more than one person."

"I didn't say that it was."

"But you're looking at me like that."

"Like what?"

Ava shrugged, unable to describe it.

"I know many people in relationships with more than one person, Ava. I don't judge anyone for their choices. It isn't my place."

Ava huffed. "It doesn't matter anyway. It's not like I can be with Trey."

"Why not?"

"Because I'm the reason they broke up."

"How is it your fault?"

"I kissed Trey," she said softly. "And now he won't talk to me."

"Is he angry?"

Ava shrugged. "I think he's confused."

"Because he's gay? Or because he likes you, and he's not sure how to deal with that?"

"Maybe."

"Ava?"

She looked up at the doctor.

"It sounds to me like Magnus and Trey are very important to you."

"They are."

"You said that Magnus won't kiss you because he's in a relationship with someone else. Only they aren't in a relationship anymore."

Ava nodded.

"This has me wondering. Do you think Magnus doesn't kiss you because he's looking out for you?"

Ava considered that for a moment, and then it dawned on her. "He's scared of me."

Dr. Briggs's smile returned. "I'm not sure he's scared *of* you, but maybe he's concerned *for* you. You said it yourself, he's been taking care of you, and you've known him for a long time. Did he know Harrison?"

Ava nodded. "They were never formally introduced, but they knew about the other. And then Harrison tried to frame Magnus for my murder. Only I wasn't dead."

Dr. Briggs's expression shifted, but before she could go down *that* path, Ava tacked on, "But I'm not ready to talk about that."

"Okay. You mentioned that you would see Magnus when you needed a friend."

"I knew he'd be there for me."

"So Magnus was aware of what you were going through with Harrison?"

Ava nodded. "He tried to get me to leave him. I wanted to. I really did. But Harrison used my mom against me. I couldn't leave. He said he'd kill her if I did."

"Have you talked to Magnus about what happened? About how he felt when he was looking for you?"

Ava frowned. "No."

"Maybe you should. It might help if you understood what he experienced during that time. It sounds like he might be taking things slow because he doesn't want to scare you."

"Magnus is the one person I trust most in this world," she countered. "He'll never hurt me."

"I didn't say he would. I'm saying he might be worried that you're not ready for a real relationship with him."

Ava shook her head. "No. It's because I'm the one who broke him and Trey up. I'm the reason Trey left. And now Magnus is just dealing with that loss."

"You take the blame for a lot of things, Ava."

"Only when it's my fault," she argued.

"Only when you *think* it's your fault," Dr. Briggs corrected. "If you haven't had this conversation with Magnus or with Trey, how can you be certain you're the reason?"

"Because I'm still there, and Trey's not," she snapped.

"From what I'm getting from you, I think there are two separate issues here. One, you've got feelings for both Magnus and Trey. And, for whatever reason, they've separated. And two, your relationship with Magnus isn't progressing as you'd like it to."

Ava considered that. "Yes. And my relationship with Trey is deteriorating."

Dr. Briggs's nodded, but she didn't chime in.

"I know we need to talk about what happened," Ava admitted. "It's just ... really hard for me to think about it. It's bad enough I have nightmares. I wake up screaming most nights, and Magnus has to console me. If I ask him to, he'll sleep on the couch with me."

"Why on the couch?"

Ava shrugged. "I guess that feels like neutral ground."

"Who's determining what is neutral ground?"

"I don't know what that means?"

"Who's suggesting that you sleep on the couch?"

"Me."

"Do you have your own bed at his house?"

"My own room," she clarified. "Magnus cleaned it out and bought me a bed so I'd have some privacy."

"What's the difference between having Magnus stay with you in the bed versus on the couch? Why do you choose the couch? Because it's neutral ground?"

"Yes."

"So, in a sense, could it be that you're keeping Magnus at arm's length?"

Ava stared in surprise. She hadn't thought about it that way. But she could see how Magnus might misconstrue it. "I hadn't considered that," she admitted.

"I think it's important for you to sit down and talk to Magnus about what happened. You might learn a few things about what he went through during that time. And vice versa. If you think he's making assumptions, then it's important for the two of you to clear the air and put your feelings all on the table. Otherwise, you'll be stuck in this vicious cycle until you do."

"How did it go?" Magnus asked when Ava came out of Dr. Piper's office.

Ava's response was a shrug of her shoulders as she got into his SUV and put her seat belt on.

"Is something wrong?"

"No." The response was curt, and he noticed she was looking anywhere but at him.

"Ava?"

"Could we please just go home?" She frowned. "I mean back to your house."

He wanted to tell her that she'd had it right the first time, but he kept his mouth shut. Whatever had transpired during that hour had put her in a sullen mood.

"Okay."

They made the thirty-minute trek not speaking. At one point, Ava turned the radio on, which did nothing to ease the tension filling the car. Magnus wanted her to open up and talk to him, but he didn't know what the protocol was. Could he ask her what had happened? Did he really want to know?

Magnus managed to stay out of Ava's way for the better part of the evening. When they got back, he went to work at the camp, helping with the evening chores. He stayed long after Gia left and waited until Billy could settle in for the evening. He was on for the overnight shift, and though Magnus had considered offering to fill in, he decided against it. He needed to talk to Ava, and if he put that off for too long, it would only put a wedge between them.

"Night, Billy. Holler if you need anything."

"Will do."

Magnus stepped outside into the humid summer night. The daytime temps were soaring into the hundreds, and the nights weren't getting much cooler. It was so hot they were resorting to letting the dogs play in the training room to keep them from getting dehydrated. And they were utilizing the swimming pool more often. Granted, it wasn't really a swimming pool since the deepest part was only two feet, but the dogs whose owners allowed them to play in it had a good time. Between splashing in the water and running through the water fountains, they found ways to entertain themselves.

But the pool was closed, and the dogs they had in residence were winding down for the evening. Sarge and Aurora were keeping Billy company, as they'd done for the past five months. Before Ava's *incident,* for lack of a better word, both dogs had spent all their spare time with him. They'd stayed at the house when Magnus was in it and at the camp when he wasn't. He'd had to stop doing that when he brought Ava back here because he hadn't wanted them to be in her way. Now he missed their company, more so because he spent his nights alone.

Magnus stepped into the house to find most of the lights had been turned off. The sun was still out, but the shadows were growing as night fell. The kitchen was dark because Ava had drawn the shades. The only light was coming from the lamp in the living room.

He headed that way and found Ava sitting on the couch, staring blankly at the darkened television.

"Ava? Are you okay?"

She slowly peered over at him. She looked surprised to see him.

He moved toward her, taking a seat on the couch, ensuring he left plenty of space between them. "What's wrong?"

Her pretty blue eyes leveled on his face for a moment. "Dr. Briggs told me we need to talk about what happened."

Magnus knew she was referring to *the incident*. That's what he'd been referring to it as because he didn't know how else to. The newspaper articles called it the attempted murder of Ava March. Every time Magnus even thought about the fact Harrison Rivers had attempted to kill her, a red haze clouded his vision. So he'd dubbed it *the incident*, although it seemed lacking in so many ways. The reality of it was it was a moment in time that had forever altered Magnus. Not nearly as much as it had impacted Ava, but he could admit—at least to himself—that he was having a difficult time coming to terms with it. He hadn't discussed it with anyone. Not even with Trey. Since neither of them had brought it up, Magnus figured Trey was burying it the same way.

"What would you like to talk about?"

Her forehead creased. "I didn't say I *wanted* to talk about it. She said we should."

Magnus held her gaze, not sure what to say to that.

Ava sighed, leaning into the cushion and turning her attention back to the TV. "Are you scared of me, Magnus?"

"What?" Now he was confused.

"Are you scared to touch me? To *be* with me?"

"I don't know what you mean." Fine, that was a deflection, but Magnus didn't think they needed to have a discussion about this. Of course, he should've expected Ava to bring it up. She'd always been that way. No topic was off-limits with her. As a kid, she was always asking questions, wanting answers. Didn't matter if the subject made others uncomfortable, she would still ask.

"Do you think I'm damaged?" she blurted, this time confronting him eye to eye.

Magnus opened his mouth to speak but snapped it closed.

Ava's eyebrows angled downward slowly as her eyes danced over his face. "You do," she whispered.

He shook his head. "That's not true." Not entirely, but he had no idea how to tell her that he would never forgive himself if he pushed for something she wasn't ready to give. They'd spent enough time together these past five months, he knew she thought she owed him something for taking care of her. Not sex, but something. And the last damn thing he wanted was for Ava to think he wanted her because of that. He wanted her, yes, but that wasn't new. He'd wanted her for years, and taking care of her had only made him fall in love with her more, but it certainly wasn't the reason he was in love with her.

"He didn't break me, Magnus," she said, her tone stern. "Harrison. He hurt me, yes. But he didn't break me. I'm not damaged goods."

"I didn't say that," he countered, feeling her ire rise.

"You don't have to. You tell me every time you refuse to touch me. You won't hug me unless I instigate it." Her eyes snapped down to the cushion between them. "You won't even sit by me until I ask you to or I move toward you."

Magnus didn't know what to say to that because she was right. He kept his distance for her benefit, not his own.

"I know there's a difference between you and Harrison. A significant one. I don't cringe when you come into a room, and I don't expect you'll raise a hand to me if I piss you off. I *know* you won't. And it hurts my feelings that you could even think I would."

"I don't think that," he snapped. "I've never thought that. But Ava, what he did to you..."

"You mean when he strangled me and left me for dead in a field?" she shouted.

Magnus flinched, the memory of how she'd looked when they found her made his throat close. He could still see the rope burn around her neck. It was the first thing he'd noticed when they'd found her at Gloria Steiner's house.

"Or when he raped me every single night I lived in that house with him because he said I was his wife and I owed it to him?"

Magnus kept his ass on the cushion, but he wanted to jump to his feet. He wanted to dig Harrison's cold, dead body out of the ground and beat the shit out of him because the bastard hadn't deserved to die the way he had. Being shot in the head while asleep had been a mercy the man damn sure didn't deserve. He hadn't paid for what he'd done to Ava. Magnus hadn't even gotten the chance to make the bastard pay for it.

And to top it off, his own family had distanced themselves. Harrison's father had made a blanket statement to the press, not confirming or denying whether they believed he was at fault. The only positive was they hadn't pointed the finger at Ava. If they'd done that, Magnus would've lost his shit.

"I hated him with a vengeance, Magnus," Ava said, her tone softer. "I wanted to leave him every single day, but I couldn't. He threatened to kill my mother, and forgive me, but I believed he would."

Magnus swallowed past the constriction in his throat.

"I don't want to spend the rest of my life remembering all that," she stated firmly. "I want to move on, and I thought I was gonna do that with you. I thought that's what you wanted."

"It is," he said quickly. "It's all I've ever wanted."

"So why won't you touch me?" she repeated, her words more of an accusation than a question.

He couldn't come up with a reason.

"What you have with Trey—"

"Had," he corrected.

Ava's expression softened. "That's what I want, Magnus. I want that undeniable chemistry. I want a man who walks in the door and can't keep his hands off me because I can't keep my hands off him. Do you know how many times I've fantasized that you come home and I'm in the kitchen making dinner? You spin me around and kiss me so hard I'm breathless. And then you strip off my shorts, pick me up, and set me on the counter so you can do to me what you did the other day. *That's* what I think about when I think of you, Magnus. I don't expect you to be gentle, because I know that when you take me, it's because you *want* me, not because you want to control me."

Now Magnus had that image in his head, and he'd be damned if his cock didn't harden.

"Once, I even imagined that..." She stopped herself and took a deep breath. "I saw you once. When you were sucking Trey's cock. It was an accident, but I saw you. I couldn't look away. I was fascinated by it. The hunger I saw on his face as he stared down at you. I fantasized that I was on my knees beside you, and we were both giving him pleasure."

"Ava..." Magnus wasn't sure he could handle more of her fantasies.

"I'm not broken, Magnus." She lifted her arms and then dropped her hands in her lap, staring down at them. "I'm really not."

"I know."

She didn't look up or acknowledge that he'd spoken. "You think I ask you to sleep on the couch with me because I don't want to be in a closed room with you. "

Since she didn't ask a question, he didn't answer. She was right, though. He had come to the conclusion that Ava felt safer with him on the couch than in her bedroom. It made perfect sense considering all she'd been through.

"That's not why I suggest the couch." She glanced at him from beneath her lashes. "It's because my bed is too small, and I don't want you to think I'm assuming anything if I ask to sleep in your bed with you."

He inhaled sharply. That had never occurred to him at all. There'd been so many times, at least recently, when he'd wanted to suggest they go to his bed so she could be more comfortable. He hadn't, and he never would have because Ava's sense of security was the only thing that mattered to him.

"What I'm trying to tell you is that I want you, Magnus. And I want you to want me, too."

She continued to stare at him, but he wasn't sure what she wanted him to say. He wanted her more than his next breath, but he didn't want to rush things. He'd learned what happened when he did that. Look at what had happened between him and Trey. They'd lasted for a year and a half because Magnus had been the one to pursue Trey.

And in the end, it had backfired in his face. Trey didn't want him because he didn't understand him. He knew he wouldn't survive if Ava came to that same conclusion later on down the road.

Ava sighed softly, then got to her feet. "Good night, Magnus."

He was still rattled, staring after her as she disappeared down the hall and into her bedroom.

Chapter Ten

Saturday, July 30, 2022

By Saturday night, Trey was getting on his own nerves. He'd spent the entire week wallowing in self-pity to the point he wanted to punch his whiny ass in the face.

Since he didn't care to get drunk alone—something he'd stopped doing a long time ago when he'd acknowledged he was on a downward slide—he decided to head down to Moonshiners. Saturday nights were the busiest for the bar, so there was a good chance he would see someone he knew. At least this way, he could play pool and carry on a conversation with someone other than himself and have a beer or two.

When he arrived a little after nine, the parking lot was full, the bar bustling. Several people on the makeshift dance floor were attempting to line dance to "Achy Breaky Heart" while onlookers cheered them on. All the stools at the bar were occupied, and there were groups crowded around the pool tables. Looked like he'd made the right decision tonight.

Trey made his way to the bar, skimming all the faces to find someone he knew, and that's when he saw them. Evan Vaughn, Slade Elliott, and the new guy, Atticus James, were sitting at a table near the back wall, engaged in conversation. Slade was grinning ear to ear while Atticus was talking. Evan looked like he wanted to be anywhere else, so Trey decided to head over, figuring he could give his old partner an out if he wanted one.

"Thanks, Rafe. Start a tab for me, will ya?" Trey told the bartender as he took the cold bottle and sauntered toward the back.

Evan's gaze landed on him first, his surprise there one second, gone the next. Trey grinned, lifting his bottle in greeting.

"Well, look who it is," Slade said with a shit-eating grin. "How the hell've you been, man?"

"Good." It was a harmless lie. "You?"

"Same ol' same ol'." Slade nodded to Atticus. "You remember the new kid."

"Kid, my ass." Atticus snorted, his eyes shifting to Trey. "I figure twenty-five's old enough to know better, young enough to do him anyway."

Ah, hell. Atticus had looked right at Trey when he said *him*. And since that's not how the saying went, Trey got the impression that Atticus was flirting. It wouldn't have been more obvious if he'd used *you* instead of *him*. He'd heard Reese grumble about Atticus a few times in recent weeks, claiming the guy had no problem openly flirting with Brantley. Reese had said the kid wasn't a real threat because he understood Brantley was spoken for, and Trey had believed him. More so when Reese relayed how his mother had hit Atticus over the head with a baseball bat the first time she saw him. Reese told him he used that to warn Atticus off anytime he started crossing the line.

The kid was obviously a natural flirt, especially since that gleam in his eyes said he was looking to throw caution to the wind tonight.

Trey took a pull on his beer and quickly assessed him. He was damn easy on the eyes with dark hair—floppy on top, tapered at the sides and back—and those mischievous green eyes. A couple of years ago, Trey would've found him just perfect for a night of sin and debauchery. These days, he didn't find even the prospect appealing. He preferred dark hair and hazel eyes with a body built to take everything Trey could dish out. This kid looked like he'd blow away in a stiff breeze.

"Magnus with you?" Evan asked, dragging Trey's attention back.

"Pull up a chair," Slade insisted before Trey could answer.

He started to reach for one at the next table, but Atticus beat him to it, pulling it over and gesturing for him to sit. If he thought that gesture was gonna get him laid tonight, the kid had better think again.

"I honestly don't know," Trey told Evan. "Probably at home."

"How're things at Camp K-9?"

Trey shrugged and bided some time by drinking his beer. "I quit workin' there last week." When Evan's muddy brown eyes turned curiously concerned, Trey tacked on, "Ava's all healed up, so Magnus came back to work. I was only helpin' out temporarily."

It was the same thing he'd told his brother, and while it wasn't the whole truth, it wasn't a lie either. Perhaps he'd hoped things might progress with them to the point he could become a permanent fixture. But then he'd basically sat back and watched Ava and Magnus fall in love with each other right before his eyes. Taking his leave seemed like the better option.

Then how the fuck do you explain that kiss?

Trey downed half his beer to drown out that fucking voice. The last thing he wanted to do was think about how Ava's kiss had knocked him for a fucking loop. It'd been unexpected, but his reaction to it more so. Since then, he'd found himself daydreaming about shit he had no business even thinking about.

"How're things at the office?" Trey asked, quickly changing the subject.

"Same ol' shit, different day," Slade answered.

"Is that your answer for everything?" Evan grumbled.

"What?"

"Same ol' shit," Evan drawled, mimicking Slade's laid-back country twang.

"It's true, ain't it?"

Trey smirked as he watched the interaction between the two. He'd heard that Slade and Evan had partnered up on the task force after Trey left. Evan was the silent, brooding type, and Slade the outgoing, never-met-a-stranger kind. The two mixed about as well as oil and water except when it came to solving cases. They had a knack for uncovering things no one else thought to look for.

The four of them spent the next couple of hours shooting the shit while Trey sucked down one beer after another. His limit of three had gone out the window when he saw a petite blond who reminded him of Ava wearing those damn cowboy boots. Since she strolled into the bar, Trey's thoughts had gone off the rails. He was doing his best to drown out the noises in his head, the ones telling him he should check in with Magnus, see how Ava was doing. He hated how he'd left things with her, brushing off her text message like it didn't matter. Truth was, he'd been as conflicted about that kiss as he was with how things ended with Magnus.

And while he was getting three sheets to the wind, Trey avoided Atticus's blatant advances. If he'd thought for one second the kid wasn't playing with him, he would've quickly put him in his place. But something told Trey that Atticus enjoyed the banter far more than he would enjoy anything else. Brantley had mentioned he was a lone wolf, but he didn't go into details. Since Trey had no desire to get cozy with anyone right now, he settled for pretending not to notice.

Like all good times, they eventually came to an end. Since Trey'd had far too much to drink to get himself safely home, he requested an Uber and let the sober driver get him from the bar to his house. He could huff it into town tomorrow to pick up his truck or, worst case, call one of his kin to drive him.

As soon as he stepped into the house, he began stripping off his clothes, eager to land face-first in bed so he could sleep it off. It wasn't until he was standing at the end of the hall and needed to make a choice about which bed he was going to sleep in that he felt that all too familiar longing hit him. He could go with the one in the master bedroom, which he'd avoided for the past few years because that's where he'd slept with his ex-husband. Or the one in the guest room, where he'd fucked Magnus damn near every night for a year.

He hated both options for different reasons, and since he was too tired to figure it out, he marched back to the living room. The couch wasn't the most comfortable place, but since he'd spent the past few months nodding off right here, he figured one more night wouldn't hurt.

MAGNUS WAS ROUSED FROM SLEEP BY THE sound of his cell phone ringing. Since he never got calls in the middle of the night, he grabbed the phone and tapped the screen to answer without focusing enough on who it was.

"Yeah?"

"Magnus."

Trey.

For some reason, Magnus couldn't find his voice to speak, but his ears weren't having a problem listening to Trey's breathing on the other end.

"I know you're there," Trey slurred. "Magnus? Can you hear me?"

He cleared his throat. "I'm here. What do you need, Trey?"

"You."

A painful tightness formed in his chest because he couldn't count the number of times he'd wished that Trey would admit that since they met. He'd clung to all that stupid hope minute after minute, month after month, hoping that one day Trey would admit what they had was real, not some convoluted fuckfest that didn't have an end date.

"Trey, you're drunk."

"So? Doesn't mean I don't need you, does it?" Trey countered hotly. "No. It *doesn't.*"

The more words Trey spoke, the more inebriated he sounded. Magnus only hoped Trey hadn't gotten behind the wheel in his current state. He'd always been smart in that regard, but sometimes Magnus didn't know what Trey was capable of. Not in a million years had he expected Trey to just up and quit—both his job and Magnus. Yet here they were.

"Trey—"

"Shut up," Trey hissed. "You're gonna listen to me."

Magnus snapped his mouth closed and took a deep breath, staring into the darkened room.

"That's more like it," Trey grumbled. "I like you better with your mouth shut." He chuckled harshly. "No, I don't. I like you better with my dick in your mouth."

Oh, boy. Trey was definitely drunk, and he'd moved on from the touchy-feely phase and right into horndog land. Magnus had rarely encountered this side of Trey because Trey had always stood by his desire not to drink. He'd once told Magnus that he'd been dangerously close to fucking up his entire life while looking at the bottom of a bottle, and he refused to do that anymore.

"Trey, listen to me," Magnus said when Trey was silent for a minute. "I know you, and when you wake up in the mornin', you're gonna hate yourself for this phone call. So I'm gonna give you a reprieve and let you go now."

"No!" Trey shouted. "Not until I tell you somethin'."

Magnus knew he should hang up. The only way this was going to end was badly. Trey was drunk enough to say things he would regret tomorrow morning, things that Magnus had been hoping to hear for so fucking long. Trey had the power to flay him open with those words, and tomorrow he'd be starting over on the process of trying to get over Trey.

A knock sounded on his bedroom door. A moment later, it opened and Ava walked in. She was wearing one of his T-shirts, something she'd started doing a couple of months back. She claimed they were comfortable to sleep in, and since he loved seeing her wearing his shirt, he had encouraged her to do so.

"Is everything okay?" she asked as she moved toward him. "I heard you on the phone."

"Everything's fine," he assured her.

"Fuck," Trey growled. "She's there, ain't she? She's in your bed." Trey grunted. "You're probably fuckin' her right now."

"Trey, that's not what's happening."

"Don't fuckin' lie to me. I've seen the way you look at her. Like she's the most precious thing in the world."

Magnus didn't bother to deny it because Ava was the most precious thing.

"First time I saw it, I wondered why you never looked at me that way," Trey grumbled, most of the words incoherent. "I was never enough for you, Magnus. You told me so yourself."

He'd never said any such thing, but he knew Trey was referring to the fact Magnus stood by his claim that he needed to be with a man and a woman. That never changed, despite how much he loved Trey. For a short time, he'd even tried to convince himself Trey had changed him because Magnus couldn't imagine his life without the man. This past week had been torture because it was the first time in a year and a half that he hadn't gotten to see him every single day. The physical ache in his chest had nearly taken him out at the knees more than once, but he was trying to push forward. After all, what other choice did he have?

"You should fuck her some more," Trey mumbled, his voice getting softer. "I don't give a shit anymore."

"Trey? Listen to—"

"Fuck you, Magnus. I don't love you anymore. That should make you happy."

The call ended, and Magnus sucked air into his lungs as he stared at the screen. He breathed past the pain as his heart shattered. Not once in all the time he'd known Trey had the man admitted that he loved him.

Not until he told him that he didn't.

AVA WATCHED AS MAGNUS LOWERED THE PHONE to his side. He looked like someone had just told him one of his dogs had died.

She didn't think before she crawled into his bed with him. She didn't ask if he was okay with it when she pressed up against his side, draping her arm across his chest. She rested her head on his shoulder and held him tightly. His heart beat fast in her ear, and his breaths were coming more rapidly. It was apparent he was trying to hide his pain.

"Was that Trey?" she asked after a few minutes of silence.

He nodded. "He was—" Magnus cleared his throat. "He was drunk."

"What did he say?"

Magnus's arm curved around her back, and he pulled her tighter against him. She clung to him as much as she could, wanting to alleviate every ounce of pain and heartache he suffered. She knew it wouldn't be enough, but she didn't want him to be alone.

"That he doesn't love me anymore."

Tears formed in Ava's eyes as she clutched him tighter. Her heart was breaking for Magnus. She'd never heard either man speak those words between them, but she didn't have to hear them to know how they felt about one another. Even when they were drifting apart, she'd witnessed those longing glances. Trey would stare at Magnus when he didn't think anyone was looking, and Ava could swear she could feel his pain. And Magnus ... the way he'd talked about Trey, sharing stories about how they met when she would ask ... there was no doubt in her mind they would stay together. How could they not with that much love between them?

And then she'd come along...

"I'm sorry," she whispered against his chest. "I'm so sorry."

"Go to sleep, Ava," he rasped.

The torment in his voice was enough to have her closing her eyes. She imagined Trey was somewhere else suffering the same fate as Magnus. Two stubborn men were unwilling to open their eyes and see what they wanted was right in front of them.

She could never replace Trey, didn't want to, but she loved Magnus, too.

For now, she hoped it would be enough.

Chapter Eleven

Tuesday, August 2, 2022

ON TUESDAY AFTERNOON, AVA FOUND HERSELF BACK in Dr. Briggs's office, sitting in the same spot on the same couch, recounting the same thing she'd said the last time she was here. When Dr. Briggs had asked her how she was doing since the last time she was in, she blurted out that Trey and Magnus had officially broken up, and it was all her fault. From that moment on, she'd been rambling incessantly, never giving Dr. Briggs a chance to weigh in.

But now, as she'd run out of things to say, she could feel the psychiatrist's weighted gaze looming.

"Ava?"

"Hmm?" She didn't look up from where she was wringing her hands in her lap.

"Do you realize you've been talking about Magnus and Trey for the better part of forty-five minutes?"

She hadn't, but it didn't surprise her.

"During our last session, we discussed that you and Magnus needed to have a conversation about what happened. Were you able to do that?"

She gave a small shrug. "I told him I'm not broken."

"And what did he say to that?"

"Nothing." Her eyes snapped up to the doctor's face. "Nothing at all. I called him to the carpet, and he wouldn't talk to me."

"Did you give him a chance to?"

Ava stared. "Why would you ask that?"

Dr. Briggs arched one perfectly shaped eyebrow behind her rectangle-framed glasses. "Because you haven't given me a chance to speak this entire time."

"I'm sorry." She sulked. "It's just … it's like I've got so much on my chest, and I need to get it off. I think about what I want to say, how I want to say it, but it never works out as I planned. It comes tumbling out."

"I'm seeing that," Dr. Briggs said with a chuckle. "And that's okay. It's important to get things off your chest. But if you want to have a conversation with Magnus, you need to give him enough warning so he doesn't feel ambushed."

Ava knew she was right. But all Ava's good intentions seemed to go right out the window when she wanted to talk about something. She'd been that way her entire life. She'd opened up to anyone who would listen. And then she'd married Harrison and spent years unable to speak for herself. Now that she was free again, it was like she was making up for lost time.

"Ava, can I ask you a question?"

She peered up at the doctor and waited.

"Why haven't you brought up what happened the night Harrison attempted to kill you?"

Ava tried to pretend she wasn't shocked by Dr. Briggs's bluntness, but when she asked questions like that, it was hard to. "I don't know."

"You've danced around it numerous times. You've mentioned how that incident brought you and Magnus together, how you were introduced to Trey because of it. But you haven't yet told me what happened."

"If you've watched the news, you probably know," Ava said, feeling ornery.

"That's not what I'm talking about, Ava, and you know it. I don't need an account of the events, I would like to know how you felt ab—"

"How I felt?" Ava barked. "You want to know how I felt? It was a living hell! Harrison hit me and kicked me and... I saw it on his face, the hatred in his eyes. He wanted me dead. No," she shouted, "it was more than that. He wanted me to suffer." She sobbed but kept her eyes locked on the doctor. "I know you want me to tell you, but I can't. I just ... can't."

"It's okay, Ava." Dr. Briggs's tone was soothing. "I'm not going to push you."

Ava tried to slow her pounding heart. She took deep breaths in through her nose, pushed them out through her mouth. When she'd calmed down some, she said, "I'm sorry for that outburst. You don't deserve that."

"There's nothing to apologize for," the doctor assured her. "Believe it or not, you're making progress."

"Thank you."

"I would like to see you again on Thursday. If you're up for it, of course."

Ava nodded even as she got to her feet.

She didn't recall anything after that. Gia had driven her to the appointment because Magnus had been busy with one of his training classes. She obviously drove her back, but Ava didn't remember anything about the drive or how she'd gotten into the house.

She'd been sitting on the couch since then, staring at the blank television. She hadn't moved in at least two hours, wasn't even sure she could.

When the back door opened and Magnus came in, Ava wanted to plaster a smile on her face and welcome him home. She couldn't even do that. She was emotionally wrung out.

Realizing there were tears streaming down her face, she quickly wiped them away, praying he didn't notice.

Of course, *that* didn't happen because the second he stepped into the living room, he asked her what was wrong.

"Nothing," she said on a sob.

Magnus took a seat next to her, but this time he didn't leave space between them. Nothing had really changed between them since the last conversation they'd had or the night she slept in his bed after Trey had drunk-dialed him, but Magnus wasn't quite as standoffish as he had been.

"Talk to me," Magnus urged, putting his arm around her shoulder.

Ava couldn't stop herself. She leaned into him, pressing her cheek to his chest and resting her palm on his stomach. For a few minutes, she just wanted him to hold her. If he would do that, she would be able to pull herself back together.

She wasn't sure how long they sat in silence, but her tears finally stopped, and her breathing evened out.

"Thank you," she whispered, patting his chest lightly before sitting up.

"Did somethin' happen at therapy?"

Ava swallowed hard, her teeth locking together. "No."

Magnus brushed his thumb over her cheek. It was a sweet gesture, causing her to risk looking at him for the first time since he came into the room. As soon as she did, the tears returned.

"Baby, talk to me."

Oh, God. *That* didn't help. It was like he was soothing a wild animal, but instead of making her feel better, it unraveled her more. How long had it been since anyone had spoken to her so gently?

She turned away from him, not wanting him to see her cry anymore. She didn't get up because she wasn't sure her legs would hold her, but she refused to look at him. The next thing she knew, she was recounting what had happened that night.

"It came on so suddenly. Or it felt that way," she began, her voice so low she wasn't sure he could even hear her. "He told me he wanted to have sex, and I told him no. I'd never told him no before. Not like that. Not to his face. But I didn't want to have sex with him. Not ever again. I was still pissed because earlier that day, he told me he was gonna have my mother committed to a mental hospital, and this time he was gonna make sure she stayed there forever." She snorted. "And the bastard thought I would have sex with him after that? I told him he was crazy."

She glanced down at her hands. "He told me he would show me crazy." Ava had to pause for a moment as the memory assaulted her. "He wasn't lying. He grabbed me by the hair and slammed the side of my head into the wall. He'd hit me plenty of times, but never in the face. Never where anyone could see. It hurt so bad."

Ava took a deep breath, wishing she could stop, but the words kept coming, although it felt like they were cutting off her air. "My legs gave out. I slid to the floor." She could still feel the queasiness that had consumed her. "He kept pulling my hair, dragging me down the hall. I pushed off with my feet to keep him from ripping my hair out." The pain had blinded her. "He laughed and said I was a stupid little girl who needed to be punished."

Ava realized she was sobbing uncontrollably. She tried to get to her feet, but Magnus banded an arm around her waist and pulled her back against him. He didn't let go, holding her tight, his forehead pressed to the back of her head.

"Tell me, Ava. I need to know as much as you need to get it out."

She stopped fighting him, covering her face with her hands as she sobbed. She was unable to stop the mortification that flowed through her. She'd been so weak that night. So powerless. No one had ever made her feel like that before.

"He did what he promised. He punished me. But it was different than the other times. He acted like I wasn't human," Ava whispered, sucking in gulps of air. "He punched me in the face, and when I hit the ground, he kicked me in the stomach, then yanked me back to my feet. I begged and pleaded. I tried to fight him off, but he would only hit me harder. The more I cried, the more he hit me. I begged him to stop. So many times."

The hell was on vibrant replay inside her head. Ava could almost swear she felt the blazing fires burning through every inch of her body.

Her voice was thick with tears as she continued. "I remember saying his name, hoping to get through to him, but that pissed him off more. He started screaming in my face, landing blows on the side of my head. I hit the floor and tried to back away from him. He stopped me by putting his foot on my leg, and when I tried to get free, he put his entire weight on that leg and lifted his other foot off the ground. The pain was so intense I screamed bloody murder. He laughed and grabbed me by the hair, told me to *stand up, you little bitch*," she said in a voice mocking his. "I tried. I told him I thought my leg was broken. He didn't care. He told me he'd break the other if I didn't shut up. I screamed every time he hit me. He would get in my face and shout for me to shut up. I couldn't. Fire blazed through my entire body."

Magnus's grip on her tightened, and Ava realized she was digging her fingernails into his arm. She relaxed her hand. "He picked me up and threw me on the bed. I tried to scramble off, but my leg wouldn't work, and the pain made me dizzy. He grabbed me by my wrist and yanked so hard I heard something snap. I screamed again, and that's when he ripped at my clothes."

Ava hated this. She hated reliving that night. The monster was dead, so she didn't understand why she had to go back there, but now that she was talking, she couldn't seem to stop.

"He clawed at me, purposely trying to inflict as much pain as possible. I couldn't stop crying, which made it worse. He wanted to see me cry. He started calling me names. Told me I was a frigid bitch. Said he was gonna fuck me until I bled. Then he shoved my legs apart. I bit my lip because fire blazed through my entire right side. I remember feeling a wash of cold move over me right after. He slapped me in the face, then shoved his dick inside me." She swallowed. "I'm not sure when the pain stopped, but I didn't feel anything anymore. It's like my mind shut down to block it all out. I was aware of what he was doing, but I didn't feel it."

Magnus pressed his face into her shoulder, and that's when Ava realized he was crying, too. It pained her that he had to relive this with her.

"After he got off, he went to the bathroom. I thought he would leave me alone after that. I couldn't move. My hand and leg were useless. I should've sucked it up and run out the door, but I couldn't. He came back fully dressed in jeans and a ratty old T-shirt. I'd never seen him wear anything like that before. I guess he didn't want to get blood on his good clothes. He told me to get up because we needed to go to the doctor. I ignored him. I just wanted him to go away."

Ava took a deep breath and forged ahead. "He told me I had five minutes to get up and get dressed. He left the room."

She sat there for a moment as some of the tension eased out of her body. She covered Magnus's arms with hers, stealing the warmth of his body. She felt safe with him, and that's the only reason she could get through this. Ava knew without a doubt that Magnus would move heaven and earth to ensure nothing ever happened to her again.

"I thought it was over," she said, some of the emotion draining out of her words. "I started to feel some relief, like maybe I wasn't going to die at his hands. That was short-lived when he came back a little while later. He saw that I was still on the bed, and he got furious. He called my name, but I didn't look at him. He screamed my name several more times in my face. I still didn't look at him. I saw him reach for the candle holder on the dresser. It was one of those tall metal ones with a thick base and a little ring to hold it. He picked it up by the tapered end and wielded it like a baseball bat. He slammed it down on my chest. I think he meant to hit me in the face. I'm not sure if he missed or if he changed his mind. I think that's what broke my clavicle."

Magnus was trembling, his arms tightly banded around her. Because she'd gotten this far, Ava decided to finish.

"I didn't even flinch, didn't cry. I think that pissed him off more than anything. I was numb. I didn't care anymore. I knew he was going to put my mother away no matter what he said. And I couldn't stand the thought of living with him another minute. He'd made sure I knew he would kill me if I ever tried to leave him. I figured I might as well let him. At least then I wouldn't have to see his face ever again."

She took a deep breath, more of her anger and fear dissipating.

"All I remember after that is him yelling and screaming. The more I ignored him, the more he shouted. I'm not sure when he got the electric shaver, I only remember looking him in the eye as he held me by my hair and began to shave my head. It didn't matter at that point. I knew I was dead, so why would I care? He left for a little while after that. I was hoping he was calling the doctor."

She took another deep breath. "I didn't consider the fact that he'd beaten me so much he couldn't risk anyone seeing me at all. Not until he returned carrying a thick rope in his hand. He clutched it so tightly, lifting it to my face. He snarled at me, said if I didn't get up, he'd make sure I never got up again. The pain had disappeared, so I didn't move. I knew when I did, the fires of hell would blaze through me again, and I'd lost the will to live at that point.

"The next thing I remember is waking up in the dark. I could feel something pressing in around me. I tried to move, but I was wrapped tightly in something. I thought it was a coffin at first. I thought maybe I was dead, and that was how you went to the afterlife. I don't know how I got out, but I did. It was dark outside. I tried to stand up, but I couldn't. I decided to crawl but realized I couldn't do that either because my wrist was broken. It was then I realized I wasn't dead. No way the afterlife would be so painful. I heard a noise. Could've been an animal, I don't know. But I got scared. There were lights off in the distance, so I started limping toward them."

"Gloria Steiner found you," Magnus whispered against her neck.

"She did. She got me to her house. I begged her not to tell anyone because I knew he would find me." Ava pressed her hand against Magnus's arm, which was still banded across her stomach. "Then you found me, Magnus. You saved me."

"You saved yourself, Ava."

She shook her head, but she didn't argue.

MAGNUS HELD AVA FOR THE LONGEST TIME. He couldn't let go. He needed the warmth of her body against his so he could reassure himself that she was alive, that Harrison Rivers no longer had the power to hurt her. If the bastard hadn't been dead, Magnus would've killed him without batting an eye. He'd never wanted to hurt anyone as much as he wanted to hurt that man for what he'd done.

Ava was the first to move, shifting his arm from around her waist, but she didn't get up. Instead, she turned around and faced him, her arms wreathing his neck.

"I'm alive, Magnus. The only way to move on is to accept that. Neither one of us can change what happened."

No, they couldn't.

"I'm not broken. Not my body and not my spirit." She pulled back and stared into his eyes. "And now that you know ... you have to let it go, too."

He cupped her beautiful face. It was ravaged with tears, her nose and eyes red, but she was still the most beautiful woman in the world.

Magnus held her stare. "You're so precious to me, Ava."

Her eyes softened. "I know."

"Do you?"

She nodded.

Magnus couldn't resist the urge to kiss her. He leaned in and pressed his mouth to hers. Softly at first as he waited for her to kiss him back. When she did, he pulled her onto his lap, cradling the back of her head as he lost himself in her, his tongue dancing with hers in a soft, sensual embrace. He held on to her, circling her in his arms to soothe himself. As far as he was concerned, this was where she belonged. Nothing and no one would ever hurt her again because he would make sure of it.

It was the first of many kisses that spanned the next few days as they fell into a routine, one that didn't involve him hovering over her so much. She didn't bother trying to hide how much she appreciated that, and he understood.

But while they were becoming closer that way, Magnus didn't make love to Ava although he wanted to. He just wasn't ready because, try as he might, he couldn't get past his conversation with Trey. When the man thought Magnus was having sex with Ava, he told him he didn't love him anymore. Trey had ripped his heart clean out of his chest with those words. Since then, he'd felt flayed open.

Taking care of Ava allowed him to forget about it for a few minutes, but the pain would eventually return. Every time his anger would get the best of him, an image of Trey's cocky smirk would pop into his head, and tears would spring to his eyes. He wanted him to come back. He loved the man so much. Magnus wasn't ready to let go of Trey completely.

Eventually, he would have to, but he hoped to heal a little before that happened.

Chapter Twelve

Friday, August 5, 2022

ON FRIDAY MORNING, TREY WOKE UP AND checked his text messages as he always did. Every other Friday was payday, and he was used to getting a message from the bank that his paycheck had been deposited, but he never received a notification. Then when he checked his account, he found that Magnus hadn't fucking paid him.

It wasn't that he needed the money, because he didn't. He was lucky in that he didn't live paycheck to fucking paycheck, but by God, when someone promised you something, Trey expected them to follow through. He figured this was Magnus's way of paying him back for what Trey had said. He couldn't recall the entire conversation, but Trey knew he'd drunk-dialed Magnus. He remembered hearing Ava's voice in the background. It had cemented the fact that Magnus had moved on, that Ava had already moved into his bed. It had only been a week, and Magnus had forgotten him already.

Well, Trey intended to remind him that when you made a promise, you fucking followed through.

Rather than call, he figured showing up in person might drive his point home. Not to mention, it would guarantee that he got fucking paid for the work he'd done. He was due, goddammit.

It was shortly after noon by the time he got to Camp K-9 because he'd spent the better part of the morning arguing with himself about what a stupid fucking idea this was. He'd acknowledged that he didn't need the money, so he knew that he was blowing this out of proportion in an effort to see Magnus again. And yes, maybe Ava. But only because he wanted to see them with his own eyes, not because he gave a shit either way.

At least, that was what was going with.

"You're an idiot," he told himself as he parked the truck in the Camp K-9 lot. "A stupid fucking idiot."

Despite that acknowledgment, he walked inside anyway, swinging the door open harder than he should have. He silently apologized to Sarge because the dog's head popped up, his ears back, obviously startled from his nap.

Magnus appeared, coming from the kennels, and the moment he saw Trey, he froze.

"You didn't fuckin' pay me, asshole," Trey barked.

Magnus's expression shifted from one of disbelief to rage in the blink of an eye. "The fuck I didn't."

"Then give me the goddamn paper check."

"You got paid by direct deposit."

"I damn sure did not, and you fuckin' know it, Magnus." Trey couldn't fucking believe that he was having this argument or that he was this fucking angry over something so goddamn petty.

"I'll prove it to you." Magnus marched around behind the counter and pulled the keyboard drawer out.

Trey waited patiently, restraining himself from drumming his fingers on the counter. Not once had Magnus ever missed a paycheck, so obviously, he'd done it on purpose. And now he was pretending that he hadn't.

Magnus leaned into the screen. "What the fuck?" His tone cooled significantly. "I know I submitted it."

"Just fuckin' pay me," Trey bit out through clenched teeth. "You got what you wanted. I showed up."

"Fuck you, Trey. I don't give a shit if you *ever* come back here."

Trey stared at Magnus in shock. If he'd been kicked in the nuts, he wouldn't have felt worse pain than that single statement caused. The look on Magnus's face said he meant it.

"You know what, keep it," Trey managed as he stood up straight and started for the door. He damn sure didn't want Magnus to see the pain he'd just inflicted.

"Trey, wait!"

He ignored Magnus and stepped out into the record heat, wishing the sun's rays would make him spontaneously combust. How could he have been so fucking stupid?

Trey reached the door of his truck at the same time Ava called out his name. He glanced over to see her coming around the side of the building. She'd obviously been in one of the play yards and probably saw him pull up.

"I've gotta go," he said, opening his door.

Unfortunately, he didn't get far when Magnus grabbed his arm and spun him around.

"I didn't mean that," Magnus ground out, stepping up to him.

Trey was too shocked to respond. He didn't even recognize the pain churning in Magnus's eyes. Evidently, it was fine as long as Trey was the one doing the walking, but the fact that Magnus didn't want him anymore ripped him up inside. If Trey hadn't been led around by his goddamn emotions, he would've been able to prevent this. And if he'd stayed home where he fucking belonged, he could keep on pretending that Magnus was secretly pining away for him and waiting for him to come back instead of playing house with Ava.

He was a fucking pussy, that's what he was.

Magnus stepped up to him, pinning Trey between his body and the truck. He lowered his voice even more. "I didn't mean it."

"I shouldn't have come here."

"I did it," Ava called out as she came around the front of the truck.

Trey peered over at her.

"I removed your paycheck from the system. That's why it didn't go through."

Magnus was about to say something, but Ava held up her hand and looked at Trey. "I needed to get you out here so we could talk. This seemed like a good option." She shrugged. "Well, the *only* option, really. What with you not responding to my messages."

Fuck this and fuck them.

Trey shoved Magnus back and reached for the door handle.

This time Ava stepped up, placing her hand over his. He glanced down at it but couldn't look her in the eye.

"Please stay so we can talk."

"Nothin' to talk about."

"Well, I have some things," she charged on. "And if you won't talk, then you can listen." She squeezed his hand. "Please."

When Trey looked back at Magnus, he saw the man staring at Ava's hand on his. Was that jealousy? Served the fucker right.

Trey released the door handle and dropped his arm.

"Thank you," Ava said softly. "Now, you two go in the house and figure out something for lunch. I'll let Gia know we'll be out of pocket for a couple of hours."

A couple of hours? Try ten minutes because that was all Trey was willing to spare. He wasn't even sure he could commit to that long.

"Go. In the house. Both of you," she repeated.

Trey frowned, glancing at Magnus. The man looked as bewildered as Trey felt. Since when had Ava started calling the shots?

Rather than argue with her, Trey headed toward the house. The least he could do was hear her out. *Then* he could go home and wallow in his self-pity. After that, he'd go to Moonshiners and drink his pain away. And perhaps he'd give another twenty-five-year-old a go.

After all, they were fun for a minute.

Provided he didn't go and fucking fall in love with them.

MAGNUS WANTED TO THROTTLE AVA, BUT AT the same time, he wanted to kiss her. And not because he genuinely liked kissing her. He did, but that was beside the point. If he hadn't spent the past week mourning the end of his relationship, perhaps he would've come up with the idea to lure Trey out here by not paying him his final check.

Then again, unlike Ava, Magnus would've known that would only piss Trey off, as had been the case. If Ava hadn't admitted it was her idea, without a doubt, Trey would've already hightailed it out of there. But for some reason, he was sticking around to hear her out. And Magnus wasn't above taking advantage of that.

"Trey, I didn't mean what I said," he told him again, closing the back door behind him. "It was the heat of the moment."

"Doesn't matter. Don't worry about it."

Easier said than done. If Magnus hadn't seen Trey's expression as soon as the barb left his mouth, he never would've believed the man had reacted that way. It was as though Magnus had punched him in the solar plexus. And that pained expression on Trey's face had nearly sent him to his knees. The last thing Magnus ever wanted to do was hurt Trey. Although he hated that things had turned out this way, he wouldn't trade a single second of what they'd shared.

"You know what? I really can't stay," Trey said as he pivoted on his heel and headed for the back door. "Just keep the money. I don't fuckin' need it, and I've got shit to do. I'm sure you and Ava do, too."

"It's not like that, Trey."

Trey stopped with his hand on the doorknob and looked back at him. His eyes were tormented, more so than usual. "It sure looked like *that* the other day."

Magnus cocked his head. "Because I kissed her after she kissed you?"

Trey's jaw clenched, the muscles bunching.

"If it makes you feel better, Ava beat herself up about that when she realized you saw us."

"Why? What does it matter? From the sound of it, y'all both moved on. That was *her* in your bed when I called, wasn't it?"

"She wasn't *in* my bed," he countered. "She came into my room to make sure everything was okay after she heard the phone."

"I bet you made it okay after that."

Magnus huffed. Arguing with Trey was like hitting a brick wall and expecting to win without busting some knuckles. "Ava cares about you, Trey."

Trey turned to face him. "But not you?"

"Of course I do, but you've already told me where I stand."

Trey's eyes moved over his face, and Magnus willed the man to say something that would tilt the world back on its axis. Because without Trey in his life, Magnus was floundering.

"You're right," Trey said through gritted teeth. "And you've told me where *I* stand."

When Trey reached for the doorknob again, Magnus lunged for him. He didn't intend to, but he couldn't help himself. "Goddammit, Trey! You're not walking away from me this time."

Magnus spun him around, slammed Trey against the door, and kissed him. Trey didn't kiss him back. Not at first. Probably because he was stunned, but Magnus didn't back down. He stepped in closer, gripped Trey's hair, letting his lips hover over Trey's as he dragged in deep lungfuls of air, breathing him in, light-headed from the kiss and the rush he always felt when he was with Trey.

"Jesus fuck," Trey growled, grabbing Magnus by the hair and dragging him back, stalking him across the room.

Magnus stumbled backward until he hit the opposite wall, then accepted Trey's weight as their mouths crashed together. And just like every other time Trey had kissed him, Magnus felt the sensation through his entire body. But rather than let Trey use him as he had so many times before, Magnus gripped him by the shirt and held him close, refusing to let him go.

Trey was the one to pull back first, pressing his forehead to Magnus's as they both fought to catch their breath.

Time stood still as they remained like that, Trey's hand fisted in Magnus's hair as though he wasn't willing to let him go. Magnus kept a firm grip on Trey's shirt because he *wasn't* willing, and he needed Trey to know that.

"I don't know if I can do this," Trey whispered.

Magnus didn't need him to explain. He knew Trey was referring to the three of them.

"And I don't know if I can't," he countered. "I've never wanted a man as much as I want you."

When Trey tried to step back, Magnus held tight.

"You can deny it all day, but we both know this isn't a one-and-done thing, Trey, no matter how many times you try to pretend it's the last time."

Trey's gaze met his, his eyes shifting back and forth. "But you still want her?"

"Yes." Magnus lowered his voice to a whisper and confessed once and for all. "I love her, Trey. The same way I love you."

Trey exhaled heavily, his eyes darting away as he tried to pull back.

"Tell me you don't care about her," Magnus snapped, jerking on his shirt before releasing it.

"Of course I do!" Trey hissed.

"And when she kissed you?"

Trey's gaze slammed into his face, a crease marring his forehead.

"Did you feel something?"

"I don't know."

"The fuck you don't." Magnus was so fucking tired of Trey's avoidance tactics. "Either you felt something or you didn't."

Trey's jaw bunched again. "Yeah. I felt something."

"Then where's the harm in seein' where it goes?"

Trey stood tall, met his stare head on. His anger and hurt made his voice louder and deeper. "Because if it doesn't work out, I'm gonna be gutted, Magnus. Is that what you want to hear? That I fuckin' love you? That I don't know if I can live without you? And that I can't trust what I feel for Ava because I've never felt it before? I'm gay, goddammit! Don't you fuckin' get that? I've never had sex with a woman. I've never wanted to!"

Magnus didn't lash out, taking Trey's anger in stride because he'd never heard a single emotion come out of Trey's mouth, and the man had nearly leveled him with it now.

"So, yeah, I fuckin' liked when she kissed me." Trey's blue-gray eyes were wild. "But was it real? Or was I tryin' to make it real so I wouldn't have to give you up?"

Magnus swallowed the lump in his throat. He honestly hadn't considered that. And truth be told, he'd never seen it from Trey's perspective.

Keeping his tone level, he decided since they were laying it all out on the table, he might as well get real with Trey.

"I'm bisexual, Trey. It's not somethin' I experimented with. I didn't play around and learn that, yeah, I can get off either way. Since I hit puberty, I've found both sexes equally appealing. And then, I *did* experiment. I dated in high school, and I didn't discriminate because I didn't fuckin' care what people thought. And then I graduated to havin' sex. Again, it didn't matter. But the second real feelings started to arise, I realized that I wanted somethin' different from most people because I fuckin' *feel* somethin' different." His voice grew louder as his frustration ratcheted up. "There's a difference between a man and a woman, and I'm not just talkin' physically. I *feel* something different for you than I do for Ava. Ultimately, it's the same, but it's vastly different.

"That's where the hole comes from," Magnus admitted, feeling defeated. "There's a hole in my life, and it comes from not gettin' what I need because you're not capable of givin' me what Ava can and vice versa." He exhaled heavily, suddenly so tired he could hardly breathe anymore. "I have tried so fuckin' hard this past year and a half to convince myself that you're enough for me because, goddammit, Trey, you *are* enough. It's not you who's broken. It's me. It was fuckin' easy to be happy with you because I fell in love with you, and the woman I've been in love with for years was married. She was off-limits, so I allowed myself to believe that *knowin'* I loved her was enough, but then...

"It's never been about findin' two people who are compatible, Trey. I want love like everyone else. And I found it, but I don't know how to have it all because, in all fairness, I never considered what it would mean to you or Ava when askin' y'all to commit to me."

AVA WASN'T SURE SHE COULD BREATHE AS she stood at the back door and listened to them.

She'd heard every shouted word—the neighbors probably had, too—which explained the tears streaming down her face. Never had she heard that kind of torment come from anyone before. Certainly not two men who'd just pledged their love for one another.

When there were no more heated exchanges, she mustered up the courage and opened the door, not bothering to hide her tears.

Magnus saw her first, his forehead creasing with worry. "What's wrong? What happened?"

She pursed her lips and shook her head. "I heard you." Ava looked at Trey. "Both of you."

He looked embarrassed, but she didn't care. He had nothing to be embarrassed about. She could understand more how Trey felt than she could Magnus because, like Trey, she only liked one gender. She'd never even wanted to experiment with women. But she wasn't the one who had to concede, because if they did give this a chance, she was getting the best of both worlds. So was Magnus. But Trey ... he had to compromise, and that broke her heart because she already loved him, and she knew Magnus did, too.

"I owe you an apology," Ava began, stepping toward Trey. "Maybe a couple if you count your paycheck."

His eyebrow quirked.

"I shouldn't have done that, but I needed to talk to you, and you refused." She held up her hands in surrender. "Doesn't make it okay, I know." Ava took a deep breath. "But I am sincerely sorry for kissing you. I shouldn't have put you on the spot like that. I only thought about what I wanted, not how it would make you feel. Can you forgive me?"

Trey continued to stare at her for the longest time. Ava was seconds away from apologizing again when he took one step toward her. It closed the distance between them and forced her to crane her neck back to look him in the eye. She gasped when he tilted his head to the side and leaned down, sealing his mouth over hers.

For some reason, she wanted to cry even as she prayed that he wasn't thinking how horrible this was because, as far as she was concerned, it was amazing. He was gentle yet dominant, his tongue urging her lips apart, licking his way inside her. When he sought entrance, she gave it freely, sliding her tongue against his. But it wasn't until his arm curled around her back and his hand cradled her head as he deepened the kiss that the emotion choked her, and she sniffled.

Trey pulled back instantly, and the look on his face was one of deep regret. "Shit. I'm sorry. I didn't mean to scare you."

"You didn't," she said quickly, reaching for him so she could bring that wonderful mouth back to hers. This time *she* kissed *him*, and he let her. His tongue danced with hers as his arm banded around her back, pulling her tightly against him. They inhaled each other until they had no choice but to pull back or suffocate.

"Oh, fuck me," Trey whispered, staring into her eyes. "I've never…"

Ava searched his face, trying to figure out what he was going to say, but he didn't elaborate. Instead, he turned to Magnus and stared for an interminably long time before he stepped forward and kissed him. They came together like freight trains colliding, their powerful bodies dueling for supremacy as Trey fought to push Magnus back against the wall. She'd never seen anything as magnificent as the two of them like this.

When they separated, they were both breathing hard. Ava was, too, although she wasn't sure why. Maybe the thermostat was broken, because she was sure it was as hot inside as it was outside.

"What do we do now?" she asked when they both looked bewildered and confused.

"I should go," Trey said softly.

Uh … *what* now? That was the exact opposite of what she'd been thinking.

He ran his fingers through his hair, brushing the long, silky strands back from his face. He looked perplexed, and she could only imagine why. Seriously … that kiss had been mind-blowing.

Ava wasn't sure why he felt the need to leave, but she wasn't sure begging him to stay was the right move. If Trey had felt even a sliver of what she'd felt during that kiss, he was probably going to have to do some self-reflection.

Before he turned to the door, Trey leaned down and pressed a kiss to her forehead. He didn't say goodbye to her or Magnus, simply walked out the door.

Ava turned to Magnus when they were alone, and she saw the lingering pain on his face. What he'd said earlier about being broken had shredded her heart. Couldn't he see? He wasn't broken. He was *human*.

It wasn't his fault that somewhere along the way, someone decided they could categorize humans. They created these boxes—male or female—and decided slot A from one box went into slot B from the other. But they didn't take into consideration that there were people who were different from them. Humans had evolved, and thank God or the universe or whatever higher power might be out there for that. Because humans couldn't be cataloged or labeled based on one man's view of the world. (And fine, she was assuming a man decided all that nonsense because women were hunting and gathering or tending house and raising babies back in the Stone Age and the olden days.) Diversity and inclusion should not be a luxury but a standard. The heart wanted what it wanted, and it couldn't be restricted to someone's definition of normal that never should've been set in the first place.

"You're not broken," she told Magnus as she moved toward him.

He stared down at her, and some of the strain disappeared. "Neither are you."

"That's still up for debate." Ava wasn't ready to say she was fixed, because she had a long way to go for that. She'd told Magnus her story, and she'd talked to Dr. Briggs about that yesterday. They had agreed that it was progress. But a few days of therapy and confessing the horror hadn't gotten rid of the nightmares, but she was taking Trey's advice and giving it her all because, for the first time in her life, Ava was able to put herself first.

"So what's for lunch?" she prompted, trying to lighten the mood.

"What sounds good?" Magnus narrowed his eyes. "Please just don't say salad."

Chapter Thirteen

RATHER THAN GO HOME AND PONDER WHAT the fuck had just happened, Trey made a call to the one man he figured might be able to give him some clarity on his current situation.

"If you could spare an hour, I'd like to buy you lunch or a drink, your choice," Trey offered when Gage Walker, Trey's cousin Travis's husband, answered the phone.

A soft chuckle sounded. "Why not both?"

"That'll work, too. You think the fam can swing it without you for a bit?"

"I'm sure Travis'll be fine. He's at home with the munchkins today."

"Just out of curiosity, have they ever wrapped him in Saran Wrap?"

"No. Why?"

"Just askin'. We did it to my dad when we were kids."

"Jesus. Y'all got ol' Frank down long enough?"

"There were seven of us. And it took every single one."

"Did your mom help?"

"Maybe," he drawled. "It still counts."

Gruff laughter sounded through the phone. "I might have to mention it to Kate."

"She can take him," Trey told him.

"So, where do you wanna meet?"

"The diner works for me."

"Cool. Give me half an hour, and I'll meet you there."

Trey disconnected the call and made the drive back to Coyote Ridge. He took his time, figuring he'd beat Gage by a few minutes. It would give him a chance to get a table and order a couple of beers.

The diner was busy, which wasn't unusual for a Friday afternoon. People seemed to have the same idea Trey did, stopping in for a late lunch or an early dinner. Either way, there were only a few tables empty, but Trey requested a booth in the back. He informed the waitress he was expecting Gage any minute and ordered two beers.

When Gage arrived, he was waylaid by a couple of people who wanted to chat with him as he moved through the restaurant. Trey watched him, grinning as he did. That was one thing about small towns: if you didn't see someone you knew when you went out, they were likely hunkered down because there was a storm, and you were the idiot out trying to buy batteries for your damn flashlight. Trey knew because he'd been that idiot. Twice.

The waitress delivered the beers at the same time Gage sat down. Neither of them needed to peruse the menu, so they ordered up the Friday special—chicken fried steak, mashed potatoes, and fried okra—times two.

"So, what's up?" Gage leaned back and put his arm across the back of the booth. "I haven't seen you in a while."

"I've been out at Magnus's place, workin' for him while Ava healed up."

"At the dog camp, right?"

Trey nodded.

"How's she doin', anyway? I haven't heard much since y'all found her."

"You helped make that happen," Trey countered.

Gage had been part of the search team they'd brought in to scour the field where Brantley had found Harrison Rivers. Turned out it was where the bastard had dumped Ava, and he'd been returning to the scene of the crime in order to cover his own ass. Trey remembered the moment he'd seen the bloody rug. He'd been with Magnus, had heard the otherworldly pain that had escaped the man. They'd feared the worst, but thankfully, the rug was the only thing they'd recovered. He hated to think what would've happened if Ava had been…

He shook off the thought. Trey couldn't even think it. It was too horrific.

"She doin' all right?"

Trey took a sip of his beer. "Physically, she's tip-top. She's seein' Piper for the other stuff."

"Piper's a good doctor. I've been seein' her for a while now."

Trey nodded his understanding even as a familiar lump formed in his throat. After Travis and Gage's wife, Kylie, was murdered, the entire Walker family—hell, the whole town of Coyote Ridge—had gone into mourning. Although it was a significant loss to everyone who knew her, Travis, Gage, and their five kids had been devastated. Sometimes it felt like only yesterday, but it had been close to a year and a half now. He knew the pain would never go away completely, and they would never get over it, but they were making their way through. The healing process had begun.

"Did it help? Seein' a shrink?" Trey prompted.

"It takes time, but she helped me work through a few things. Both in coping with the loss and my relationship with Travis."

"Speakin' of…" Trey took a sip of his beer. "I wanna ask you a personal question."

"Shoot."

Trey had to conjure up all the courage he could to get the question out, but he managed. "When you and Travis … got together, how'd you come to terms with it?"

"You talkin' about the fact I was straight, Travis and Kylie were married, or that Travis wanted to be with a man and a woman?"

Trey grinned. "First and last, I guess."

Gage's eyebrows lifted slowly. "It might be easier if you give me some context."

Trey wasn't keen on spilling his personal life to just anyone, but he figured it was only fair considering what he was asking. "Magnus and I have been ... seein' each other for a while."

"Okay. Is it serious?"

Trey nodded, refusing to deny it.

"But...?"

"He's bisexual," Trey stated. "But it's more than that. He's like Travis."

"Ah. Meanin' he's not complete without a man and a woman?"

"Yeah. That's what he claims." Trey peered down at his beer bottle.

"I know firsthand that it's not somethin' Travis claims, Trey. What he gets from me and what he ... got from Kylie ... two very different things."

Trey nodded. "Magnus actually laid it out to me in a way I understood today, so I'm not askin' you to divulge Travis's psyche."

Gage laughed. "Good thing. I've been married to the man for goin' on nine years, and I haven't scratched the top layer yet."

Trey huffed a laugh. "Hell, I've known him all my life, seen him at a million family functions, and I haven't figured him out."

"Fair point."

"Magnus is in love with Ava," Trey blurted. "Has been for a long time. They grew up together, have a shared history and whatnot. But she was married, so he considered her off-limits."

"And now she's not? And they've gotten closer?"

Trey nodded.

"And you and Magnus...?" Gage wagged a finger back and forth.

"It's rocky right now. Although I've denied it a million times, I love him."

"But you don't wanna share him."

"Partly, yeah. The other is that I've..." This was the hard part, but Trey forged ahead, lowering his voice. "I'm thirty-eight fuckin' years old, and I kissed my first woman last week."

Gage grinned. "I assume you mean Ava."

"She kissed me."

Gage's eyebrows rose. "And…?"

"I didn't throw up."

Gage barked a laugh loud enough to draw attention from others. Trey couldn't help it, he laughed, too.

"Seriously," Trey amended. "I liked it. But when it first happened, I wasn't sure if it was because I'm not ready to let go of what I have with Magnus."

"That makes sense, sure."

"What I want to know is … how did you know Travis was it for you?"

"First off, if you know our history, you know I hated him. Hell, I'm the one who outed his secret marriage to Kylie by bringin' her to Coyote Ridge."

Trey had heard the tales.

"I fought my attraction to him tooth and nail, but in the end, there was no denyin' it. I wanted him, but that's because I wanted *him*. I fell in love with Travis Walker, not *a* man."

"That's my problem," Trey admitted, using his fingernail to peel the label off his beer. "I felt somethin' when Ava kissed me the first time, but even more so today." He met Gage's eyes. "I can't name another woman who's ever captured my attention or made me wanna switch sides. Or play both, as is the case with them."

Gage set his beer down and leaned forward. "Gay or straight, you love who you love, man. And I love Travis with all that I am, but I can tell you, I've never looked at another man that way."

"Or been in a relationship with two people?"

Gage's eyes dropped to the table.

"Do you think you and Travis will ever…?" Trey couldn't get the words out.

Gage's eyes snapped up to his face. "I'm surprised you asked me that."

"I didn't mean to overstep."

Gage waved his hand where it rested on the table. "It's not that. I think it's on everyone's mind. No one's ever had the guts to ask." He exhaled slowly. "It's far too soon for me even to consider that right now, but who knows what the future might bring. Right now, our only focus is on the kids." Gage leaned back in his seat. "I still miss Kylie every minute of every day, and though it no longer feels like there are shards of glass rippin' and slicin' through my insides, I still ache. I don't wake up in a cold sweat anymore, though, so I figure that means the healin' has begun."

Trey felt a knot form in his throat, but he swallowed down the emotion.

"I can honestly tell you, Trey, I had the best of both worlds, and I was fuckin' blessed to have them both, even for a short time." Gage's voice lowered, but there was more conviction in it when he said, "If I had a chance to do it all again, the only thing I'd do differently is I would've done it sooner. I'd give anything to have had more time with her. So if there's a chance for you to find that with Magnus and Ava … goddamn, man, what the fuck are you sittin' here with me for?"

"I'M GONNA TAKE A BATH," AVA ANNOUNCED, drawing Magnus's attention away from the television. "If you don't mind, that is."

"Why would I mind?"

"Because I'm gonna use your bathtub."

Her smile was devilish, and Magnus couldn't help but smile back. "What's mine is yours, little one."

She leaned over and pressed her lips to his cheek. "Exactly."

Magnus had to practically sit on his hands to keep from reaching for her. He wanted to. God knows he wanted to, but after what went down with Trey earlier, he was trying to take things slow. Until he knew where he stood with Trey, he wasn't sure which direction they were headed. It shouldn't matter because he should be focused on Ava, but Trey had thrown him for a loop. And now Magnus was battling the guilt over what he'd wanted all this time.

When Ava disappeared down the hall, Magnus glanced at his phone. He considered texting Trey or, better yet, calling him so he could hear his voice. He wanted to make sure he was all right. Trey had left so quickly that Magnus wasn't sure what his state of mind was.

He resisted the urge, settling back on the couch when he heard the water rushing through the pipes in the wall. His bathroom shared a wall with the living room, so it was hell watching television while Ava filled the tub. Until she'd come here, he hadn't even noticed because he'd never been in both rooms at the same time. Not to mention, he'd never taken a bath. He'd had the tub installed because the contractor had told him it was better for resale value. Since Magnus wasn't sure he wanted to stay in this house for a lifetime, he'd given him the go-ahead.

When his phone chimed a short time later, he glanced at the screen to see a notification that someone had come onto the property. Gia was on overnight at the camp, and the daytime help had gone home after all the daycare pups had been picked up by their owners. He wasn't expecting company, but that didn't mean anything. People were constantly dropping by, most of them seeking information about the camp.

Getting to his feet, he headed to the back door so he could see if someone was coming to the office. It could be Gia's husband was bringing her dinner. Randy was known to do that from time to time. So Magnus opened the door and leaned against the jamb, waiting for headlights to appear beside the house. A minute later, Trey's truck pulled up near the back deck of the house, and Magnus stepped outside to greet him.

Magnus couldn't ignore the thrill that raced through his bloodstream or the nerves that rioted in his stomach. This was certainly unexpected, but he wasn't sure this was a positive thing. You never knew with Trey.

He walked over to the railing and leaned on his hands, waiting for Trey to get out. When he did, Magnus inhaled deeply. He looked good. More specifically, he looked calm. He was still wearing the same T-shirt and jeans he'd had on earlier, work boots on his feet. His long hair was down around his face, and he brushed it back by dragging his hand through it as he approached.

"Hey."

Magnus stood tall. "Hey back. What's up?"

Trey didn't answer as he came up the steps. He still didn't answer as he walked right up to Magnus, gripped his head firmly, and pressed his mouth to his.

Sometimes this man did things that surprised him. This was certainly one of those times. Trey wasn't known for being gentle. Not when it came to their intimate interactions. So this was a new one, but Magnus damn sure wasn't complaining.

"Where's Ava?" Trey asked when he pulled back.

"Takin' a bath."

Lines formed at the corners of Trey's eyes when he smiled. "Have you showered yet?"

Magnus frowned, not sure what prompted that question. "No. Why?"

"Neither have I."

Magnus didn't have time to say a word because Trey took his hand and led him into the house. He barely managed to lock the back door before being tugged down the hallway and into Magnus's bedroom.

The water had been turned off, but Magnus could hear a gentle splash every now and then as Ava shifted around.

He considered announcing their presence, but then Trey was kissing him again, harder this time, exerting his dominance as he held Magnus's head firmly between both hands. Magnus knew his lips were going to be bruised, but he didn't give a shit. He'd sported plenty of bruises since he met Trey, and he didn't regret a single one of them. He welcomed the way Trey bit his lower lip, then licked away the sting, and the way he licked into his mouth so deep their teeth bumped. He'd never met a man who could kiss like Trey. So sure of himself and always focused in the moment.

"Take off your clothes," Trey breathed against his mouth, his words so softly spoken Magnus barely heard them.

His eyes bounced over Trey's face. Magnus had never said no to this man, nor had he ever wanted to, but he was hesitant this time.

Then Trey leaned in and pressed his lips to Magnus's ear. "It's not over. And I'm not gonna run."

When he pulled back, Magnus met his gaze again. He had no idea what Trey's intentions were, but he didn't care. That was more than he'd ever gotten from Trey before, so he didn't ask. Doing anything with Trey while naked was sure to be a good time.

Keeping his eyes on Trey's face, Magnus took a step back and stripped off his shorts and T-shirt while Trey made quick but silent work of stripping out of his own.

Once they were naked, Trey took his hand again and tugged him toward the bathroom. He didn't say a word as they traipsed through to the shower. Magnus glanced over at Ava to see she was watching them, her mouth hanging open. She didn't speak, nor did she look away. Not when Trey turned on the water and not when Trey pulled Magnus in for another scorching kiss.

It took a minute for the water to heat, but as soon as it did, Trey moved them beneath the spray, their lips still fused. Magnus couldn't resist running his hands over the hard planes of Trey's chest and up the smooth contours of his back, enjoying every moan that rumbled in Trey's chest as he did.

"I want you on your knees," Trey said after they'd warmed up with that brief make-out session.

At least he was no longer whispering.

Magnus didn't hesitate, lowering to his knees directly in front of Trey. If Trey shifted just right, the water would hit Magnus square in the face, but even that didn't bother him. And certainly not when Trey fisted his cock and angled it at Magnus's mouth. His other hand gripped a handful of Magnus's hair as he pulled him forward. Magnus took care of the rest. He teased and tormented Trey's cock, doing everything he knew would drive the man crazy. He'd learned a lot about what Trey liked over the past year and a half, and he wasn't above using everything in his arsenal to bring the man to his knees. Figuratively, if not literally.

"Fuck ... Magnus ... fuck, that feels good." Trey's hand tightened on his hair. "Take more."

Magnus leaned in, taking Trey's cock to the root, the head sliding into his throat. He couldn't do it for long without gagging, but Trey knew that, pulling back before pushing in deeper.

"Don't make me come. Not yet."

Heeding Trey's command, Magnus backed off, but he didn't stop licking and laving, enjoying himself in the process. He loved sucking Trey's cock because the man was so vocal about it. He didn't have a problem telling Magnus what he liked or wanted.

When Magnus brought him to the brink once more, he released him from his mouth and glanced over at Ava. She was watching them intently, her little nipples pebbled, her skin pink from the heat of the water. She looked so fucking good like that.

"Don't stop on my account," she said when she realized Magnus was staring at her.

"You heard her," Trey grunted, gripping Magnus's hair again. "This time, I'm gonna come down your throat."

TO SAY SHE'D BEEN SURPRISED WHEN TREY and Magnus strolled into the bathroom would've been an understatement.

Ava had been at a loss for words when she saw Trey come through the door, all two hundred naked pounds of sexy man walking in like he didn't have a care in the world.

She knew for a fact that Trey considered himself old, although, at thirty-eight, he was far from it. It likely had more to do with the fact that he was considerably older than Magnus. By eleven and a half years, to be exact. Which made him fourteen years her senior. What Trey didn't realize was that he wasn't old, merely mature. He'd lived and learned and had those experiences to fall back on. He was past making mistakes and pretending he hadn't. To Ava, that was an incredibly appealing trait.

To look at him from the neck down, Trey could easily pass for … a much younger man. Virile and strong, he had a body honed from hard work rather than time in a gym, although he'd told her he did that, too. The same way Magnus did, utilizing one of the storage spaces in the main building where he kept all his weight equipment.

And then there was Magnus.

Ava had been in love with Magnus for so long, she figured it wouldn't matter if he had a paunch and was losing his hair at this point. She would still love him. But Magnus was a far cry from that. She'd noticed these past few months that he'd gotten significantly bigger in the muscle department, his chest broader, his arms and legs thicker, his butt perfection. And though there were many things about him that reminded her of the boy she'd crushed on when she was a little girl, Magnus had matured quite a bit. He was no longer the playboy who bucked the system because he felt more at peace when everyone thought he didn't give a shit about anything. Magnus cared more than most people would ever know. She'd seen that side of him through the years.

She considered herself a lucky girl to have a firsthand account of these two men in their birthday suits. But that didn't hold a candle to watching them *together*.

It was almost necessary to run cool water into the tub just to keep from overheating as she watched Magnus take Trey's cock into his mouth. He was kneeling on the floor at Trey's feet, one hand wrapped securely around Trey's shaft, the other fondling his balls while he bobbed up and down on him like it was his favorite thing in the world to do. She'd told Magnus that she had fantasized about kneeling beside him while they worshipped Trey's cock together. She wondered briefly if he remembered that. Probably not, because he had more important things to focus on. Like making Trey come.

And man, did she want to see that. It excited her to watch Trey and the way he admired Magnus before him, one hand buried in his hair as he held him there, urging him with words and a powerful shift of his hips to take him deeper. It was obvious Magnus enjoyed what he was doing even though Trey was being forceful about it. She'd go so far as to say Magnus liked the aggression because it made the encounter hotter.

Ava had never known an intimate act to be pleasurable. She'd been with one man in her lifetime, and Harrison hadn't been gentle or loving. The night he took her virginity, he'd made her dress in slutty lingerie, and then he'd practically ripped it from her body. Not in a sexy way, either. She'd felt violated and scared throughout the ordeal, but Harrison had assured her it was okay because, one, she was his wife, and two, he knew what he was doing.

It wouldn't be that way with Trey or Magnus. Even as Trey yanked on Magnus's hair, fucking his mouth like it was his right, he was attentive and careful. For the first time in her life, she wanted to experience sex with someone who would put her needs first, and she knew Magnus and Trey would give her that.

"God, Magnus…" Trey grunted. "That's it … I'm gonna come." A rough groan sounded in his throat as he tipped his head back, the cords in his neck standing out in stark relief. "Fuck, yes."

Ava stared unabashedly as Trey's body jerked, his cock deep in Magnus's throat. He was beautiful, and he made the act beautiful, too.

Figuring it was over, Ava tried to avert her gaze as Magnus got to his feet. When Trey cupped his head and kissed him softly on the lips, keeping him close, she saw exactly what Trey tried to hide from everyone, including himself. There was so much love in that embrace that it made her chest tighten. They remained like that for a few minutes, and when they separated, they both looked her way. She'd been busted staring, but neither seemed to care.

Magnus's eyes were soft and kind as he stared at her through the glass partition. "Care to join us?"

There was enough teasing in his tone, she knew he was leaving it completely up to her.

"Only if you'll wash my hair," she countered, batting her lashes so he knew she was joking, too.

"It would be my pleasure." He waved her over.

Ava took a minute to release the drain on the tub before standing tall. When she did, the remaining bubbles clung to her body, slowly sliding down. Magnus and Trey both noticed, their eyes hot as they watched her.

Carefully, she stepped out of the tub and padded the few feet to the shower, stepping inside to join them. She loved Magnus's shower because it was huge, a luxury he'd told her he'd always wanted. It was big enough for three people, although there wasn't much more space than that.

Trey stepped to one side so she could move beneath the spray. As she leaned her head back to wet the short strands, she felt his eyes on her. When she tipped her head up, she opened them to see his expression was of awe and surprise. She wondered if it was because he felt something for her or because he was realizing he didn't.

"May I?" Trey asked, his voice a sexy low rumble in his throat. Ava nodded.

Magnus passed him the strawberry-scented shampoo, and Trey squeezed some into his hand. He stepped around behind her, keeping some space between them so he could lather the shampoo on her head. He was gentle and thorough, making her moan when he kneaded her scalp with his fingertips.

The entire time she watched Magnus. He stood before her, keeping nearly two feet between them. It was his way of not scaring her, although he would never admit he was still doing it even though she'd called him out on it. She'd figured out long ago that Magnus treated those he cared about with the utmost respect and concern. Her especially.

He reached for her body puff and the soap she preferred. She moaned softly as Trey used the hand sprayer to rinse the soap from her hair while ensuring water didn't get into her eyes. The action was so gentle she could feel tears building behind her sinuses. No one had ever treated her quite so reverently. Not her mother, because she'd been too mentally imbalanced to know better, not her father, because he'd left Ava when she was very little, and certainly not the monster she had married.

When Magnus had the soap lathered on the puff, he stepped forward and began rubbing it lightly over her skin. His gaze followed the movement. And while he watched the soap build on her skin, she watched him.

His movements soothed her to the point she worried her knees were going to give out. She should've known it didn't matter, because when she swayed, Trey stepped up behind her, giving her something to lean on. The smooth, hard plane of his chest pressed to her back as his hands cupped her elbows. She felt the lightest swipe of his thumbs over her skin, and it made her want to cry again. She prayed this was not something he was forcing himself to do because of Magnus. She ached for him so much, the last thing she wanted was for him not to be able to reciprocate.

Magnus took his time, thoroughly washing every inch of her from her neck to her toes, then used the hand sprayer to rinse her.

By the time he was finished, her entire body was taut as a bowstring, her nipples painfully erect, her clit pulsing with an ever-growing need for friction.

"Please," she whispered to Magnus.

His eyes slammed into hers, and she saw the worry. He was hesitant, and she couldn't blame him. Magnus had been by her side for months, and she knew he blamed himself for what happened to her. She'd assured him time and time again that there was nothing he could've ever done to change things. Ava had married Harrison, and it had been her choice. That was pretty much the last decision she was allowed to make for herself until Magnus saved her.

No one could've predicted that Harrison would snap or that he would try to kill her. At the same time, Ava knew no one in her life would've dedicated the time and energy to search for her the way Magnus had. Or that he'd be the one to give her the freedom to decide how she was going to live her life.

She loved him for that.

And so much more.

Chapter Fourteen

WHEN TREY CAME HERE TONIGHT, HE HADN'T been sure what would happen. He also hadn't been sure how he would feel about it.

This was new to him—having multiple partners *and* any sexual interaction of any kind with a woman—but he could willingly admit that it wasn't uncomfortable or awkward. He didn't feel out of his element or like an outsider. There was something oddly *right* about the three of them here, now.

It'd been a gamble to walk into the bathroom with Magnus, both of them naked. He figured Ava would either stay or go, that Magnus would either participate or not, and Trey would either shrivel or not. The good news was Ava hadn't gone, Magnus had participated, and Trey certainly hadn't shriveled up. Quite the fucking opposite, in fact.

Now, as the three of them stood in the shower, the water no longer hot but decently warm, he watched Magnus's expression when Ava made her plea. He didn't know what she was asking for, but based on Magnus's countenance, he was hesitant to give it to her. It told Trey their relationship hadn't progressed as far as he'd thought it had, despite his accusation. Knowing he was part of it from the beginning settled some of his chaotic thoughts and reassured him in ways he hadn't realized he needed.

Trey slid his hands from Ava's elbows to her wrists and guided her toward Magnus. They shifted forward, closing the distance since Magnus seemed too shocked to move.

Trey guided her palms onto the smooth, impressive wall of Magnus's chest. Slowly he moved her hands beneath his as they touched him. The longer they did, the more Ava leaned into him. He wasn't sure if it was to get closer or because her knees were weak. It didn't matter because it meant she trusted him, and Trey needed that trust. After what she'd been through, Trey understood Magnus's reluctance, but Trey also needed to feel included. If there was any chance of this working, he knew it wouldn't be with the three of them in two separate relationships. Trey damn sure wasn't prepared to share a lover like that. He was far too possessive to spend a lifetime imagining the man he loved making love to *anyone*. If that was going to happen, Trey damn sure didn't intend to be somewhere else.

As Ava began to caress Magnus with a firmer touch, Trey removed one of his hands so he could reach out and cup the back of Magnus's neck. He urged him closer until Magnus finally took that final step that would bring him toe to toe with Ava.

Trey watched as Ava reached up and pulled Magnus down, their lips melding together. Everything seemed to go in slow motion. Time stood still; the earth stopped rotating as they kissed. Trey expected to feel left out, but he didn't because Magnus's hand had reached around Ava and pressed against Trey's side. He gripped him tightly as though he needed to know he was there, and his presence seemed to settle Magnus more.

Trey leaned down and pressed his lips to Ava's shoulder, smiling when she tilted her head to the side to allow him better access. Magnus continued to kiss her while Trey explored uncharted territory. Her skin was baby-soft, so unlike Magnus's, and her reactions weren't nearly as guarded. He liked the way she smelled, the way she tasted. But he really liked her soft sighs as he dragged his lips along her shoulder.

She was so small, so fragile, he worried he might hurt her, so he took all his cues from her. At one point in his life, when he was young and fantasizing about sex before he'd taken the plunge, Trey had figured he would be able to make it through a sexual encounter with a woman if he had to. Then again, at the time, sticking his dick in someone had been his primary goal. But with Ava, this didn't feel forced. He enjoyed touching her far more than he'd imagined he would.

"If you want more," Trey whispered near Ava's ear, "you're gonna have to ask for it, girl."

She shivered as Magnus drew back, releasing her lips before meeting Trey's gaze. The uncertainty made his hazel eyes darken. Trey couldn't commit to everything—not yet—but he'd assured Magnus he wasn't running. For now, he was willing to explore this with them.

The water was getting colder by the second, and he didn't want Ava to get chilled, so Trey reached around and turned it off.

"Get her a towel," Trey instructed when Magnus seemed rooted in place.

Magnus's eyebrow arched, and Trey grinned. Who would've thought Trey would be the clear-headed one? Magnus was obviously too stunned to process anything at the moment.

Trey helped him along, stepping out of the shower and grabbing towels for all of them. He tossed two to Magnus, hoping the man would get with the program. It took a second, but he seemed to realize what he needed to do. Trey wiped the water from his own body as Magnus began to dry Ava. His movements were careful and slow, as though he was tending to a wounded animal. And all the while, Ava watched Magnus with her heart in her eyes and a flush to her cheeks. She wasn't as fragile as they believed her to be. No, Ava March was strong and resilient. She was a fighter, and with time, Trey expected she would come into herself and surprise them all.

He wanted to be around when that happened.

When Magnus had dried Ava and himself, he took her hand and led her to the bedroom. Trey stepped back as they passed. He was debating whether to leave when Ava grabbed his hand, urging him to follow.

Trey stared at her backside as he walked, realizing there was something distinctly appealing about her petite body, the smooth rounded globes of her ass, her narrow waist, the flare of her hips. He found himself wanting to kiss along every curve, to see if her skin was as soft everywhere.

Perhaps if Magnus could get with the program, that would happen.

Or it wouldn't.

Trey figured they had plenty of time. This was only the beginning, after all.

"ARE YOU SURE ABOUT THIS?" MAGNUS ASKED Ava as they stepped into his bedroom.

She nodded.

"I need you to tell me," he urged.

Although Magnus wanted nothing more than to feel this woman wrapped around him in every way, he wasn't willing to rush it. And he didn't want Ava to, either.

"More than sure," she whispered, not an ounce of uncertainty in her tone.

"Then come here, sweetheart," he growled low in his throat as he pulled her toward him. She bumped into him, her hands curling around the back of his neck as he leaned in for a kiss. Her mouth was sweet and soft, her sexy moans making his cock throb.

With his arm banded around her, Magnus took her down to the bed, moving over her but careful not to crush her beneath his weight. She continued to hold him to her, her fingers tightly curled behind his head.

He was aware of every beautiful inch of her beneath him. All that soft, smooth skin, her beautiful tits. He cupped her ass with one hand, sliding it toward her thigh as he settled his hips between hers. He loved the way her other leg wrapped around his. It brought them closer, his cock nestled at the juncture of her thighs. He could feel her slick heat against him, and it was enough to make his cock pulse and his spine tingle. God, he'd never wanted a woman the way he wanted Ava.

"I need to feel you against me," he breathed over her mouth. "I want to be inside you."

"Then you should be inside me," she replied with a smirk.

Damn, she never ceased to amaze him. Magnus never would've figured he would be the one to get stage fright, but that was what had happened in the bathroom when he realized where they were headed. For a moment, he'd felt like a teenager with a hard-on and no fucking clue what to do with the damn thing. And here Ava was, encouraging him to claim her.

Her eyes danced back and forth over his face, and Magnus smiled, wanting to reassure her. His smile grew when she lifted her hips and caressed his cock with her slick pussy. He groaned low in his throat.

"In a hurry?" he teased.

"As a matter of fact…"

Magnus slid one arm beneath her back, pressed his lips lightly to hers. She kissed him softly, then squealed with laughter when he rolled to his back, taking her with him.

"Fuck," he said with awe, staring up as she straddled his hips. "You look perfect just like this."

The way she sat astride him, her tits ripe for the taking, those little nipples taut and inviting his mouth to savor. He was ready to indulge, to make this last all night, but the moment her cool fingers brushed over his cock, the laughter died. Magnus groaned because it felt so good for her to touch him.

It was an accident on Ava's part, proven by the way she stared down at his cock as though she was surprised to see it.

"Trey?" Ava peered over her shoulder. She cast him a smile before crooking her finger and then patting the bed beside Magnus.

Magnus studied Trey's face, trying to read him, to gauge his comfort level. There wasn't an ounce of hesitation, only heat and curiosity, expressed by the quirk of one eyebrow and the curl of his mouth.

"Are you sure?" Trey asked Ava as he put one knee on the bed.

She countered with, "Are *you*?"

"Touché." Trey's grin widened, his eyes narrowing as he glanced at Magnus.

When Trey came down beside him, Magnus leaned toward him, wanting his kiss, needing to know he was here with them. This was new on every level. For all of them.

Trey's kiss was laced with passion and the dominance Magnus had come to crave. He took over, pressing two fingers to Magnus's jaw to keep his head turned as he ate at his mouth. Magnus could taste the man's hunger, his need. Trey was raring to go despite the fact he'd come in Magnus's mouth a short time ago. Based on their history, Magnus knew Trey never required much time to recover.

Magnus grunted his surprise, jerking back from Trey when Ava curled her fingers around his cock and stroked from root to tip. He gasped for air as the pleasure assaulted him.

She smiled. "I didn't hurt you, did I?"

Oh, the little minx was teasing him. He liked that she was because Magnus wasn't sure she was ready for this. After all that she'd endured with Harrison, Magnus had been positive it would take much longer for her to get to a point she could trust anyone. It humbled him that she trusted them.

"Not even a little," he said, tucking his hands behind his head and staring up at her. He admired the lift of her pert little tits, the way her pebbled nipples pointed slightly upward, tightening a little more as she stroked him. She inched backward, moving over his thighs so she could get a better grip. She alternated between using one hand and then two. Her chest moved up and down, picking up speed and matching the pace of her hands.

Trey propped himself up on his elbow, resting his head in his hand, his full attention on the way Ava was stroking him. Magnus's cock jerked and twitched just from the fact Trey was watching. Magnus was so focused on Ava that he flinched when Trey's hand moved over his hip. He glanced down to watch as Trey cupped his balls while Ava continued to stroke him. This had to be what heaven was like because, fuck … Magnus had never been this turned on before.

But then Ava angled Magnus's cock toward Trey, and his lungs seized up. Trey leaned in, blocking Magnus's view as he took him all the way into his throat.

"Oh, dear God," he groaned, his head falling back on the bed. Oh, that wicked fucking mouth. Magnus peered up to see Ava staring down, her view not restricted when she eased to Magnus's other side, taking a position that mirrored Trey's.

Dropping his head to the pillow again, Magnus closed his eyes as he let the sensation of Trey's mouth take over. He pumped his hips to increase the friction, but Trey stopped him by firmly gripping the base of his shaft.

All thought was obliterated when Trey's assertive mouth was replaced by Ava's soft lips brushing over the head of his dick. Lights danced behind his eyelids. He wished he could see her. He wanted to watch as she explored him. Trey must've realized that because he pulled back to enjoy the sight the same way Magnus did.

Her small hand took the place of Trey's, lightly stroking as she teased the head of his cock. She didn't take him in her mouth, but Magnus didn't care. He could come just like this with her licking the head. Hell, he might be able to come from her breath alone.

She peered up to meet his gaze, her expression curious. Likely trying to see if he enjoyed what she was doing.

Magnus placed his hand behind her head, lightly guiding her toward his cock. His goal wasn't to force her but to let her know he didn't want her to stop. She smiled before turning her attention to his cock once more. This time she opened her lips around him and shifted forward, enveloping him in the heaven of her mouth.

He ground his teeth together as she licked and laved, learning every ridge with her tongue. The pleasure was overwhelming, but he endured because of the expression on her face. She was enjoying herself. He loved that she was, even if he was positive this was the sensual assault that was going to kill him.

"Oh, Jesus," Magnus grunted, lifting his head off the pillow. "Ava ... baby ... keep it up, and I'm gonna come. If that's what you want ... keep goin'."

He was leaving it entirely up to her. If she wanted him to come inside her, he was freely offering that, too, but it was a choice she would have to make.

Ava lifted her head, her eyes shifting between him and Trey momentarily.

Magnus waited, his heart in his fucking throat.

AVA LOOKED AT TREY AND SMILED.

"Not yet," she told Magnus. He would come, she would make sure of it, but she wanted to do something else first.

She got to her knees and positioned herself between Magnus's legs, forcing him to spread them. She never took her eyes off Trey, though, and she noticed he was tracking her every move.

Using the same words Magnus had used on her in the shower, Ava gestured toward his cock and said, "May I?"

He grunted, slowly rolling to his back and shifting closer to Magnus. His eyes were a little wild as he stared at her, his chest rising and falling rapidly. She wasn't sure if it was arousal or fear. She hoped it was the former because the last thing she wanted was to freak him out, but she also didn't want to leave him out.

His gaze snapped to his cock when Ava leaned forward and curled her hand around him. He wasn't as big as Magnus, but he wasn't a small man. Her fingers touched at first, but the longer she stroked him, the harder he became until he was impressively large. Harrison hadn't been well endowed, and even during those few instances when she was willing to take him inside her, he had never pleasured her that way.

"Fuck," Magnus whispered, shifting so he could watch.

Ava spent several minutes easing Trey into it, learning every inch of his cock by touch. She teased her fingers over his balls the same way he'd done to Magnus. She cupped him gently, watching to see his reaction.

"Oh, Ava..." His head fell back, his chest expanding as his neck tightened. "It's..." He trailed off, his hips beginning to pump, driving his cock into her fist. She tightened her grip a little, grazing the head with her thumb. A pearly drop of precum had pooled on the tip, and she had an overwhelming urge to lick it off.

So she did.

"Fuck me," Trey hissed, his head snapping up, eyes opened.

Ava kept her gaze locked with his as she licked the head, curling around the wide crest, then trailing down the underside. She wasn't sure what he liked, but she was intent on finding out. He didn't stop her, nor did he reach for her the way Magnus had. His hands were fisted at his sides, much the way hers had been the other day when Magnus had made her come with his mouth.

Her pussy clenched at the memory, liquid heat pooling between her legs.

"Stop," Trey snapped. "Not yet, girl. Please."

Ava grinned, releasing him as he'd requested. She had to admit that the first time he'd called her that, a few minutes ago in the shower, she'd been so turned on it was a wonder she hadn't melted into a puddle. There was something intoxicating about his gruff voice and that silky drawl that made her want to hear all the dirty words in his vast arsenal.

"It's my turn," she decided because she knew that was what Magnus needed to hear. He was hesitant, but Ava was ready. She had been for a while now, no longer living under the weight of her past. She wanted something real, something good to replace all those negative memories, and Magnus and Trey were willing to give her that.

"Condom," Magnus urged when she straddled his thighs.

Trey was instantly on his feet, reaching for the nightstand.

"I'm clean, Ava," Magnus said, his tone reassuring. "But you're not on birth control."

"Actually, I am," she corrected him. "Two months ago, I had my prescription refilled. I had them mail it here."

Trey turned back to them, a condom in hand.

Magnus's eyes flashed with something she'd never seen before. "Are you saying…?"

"I want to *feel* you." She stared deep into his pretty hazel eyes. "No barriers."

"I want to feel you, too," he rasped, holding her stare as though it was a lifeline.

Trey tossed the condom on the nightstand and moved behind her to the end of the bed. The mattress dipped, and Magnus brought his legs together as Ava shifted forward, taking him in hand. She wasn't sure he would fit, but by God, she was going to try.

"Slow," Magnus growled as she leaned forward, planting one hand on his chest.

She lifted her hips and guided him to the slick entrance of her pussy. Once it was positioned against her, she leaned forward and planted her other hand on his chest, slowly easing down on him. She could feel the delicious stretch as he slid in inch by glorious inch. When it became too much, she eased off but tried again. Each time, her pussy grew wetter, slicking him more and allowing him to slide deeper.

And when Trey's hands slid over her back, she moaned, her pussy spasming around Magnus's cock. She loved that he was touching her. She craved that touch and so much more. The entire time, Magnus remained motionless, his jaw clenched tight, his breaths rasping out of his nose. Ava remained in control, taking what she needed from him. It was the most intense moment of her life, and she got lost in the sensations. Trey's hands moving over her, Magnus's cock gliding against sensitive nerve endings … she'd never felt anything so intense.

"Lean back, girl," Trey rasped near her ear.

Ava stopped moving, sitting up as Trey's arms banded around her. He remained at her back, straddling Magnus's legs.

Magnus's entire countenance changed as Trey pulled her back against him. When she relaxed into him, his big hands covered her tits. He kneaded them gently but thoroughly.

"Oh, God," she whimpered, rocking her hips in an attempt to get Magnus to move. She needed more.

"She likes that," Magnus acknowledged, lifting his hips and pushing his cock inside her. "Her tight little pussy is strangling me."

She loved his dirty words. Ava moaned, her pussy spasming relentlessly. She wanted him to say more because the vulgarity and the scorching heat in his eyes turned her on.

"Show me what you like," Trey whispered in her ear, his beard tickling her neck.

Ava slid her hands beneath his, taking over. She plucked her nipples and moaned again, both men watching what she was doing. Trey took over, teasing her nipples, making them pebble even more before he tweaked them the way she had. All the while, Magnus rolled his hips, fucking her from beneath.

"Magnus … Trey…"

"We've got you, baby," Magnus said through gritted teeth.

Trey's hands curled under her ass, gently lifting her and then easing her back down. It was incredible, but still not enough.

"Please … more."

Magnus took over, gripping her hips, rocking her on his cock while Trey began pinching her nipples. Each time he did, she felt the tension grow until she was positive she was going to shatter into a thousand jagged pieces. And the moment Magnus began fucking her deeper, driving up into her, Ava soared right over into the abyss.

"Oh, fuck… That's it, baby. Come all over my cock." Magnus grunted, continuing to fuck her as his neck muscles tightened.

And when he came, he shouted her name in a way that made her heart leap in her chest.

Chapter Fifteen

Saturday, August 6, 2022

TREY WOKE IN AN UNFAMILIAR BED WITH an unfamiliar body pressed against him. It only took a second for him to remember where he was and who was sharing that bed with him. He immediately settled, letting the memory of last night run through his head. He relaxed even more, more at ease than he had been in months.

He turned his head to the right and saw Magnus staring back at him, his head resting on the pillow, his dark hair tousled. His eyes were open, his expression one Trey didn't recognize. He looked almost … satisfied. That seemed an appropriate word to describe it. After last night, Trey imagined he probably was. Magnus had finally gotten a taste of what he'd always wanted.

Trey found it interesting that the friendship he'd developed with Ava over the past few months had translated into something unexpected. Like Gage had said when he referred to Travis, Trey wasn't sure he would feel the same for any other woman, but he couldn't deny he had a connection with Ava. One that made him yearn for something he'd never wanted before.

As he continued to stare at Magnus, neither of them said anything because Ava was still asleep between them. At some point during the night, she'd turned toward Trey, and now her arm was over his chest, her head resting on his arm. He wasn't sure how they'd ended up like this, but whatever. Trey had never been one to cuddle in bed. Not with anyone except his ex-husband, but that hadn't lasted long before Paul told him he was clingy. Since then, Trey had avoided it, but if Ava wanted to cuddle, he was more than willing.

When *that* had happened, he didn't know. It felt like only yesterday when he'd wondered whether he could even get hard enough to fuck a woman. And here he was, his cock swelling because Ava was draped over him. He recalled the way she'd ridden Magnus last night, so uninhibited, so fucking beautiful. His conversation with Gage had brought clarity, but last night with Ava and Magnus had cemented it for him. Perhaps he'd never had any sexual attraction to a woman before, but Ava wasn't just any woman, so he figured these foreign urges were warranted. Last night, when she'd been sitting astride Magnus, Trey had wanted to know what it felt like. He'd wanted to experience the slickness of her pussy as it sheathed him.

He would, he figured. At some point. But right now, he had something else in mind.

He met Magnus's gaze again and smirked. The responding grin told him Magnus knew exactly what Trey was angling for. Although they had rarely shared a bed through the night—only a few times, in fact, and most of those when they were searching for Ava—Trey had found he liked waking up to Magnus. More specifically, he liked waking up to the opportunity to use Magnus's phenomenal body for his own pleasure. He could count on one hand how many times he'd rolled Magnus over, rimmed his asshole until he was good and awake, and then sated his urges by burying his cock into the man's tight ass. He'd loved those mornings more than any other.

Trey eased himself out from under Ava. He sat on the edge of the bed, reaching for the lube and removing the cap before walking around to Magnus's side of the bed. As he did, Magnus slowly rolled to his back, following him with his gaze.

Trey leaned over him, pressing one knee into the mattress and a light kiss to Magnus's ear, then whispered, "Stand up and bend over the bed."

Magnus's eyes flashed so hotly it was a wonder they both didn't go up in flames. Trey knew Magnus loved when Trey used him, especially in the morning. He'd go so far as to say Magnus craved it as much as Trey did.

Magnus slid out of bed when Trey took a step back.

He admired the flex and pull of Magnus's back muscles as he leaned forward, resting his elbows on the mattress. The position put his head near Ava's thigh. There was no doubt she would be woken shortly, but Trey didn't care. Right now, he wanted Magnus, and waiting wasn't an option. Nor was going into another room. He figured if he could watch Ava fuck Magnus, she could watch Trey fucking him.

Trey lightly slapped Magnus on the ass, using his foot to push his legs wider. Magnus complied, spreading his feet apart. Trey stepped up behind him and slid his hand between his legs, fondling his balls.

"Fuck," Magnus crooned, arching his back downward to give Trey more access.

He caressed him briefly as he drizzled the lubricant along his crack. He fondled and teased, tugging on Magnus's cock as he thrust two fingers into his ass, watching that tight ring stretch around his digits. His cock was already stiff, but it hardened even more in anticipation.

Magnus groaned, pressing his face into the mattress as he pushed back against Trey's hand. Trey admired the way Magnus fucked himself on Trey's fingers. It was so damn hot.

"Careful, or you'll wake Ava," Trey said, his voice soft.

"Ava's already awake," she replied as she rolled over, curving her body around at the top of the bed and tucking a pillow under her face. From her viewpoint, she could see what Trey was doing, which, if her smile was any indication, was her intention.

The more Trey fingered Magnus's hole, the more her jaw opened until her lips formed a perfect O, and her beautiful blue eyes were blazing with lust.

"More..." Magnus growled. "Fuck me, Trey. Now."

He smacked Magnus's ass firmly. "I say when I fuck you."

Magnus grunted; Trey grinned and looked at Ava. She was smiling, clearly amused. Trey was looking at her when she noticed the tube of lubricant sitting on the bed.

She reached for it, then looked up at Trey. "Can I help?"

He had no idea what she was offering, but he nodded. Whatever it was, he wanted to see it.

"A little or a lot?"

"A generous amount," he answered.

She squeezed a quarter size drop in her hand and then lifted it for him to see.

Christ, she was so fucking cute. This woman's innocence and curiosity turned him on in a way he'd never experienced.

"A little more," he said simply because he wanted to watch her add more.

She did, then began spreading it over her fingers and her palm, coating one hand.

Trey was expecting she would want to lube Magnus, so he was startled when she reached for Trey's cock. He hissed, the sensation overwhelming to the point he felt electricity arc down his spine. She began stroking his length, generously coating every inch of him while driving him out of his ever-loving mind.

He grunted as he pumped his hips. Her touch was far too light to get him off, but damn did it feel fucking amazing. He liked how small her hand was, how gentle her grip. Unlike Magnus, who knew exactly what Trey needed to get off, Ava's goal was to pleasure and tease.

"Is that good?" She released him, and the coy smile on her face made Trey grin.

"Perfect."

Without warning Magnus, Trey pulled his fingers out and guided his cock home. He couldn't count how many times he'd fucked this man, but it was always like the first time. It was as though Magnus had been made just for him. Trey admired the way his hole stretched beautifully around him. Once the head of his dick breached the ring, he drove in deep, slamming his hips forward. He retreated slowly, then sank into the blistering-hot depths of Magnus's body again, a grunt escaping as he did.

"God, that's hot."

Trey's eyes snapped over to see Ava watching as he impaled Magnus. He wasn't gentle because he didn't have to be. Magnus had long ago shown Trey what he preferred, and being fucked hard and rough was their pace of choice.

He stepped in closer, shortening his thrusts as he pulled Magnus's hips back. He drove into him, watching the play of muscles in Magnus's back and shoulders, the way he fisted the blankets. His muted grunts and pleas for "harder" and "more" spurred Trey on. For a brief moment, Ava faded from the equation because Magnus was the only one Trey could focus on.

"Are you gonna come for me?" Trey barked.

"Harder," Magnus grunted as he turned his head to the side, lifting one knee onto the bed, changing the angle of penetration, opening himself more.

Trey's eyes crossed from the pleasure, but he kept slamming his hips forward, unable to stop. He was so fucking close. Dangerously close. It would've been easy to give in, but he wanted Magnus to come first. Hell, he insisted on it.

"Oh, Jesus," Magnus growled softly. "Trey ... fuck me ... so good ... never stop."

Trey's chest tightened with the request. He knew what Magnus was requesting, and in that moment, for those few seconds, he wanted to promise he would never stop. He wanted to promise he would be there to fuck him every day for the rest of their lives. Unfortunately, Trey wasn't there yet. He wasn't sure he could commit to this, no matter how good it felt when Ava touched him. There were too many variables and too many unknowns for Trey to trust that this would work for them. Being willing to try was his only option.

Still, he wanted to reassure Magnus in some way. Something he'd never done before. He mumbled, "Never," hoping that lie wouldn't come back to bite him in the ass.

Magnus drove his hips back, taking Trey to the root. A garbled groan escaped him as his body clamped down on Trey's cock.

"Oh, fuck, I'm coming," Magnus cried on a strangled moan.

The mind-numbing friction tipped Trey right over the edge. He slammed his hips forward and came with Magnus's name on his lips.

MAGNUS WASN'T SURE HOW HE MADE IT through the shower. Although he'd remained in bed long enough for Trey to shower first, his legs were so damn weak he wondered how they hadn't given out on him. Never had he been this sated from sex. Between last night and this morning, he'd been fucked by Ava and Trey and suspected he would be riding this high for some time. At least, he hoped he would.

He managed to dress, pulling on a pair of cargo shorts and a T-shirt. He grabbed his work boots and socks on the way to the door.

Magnus stopped just outside the door to the kitchen when he heard Trey's voice.

"Oh, it's true. Cal set the kitchen on fire, and Bryn flooded the upstairs bathroom twice. Griffin and Tori were notorious for overflowing the washing machine. But Brantley won the award when he put dish soap in the dishwasher. It took two weeks to get rid of the soap film on the linoleum floor."

Ava laughed. "And your parents didn't tell y'all to go live in a barn?"

Trey's gruff laugh echoed out into the hallway. "I'm sure they wished we would."

"I always wanted a big family," Ava admitted. "But it was only me."

Magnus loved that they were carrying on a conversation so easily. He remembered all those times Trey fucked him and how Magnus had wished Trey would open up and share pieces of himself afterward. It hadn't happened until after they'd rescued Ava. For a brief time, Trey had let him in. Magnus knew Trey had been doing it to keep Magnus's mind off of Ava's injuries, but he appreciated it all the same.

"Please tell me you're not lettin' him cook," Magnus said as he stepped into the kitchen. He stopped in the doorway, propping his ass against the jamb, and pulled on his work boots, not bothering to tie them.

"Of course not," Ava said, smiling at him over her shoulder. She was standing at the stove, a skillet filled with eggs in front of her. "Hope you're hungry."

"I am, but I need to go help Gia with the mornin' chores. Won't take long, so save me some." Magnus glanced at Trey. "You wanna help?"

Trey's eyes were wary, but he nodded, pushing off the counter where he'd been leaning back against it.

"I'll wait fifteen minutes and start some biscuits," Ava announced. "See y'all in thirty."

Unable to resist, he backtracked to her and pressed a quick kiss on her mouth. The smile that he earned in return only intensified his good mood.

"How're you doin' this mornin'?" Magnus asked as he and Trey made their way to the Camp K-9 building.

"Fine. Why?"

"Just wanted to make sure you were good with what happened last night."

Trey grunted. "I really don't wanna talk about it."

The way he said it pulled Magnus up short. He turned to face Trey, staring into his eyes, trying to read his meaning. "You regret it."

Trey stepped up to him, gripping his chin between two fingers. "Not for a second." He lowered his voice and leaned closer to Magnus's ear. "But if you start talkin' about it, I'm gonna get hard again, and you're gonna have to take care of me when you should be focused on the chores."

Magnus's cock kicked hard in his shorts. He knew that gruff whisper had been for effect since no one was around to hear them. And that alone sent a chill down his spine.

"Any time, any place," he countered, feeling bold and elated by Trey's admission.

"Careful, Magnus, or you'll find your ass stuffed full one more time."

"You can't get enough of me. Admit it."

Trey was looking into his eyes, so Magnus saw that brief moment of hesitation, but then Trey's eyes cleared. "You're right. I can't."

Magnus couldn't explain what it felt like to have the man you loved admit something he'd refused to acknowledge for so long. It was the most incredible high in the world.

"So it's a good thing I can take you whenever and wherever I want," Trey noted with a smirk.

He refrained from telling Trey that he was his forever. Magnus didn't want to push too hard. Trey was opening up, but Magnus knew from experience he could shut down at any minute. So instead, he said, "You're right. You can. But you'll have to catch me first."

Trey grunted a laugh, clearly taken off guard by Magnus's retort, the mood still light and comfortable. It remained that way throughout the morning while they did chores, when they shared breakfast with Ava, and when all three of them went back to the kennels to pitch in for the day.

It wasn't until later that evening, as they were getting the dogs tucked away for the night, that a feeling of foreboding made the hair on the back of Magnus's neck stand up. He had a strange feeling that the other shoe was about to drop.

Chapter Sixteen

Tuesday, August 9, 2022

AVA SAT ON DR. BRIGGS'S COUCH, FILLING her in on what had happened since her last visit.

Of course, she purposely omitted a few private details, but she did admit that the three of them had been intimate several times since, and Ava was now sleeping in Magnus's bed every night. Unfortunately, Trey wasn't staying the night every night, but he'd been there again last night since he had agreed to drive her to this appointment.

"And the nightmares? Are you still having them?"

Ava had to think about that for a second. She frowned as she met Dr. Briggs's gaze. "Actually, no. Not…" She tried to recall the last one she had. "It's been a few days."

"That's a good sign."

A nod was all she could muster because she was still confused to realize she hadn't had a nightmare. She'd gotten so used to them that after a while of trying not to go to sleep to avoid them, she'd given up and resigned herself to having to relive the hell of that night on repeat.

"What's on your mind, Ava?"

"Why?" she asked. "Why am I not having them?"

"It could be that you're in a good place right now, and your subconscious is settled. Or it could be that opening up to Magnus, letting him know what happened, has eased some of your stress. You've been dealing with this all by yourself for a very long time. Sometimes we need to get it out so we can process it."

Ava smiled, letting that comfort her.

Unfortunately, her new lease on life didn't last as long as she'd hoped it would. After her appointment with Dr. Briggs, Trey offered to take her to lunch. Since she couldn't imagine refusing an opportunity to share a meal with him, she agreed.

Now, as they were seated at this cozy little diner in his hometown of Coyote Ridge, a place Trey was clearly comfortable, Ava had an eerie feeling that she couldn't shrug off.

"What's wrong?" Trey inquired, his eyebrows V'd as he studied her.

"Nothing. I mean, I don't know."

Trey was about to say something, but his attention was diverted to something or someone behind Ava.

"Hey," Trey greeted.

Clearly a some*one*.

A moment later, a pretty brunette with board-straight hair and striking green eyes stepped into Ava's view. She smiled widely as she put a protective hand on her protruding belly.

"It's good to see you," the woman said to Trey.

"Same," he said, his eyes softening with … affection? "How've you been?"

"Really good. All moved into the house." She patted her belly lightly. "Now, it's just a matter of time."

For a second, Trey seemed confused, but then he met Ava's gaze.

"Oh, sorry," he mumbled. "Ava, this is Jessica James. JJ, meet Ava."

"Please, call me JJ. Everyone does."

"It's nice to meet you," Ava said, although she still had no clue who the woman was to Trey. She'd heard the name JJ mentioned a few times, but she'd always figured it was a man's name.

"It's good to see you again, Ava," JJ noted, her expression warm and friendly. "I work for Sniper 1 Security. More specifically, the Off the Books Task Force. We led the search for you when you were missing."

"I'm sorry," Ava said, trying to recall when they'd met. "I don't remember meeting you."

"You were in the hospital." JJ glanced at Trey. "My fiancé and I stopped by to see how you were doin'."

Well, that explained it. More than likely, Ava was doped up on pain meds. She didn't remember much about the first couple of weeks she was there. All the tension eased out of her shoulders, and she managed a smile. This time, it was genuine. "From what Trey told me, you were instrumental in locating me."

"I wouldn't go that far," JJ said, shifting to her other foot. "But I'm happy it turned out … I'm just glad you're better."

Ava knew she was dancing around the events, unsure how Ava might react to the fact Harrison was dead. Truth was, she was happy. She felt safer without him in this world, but she missed her mother dearly. Since she couldn't think about one death without the other, Ava had convinced herself that Renee March had avenged her by killing Harrison before taking her own life. The ache in her chest still blossomed when she thought about it, but thinking of her mother as her savior in those last moments helped to ease it a little.

"I'm glad he won't be able to do it again," JJ added before looking at Trey. "Anyway, I—"

Before she could think about it, Ava reached out and touched JJ's wrist. "What do you mean *again?*"

JJ's green eyes leveled on her face, and there was a hint of uncertainty in them. She glanced at Trey and then back.

"What aren't you telling me?" Ava prompted when it was clear JJ was hedging.

JJ glanced at Trey again. Ava looked over in time to see him nod his chin curtly.

"Mind if I sit?" JJ prompted, urging Trey to move over on his side of the booth.

He scooted toward the wall as JJ took a seat, putting her directly across from Ava.

"You said again. He's done it before?"

JJ clasped her hands together on top of the table. "When I was diggin' into Harrison's past, lookin' for clues that might lead us to find you, I uncovered some … anomalies."

Ava shook her head. "I don't know what that means."

"I pulled at strings to see what I could uncover, and I learned about another woman who'd disappeared. Technically, she's still missing. Since it's been over a decade, I honestly don't think we'll ever find her."

Ava couldn't hide her surprise. "Because she's…?" She swallowed down the bile that rose in her throat. "Are you saying what I think you're saying?"

JJ nodded. "Yes. I believe Harrison killed her and hid the body. I've been searchin' for months now, tryin' to unearth even the tiniest trace, but the trail ends about the time Harrison moved to Texas."

Ava stared at JJ as she processed this information. She had to appreciate how straightforward this woman was. Most people she encountered treated her like a child, dancing around the message instead of laying it out for her. It made her admire JJ a little.

"Who was she?"

"Her name's Shayla Andrews. I came upon her when I was goin' through Harrison's education history. I was followin' his actions on paper to see what he did after college. I located an application for a marriage license in Colorado. It was never filed, so they were never actually married. I was hopin' that was because her parents wouldn't grant permission. She was only sixteen, and he'd recently been arrested for inappropriate actions with a minor. I kinda thought it was a shotgun weddin' thing—that one led to the other, and he was bein' forced to marry her since she was underage, but I have no idea. I'm not sure if the two are even related, to be honest," JJ clarified. "I just found it odd that I could never find her after that. It's like she vanished in thin air."

"When was this?"

"Harrison was twenty-two," JJ answered. "At the time, he was still using his birth name. Franklin Harris."

That would've been a decade ago, which meant—

"Wait, you said his birth name?" She shook her head and glanced at Trey. "I … I don't understand."

JJ continued. "Harrison Rivers was one of Franklin Harris's aliases. Probably came up with it when he got his first fake ID. He'd used it a few times before he came to Texas, but it wasn't until he got here that he legally changed his name. I'm not sure if he was runnin' from something or if he just wanted to build on that persona so he could run for senate. His father and grandfather are career politicians."

"His father's still alive?"

JJ frowned. "Yes." She glanced at Trey quickly, then back to Ava. "You didn't know that?"

Ava shook her head. "He told me his parents were dead. Killed in a freak accident when he was little." She glanced at Trey. "Did you know about this?"

"I knew of the alias." His gaze shuttered. "And that he has a family."

Ava let that sink in.

"But only because they issued a press release after his death."

Press release? Why didn't Ava know about this?

JJ quickly came to his defense. "I never told Trey the details. He was with Magnus during the search and … well, you know he stopped workin' for the task force. I was hopin' to find out what happened before I brought it back up."

Trey reached his hand across the table. Ava stared at it for a moment, then reached for him. He squeezed her fingers gently, not letting go. It was a simple gesture that made her chest ache with so much love for him.

"I'm still searchin', but I'm runnin' out of ideas."

"Did you talk to her parents?"

"I have not," JJ admitted, and Ava could see her reluctance to say as much. "I haven't gotten up the nerve yet. I don't want to cause them any more pain. If she did disappear ten years ago … I didn't want to give them false hope."

"What about closure?" Ava prompted. "If they don't know what happened, it might ease their minds to know at least."

Ava would want to know if it were her child who'd gone missing.

"Will you at least keep looking?" Ava implored.

JJ's eyes softened as she nodded. "I will. And if I find anything, I'll be sure to let you know."

That was the least she could ask for. "Thank you, JJ."

TREY DROVE AVA BACK TO MAGNUS'S AFTER they finished their lunch. She'd been quiet since learning those things about the man she'd been married to. Trey could tell it bothered her, but he also got the feeling she was trying to shrug it off. He wasn't sure whether he should bring it up or let it go, so he opted for the latter. With any luck, JJ would find something, and Ava could get the closure she mentioned the girl's parents needed.

He should've known that Ava wouldn't be able to let it go for long, though. It wasn't in her nature. She was far too inquisitive to let such a vital matter get swept under the rug.

"I think I need to go back to my house," Ava declared as they were sitting down to dinner, the three of them in Magnus's small breakfast nook.

Magnus's fork hit his plate with a clatter, his eyes slamming into Ava.

"I don't mean to live there," she said quickly. "I just..." Her narrow shoulders lifted and dropped. "I think it's time I see it again."

"Trey already got everything you asked for," Magnus said, clearly not approving of her request.

"I know." She smiled at Trey. "And I'm grateful. But I still want to see it."

"Did you talk to Dr. Briggs about doin' that?" Magnus asked.

Ava looked down at her plate, forked a bite of beef stroganoff into her mouth. She shook her head as she chewed.

"Do you think you should?"

Trey knew Magnus was only worried about the effect seeing the home where her mother and husband died would have on Ava. Not that there were any traces, because the crime scene had been cleaned for the most part. The mattress where Harrison had breathed his last breath had been destroyed, and the hardwood floors had been stripped, removing all the blood. It was no longer a gruesome scene, but it didn't look the way it would when people lived there. Then again, it had been months since Trey had been out there, so who knew what it looked like now. Magnus had been paying the utilities and for a cleaning service to come in once a month, but that was only because he wasn't sure whether Ava would ever want any more of her things. Harrison's estate had paid the house off, and all the bank accounts had been changed to Ava's name. It had required Ava to grant Magnus power of attorney to get it all done, but Trey had understood the request. Magnus was looking out for Ava. Always had been.

Rather than argue, Ava looked at Magnus, her heart in her eyes. "I'd really like to. But I'd like you both to come with me."

Magnus glanced at Trey.

Trey nodded. He wasn't sure it was a good idea, but Ava was the only person who could determine that. They'd coddled her long enough. Now that she was seeking therapy, Trey had noticed a significant difference. The strong, resilient woman he knew her to be was emerging. Pretty soon, she wouldn't be backing down at all. He liked the idea but doubted that was the case for Magnus. He was overprotective when it came to her. Rightfully so, perhaps.

"Okay, just tell me when."

Ava's eyes flashed with warmth. "Thank you. If it'll make you feel better, I'll talk to Dr. Briggs on Thursday when I go back."

Magnus nodded, then exhaled heavily. His relief evident.

After dinner, Magnus took the duty of cleaning the kitchen since Ava had cooked, so Trey took the opportunity to sit on the couch with her and watch TV. He honestly couldn't say what was on, because from the moment they'd sat down, Ava had been pressed up against him, the sweet scent of her hair teasing his nose.

He felt like a teenager on the first date. He was tempted to put his arm around her but resisted the urge, only to be tempted again and again. He finally mustered the nerve when Magnus joined them, taking a seat at the opposite end of the couch. His actions were thwarted when Ava lay down, putting her head in Trey's lap and her feet in Magnus's.

"This is more like it," she said, turning her head to the side to watch television.

Trey wasn't quite on the same page. Her head resting in his lap … it was making his dick hard, and she was only touching his thigh. Something about seeing her like that … it stirred him. But it was when she looked up at him and grinned that Trey's cock roared to life. An image of her smiling down at him like that while his face was buried between her thighs flashed in his mind's eye.

"If you keep lookin' at her like that, *I* might spontaneously combust," Magnus declared with a laugh.

Trey glanced over at him, then reined in the lust that threatened to send him into free fall. "I should probably get goin'."

"No," Ava snapped, hopping to her knees before he knew what she was doing.

The next thing Trey knew, she was straddling his lap, laughing as she did.

"It's my job to keep you right here for the rest of the night," she told him as she placed her hands on his shoulders, lightly restraining him. It would've been the work of a moment to pick her up and set her aside, but even Trey wasn't stupid enough to do that.

"I'm not sure right here works for me," he told her honestly. "Perhaps somewhere with more room to move around."

Ava's blue eyes glittered with promise. "That can be arranged. What did you have in mind?"

Rather than tell her, Trey gripped her ass in his hands and got to his feet. She wrapped her legs around his waist and her arms around his neck, giggling as he carried her down the hallway to Magnus's bedroom. He didn't bother looking back to see if Magnus was following. He was smart. He would join them sooner or later.

Before he could set her on the bed, Ava's arms tightened around his neck, her lips brushing his. Trey had gotten familiar with her kiss these past few days, and he found when he wasn't kissing her, he was often thinking about it. Her lips were so soft, so gentle, it caused an ache inside him he'd never felt before. The tenderness in her touch was foreign but ridiculously appealing at the same time. Trey had always been attracted to masculine men. And while there'd been some tender moments during a few of those relationships, they'd never felt quite like this.

"That's better," Ava said, opening her eyes when Trey eased her down on the bed and settled himself over her.

"Is it?"

Her eyes glittered.

Trey lifted her T-shirt, revealing her stomach. He pressed soft kisses around her belly button, then drifted higher, sliding his tongue over her ribs, licking her along the way.

"Trey…"

Yeah, he liked the way she said his name.

Trey pushed her T-shirt higher, admiring every inch he uncovered.

"I want to suck these little nipples," he groaned, nipping them through the satin bra.

Ava arched her back and unhooked her bra. Trey sat back and watched as she pulled her shirt and bra off, tossing them aside. He stared at her tiny pink nipples and the gentle swells of her breasts. His mouth watered.

"You're so beautiful," he whispered. He didn't mean to speak the words aloud, but once they were out, he couldn't recall them.

"You make me feel beautiful," she said, sliding her hands up his arms as she stared up at him.

"I want to taste you, girl," he admitted, his voice gravel rough. That seemed to always happen around them.

She moaned softly, thrusting her chest up as she cupped one of her tits.

He fucking liked to see her touching herself. There was something insanely erotic about it. He'd never noticed that before. Not with anyone he'd ever been with. Not even Magnus. And Trey had admired the man jacking off more than once. For some reason, this was different. The way her fingers lightly grazed her smooth skin, like she was caressing delicate glass...

When she cupped herself and lifted as though offering him a taste, Trey leaned down and swirled his tongue around her nipple, loving the way it hardened beneath his ministrations. All thought fled after that, his focus solely on making Ava moan and whimper, the sounds spurring him on. Trey didn't know when he'd removed her shorts, but at some point, he'd stripped her bare, and now that she was naked beneath him, he knew he couldn't resist her. Hell, he no longer wanted to.

He sucked one of her nipples into his mouth, then released it with a pop before meeting her eyes. He saw only approval and lust shining back at him, which he took as permission. He trailed his lips from the center of her chest down to her belly button. He kept going until he reached her smooth mound. He'd honestly thought he would be hesitant about this part, but Trey didn't pause for a second, sliding his tongue along the seam of her pussy.

Ah, hell, she tasted good.

Ava cried out, her knees spreading wide, revealing the glistening pink flesh between.

He groaned, the temptation overwhelming him, but he didn't want to rush, so he took his time, massaging her soft flesh, admiring all that he revealed. Using his thumbs, he spread her pussy lips, revealing the tiny bundle of nerves nestled within. Trey leaned forward, keeping his eyes on her face as he swiped the tip of his tongue over it a few times.

"That..." Ava sighed. "That feels so good."

Trey took his cues from her, flicking her clit with his tongue, circling it before suckling it between his lips.

"Oh, God," she whimpered, her hips bucking.

He could get used to this. Her taste and the sounds she made went right to his head.

Trey spent the next few minutes worshipping her pussy, getting intimately familiar with what made her moan and what made her sigh. When he pushed two fingers inside her while he flicked her clit rapidly, he felt the tension build inside her.

He worked her that way until she cried out, her smooth inner walls clamping down on his fingers.

And before he could even contemplate what he was doing, Trey stood tall and stripped off his clothes. He couldn't wait another second before he claimed this woman. The urge was far too potent to deny any longer.

MAGNUS HAD PURPOSELY GIVEN AVA AND TREY a few minutes alone.

He'd known exactly what would happen if he did, and he was right. He had remained in the living room as long as he could before his resistance faded. When he reached the bedroom, he found Trey's face buried between Ava's thighs. She was writhing on the bed, crying out his name as he feasted on her sweet cunt.

Magnus had been momentarily stunned, unable to look away from the erotic sight. He'd never witnessed anything as arousing as Ava having her pussy eaten by Trey. She'd come so beautifully, crying out Trey's name.

But when Trey stripped off his clothes and joined Ava in the bed, Magnus got with the program. He quickly kicked off his boots and stripped out of his shorts and T-shirt before walking over to the opposite side of the bed where Ava's head was.

She turned her head and smiled over at him. "Nice of you to join us."

He grinned, stroking his cock leisurely. "Nice of you to wait for me," he countered with a laugh.

"Couldn't help it." She lowered her voice like she was sharing a secret. "He's got a wicked mouth."

"Trust me, I know."

Magnus looked over at Trey, their gazes meeting momentarily as Trey positioned himself between Ava's thighs. He wasn't sure he'd ever seen anything as carnal as the expression on Trey's face. He was holding himself back despite how badly he wanted this.

Not wanting him to stop, Magnus crawled up on the bed, kneeling beside Ava's head.

"It's time for me to catch up," he declared. "You can suck me while Trey fucks you."

She moaned, reaching for him like she couldn't hold herself back. Magnus thrust his hips forward while Ava lifted her head and took him between her lips. It was all he could do to look away from her sweet mouth surrounding him, but he refused to miss Trey taking her for the first time. He glanced over in time to see Trey pressing his hips forward, the head of his cock slipping inside Ava. He penetrated her slowly, sliding in deeper and deeper, a rough grumble sounding in his chest.

"Fuck ... so tight," Trey growled, the cords in his neck straining, his muscles tense as he leaned forward on one hand.

Magnus watched where they were joined, his cock throbbing more insistently each time Trey retreated and slid in, his cock glistening with Ava's juices.

Trey surprised them all, pulling out and gripping his cock tightly. "Not yet," he growled.

Magnus couldn't resist the urge to be part of this with Trey. He reluctantly pulled his cock from Ava's mouth so he could bend over and suck Trey's cock into his mouth.

"Oh, fuck!" Trey growled, gripping Magnus's hair painfully tight. "Don't you dare make me come."

Magnus had no intention of doing that. He merely licked every drop of Ava's sweet flavor from him and then pulled back. When he did, Trey's chest was heaving, but he looked calmer. He guided himself back inside her, driving in deeper, faster than before.

Ava lifted her hips to meet his thrust, and Trey's gaze snapped to her face.

"You feel so fuckin' good."

"So do you," she whimpered. "Make me come, Trey. Please ... make me come."

Magnus could see the restraint tightening the lines of Trey's face. He was trying to hold back for as long as he could. Trey pumped his hips a few times, then pulled out. Magnus took over, licking him clean again before Trey was once again buried inside her. They repeated it several more times, and each time Ava begged and pleaded for more.

Finally, Trey pushed inside her and held himself still for a moment. He took a deep breath then leaned forward, bracketing Ava's head between his hands.

"Hold on, girl," he growled, his voice gravel rough.

Magnus sat back on his haunches and watched as Ava dug her nails into his triceps while Trey began fucking her. He grunted and groaned, the sounds ripped from his throat, but he didn't stop. And Ava never stopped begging for more.

"You better come for me, girl," Trey said, this time the words more of a command than a request.

Magnus saw the flash of lust in Ava's eyes. She liked it.

Trey gripped her hips, driving into her, slamming in balls deep every time. Magnus witnessed the moment of no return. It happened when Ava threw her head back and screamed, her body tensing beneath Trey's much bigger body.

"Goddamn, Ava … fuck…" Trey followed her over, his hips slamming forward as he drained his balls deep inside her.

Never had Magnus seen anything as hot as that.

Trey fell to the bed beside Ava, his head landing on one of the pillows. Ava was breathing hard and smiling, glancing between them.

"You look like you're ready for more," Magnus told her.

"I don't know … I'm not sure anything can top that." She looked at Trey. "That was … amazing." She peered back at Magnus. "But you're welcome to try."

Magnus barked a laugh, thrilled by her teasing. "Oh, I'm certainly gonna try."

He waited until she was looking at Trey again before he reached around her, sliding his arm over her thighs and then under her back. He flipped her over onto her stomach, smiling when she giggled and tried to crawl forward. He stopped her with a firm grip on her hips, pulling her back.

"You're gonna take my cock while you lick all your juices off Trey's."

She peered back over her shoulder, her expression one of intrigue. "It would be my pleasure."

Magnus groaned. The sexy minx was going to drive him insane.

When she leaned in to lick Trey's cock, Magnus dragged the head of his dick along her slick pussy, teasing her before pressing the tip into her tight little hole. He pushed in deep.

Ava's back arched, her head tipping back. "Oh, God, yes."

Trey groaned, and Magnus realized he was watching him. His eyes were hot as he locked onto Magnus's hips when he began thrusting into Ava.

"One of these days, I'm gonna fuck you while you're fuckin' her," Trey said, his tone rife with promise.

Oh, shit. Magnus nearly came from the mental image alone.

Trey's eyes shifted to Ava as she continued to lick his cock as he lovingly cupped the back of her head.

"And one day, girl, I'm gonna fuck your tight little ass while Magnus fills your pussy like he's doin' now."

Ava hummed around Trey's cock.

"Fuck. You'll make me come again if you're not careful," Trey warned her.

It was too much for Magnus. Seeing them like this, hearing Trey's dirty promises. This was everything he'd ever wanted, and while he was terrified to get his hopes up, it felt like they were moving forward.

"Don't you dare come until she does," Trey barked. "You make that pussy come all over your cock first."

Magnus sucked air into his lungs as the tension coiled tightly inside him. The man had a way of making Magnus lose what little control he had.

"And you, girl." Trey caressed the back of Ava's head. "You better come for us."

Ava whimpered, lifting her head. Trey gripped his cock and stroked it slowly. It was clear he wasn't looking to come again, but he was right here in the moment with them. Their eyes met and held as Magnus fucked Ava hard. He held her hips, ramming into her, using her sweet cunt while she rocked back against him, urging him to fill her.

"Oh, fuck ... Ava ... you better come," Magnus warned. "You better come all over my dick."

She slammed her hips back. Once, twice. He felt her inner muscles clamp down on him. He gritted his teeth and fought the nearly painful urge to come.

"That's it, girl," Trey urged. "Come for us."

She whimpered and rocked harder. Magnus thrust deeper, savoring every delicious caress of her tight little pussy on his cock.

"Right ... fuckin' ... now," Trey barked.

Ava screamed, and Magnus nearly bit his tongue. She locked down on him so tight he could hardly breathe as she ripped his orgasm from him. He held himself deep inside her until every drop was drained from his balls.

When it was over, he fell to his side and smiled up at the ceiling.

He wasn't sure it could get much better than that. Of course, he would soon learn that once Trey was on board, there was no stopping him.

Chapter Seventeen

Wednesday, August 10, 2022

MAGNUS WOKE EARLY THE NEXT MORNING—TWO hours before he usually did—slipping out of bed before Ava or Trey stirred. He pulled on shorts and left the room, silently closing the door behind him.

He'd traded his overnight shift with Billy last night for one reason only. This.

He flipped on the lights in the kitchen, opened the pantry door, and dug in the back for the box of pancake mix he'd bought last week without Ava knowing. If she had seen it, she would've offered to make him some, and while he did enjoy pancakes on occasion, he preferred waffles. What she wouldn't have realized was he'd bought them for her. That and the chocolate chips he'd stashed in the small cabinet over the refrigerator after he heard her mention she was craving chocolate. Knowing Ava, she would've sniffed them out, found them and the pancake mix, and his surprise would've been ruined.

Today was Ava's birthday, and while she hadn't brought it up and he hadn't mentioned it, he'd been gearing up for this day for a while now. It would be the first birthday he'd spent with her since she turned ten. Only on *that* birthday, Magnus wasn't the one who made her chocolate chip pancakes—something she claimed was her favorite—Magnus's mother had.

This year Magnus intended to do that for her.

Unfortunately, he sucked in the kitchen, and it didn't help that he was trying to be quiet. It would ruin everything if she walked in before he had them made. Not for the first time in the past few months, Magnus wished he would've paid more attention when his mother tried to teach him to cook when he was a kid. The basics, at least. Instead, he'd been too busy helping his dad or hanging out with friends to do something so domestic. But the truth was, he didn't so much care that he would've learned how to cook as much as he would've had more time with his mom.

Magnus opened the box while skimming the instructions on the back. It sounded relatively simple, with the exception of the actual cooking part. Or so he thought before he took a look at the lumpy batter in the bowl. No way could that be edible, cooked or not.

He was beginning to get frustrated when he heard footsteps coming down the hall. He stopped moving, hardly even breathing, as he waited for her to appear. His relief was potent when Trey stepped into view.

"What're you doin'?" Trey mumbled, wiping his hair back from his face.

"Makin' Ava pancakes," he whispered. "It's her birthday."

Trey's eyebrows launched skyward. "No shit?"

Magnus pointed at the lumpy shit in the bowl. "Problem is, I fucked it up already."

"Here," he offered, pressing his hand on Magnus's chest and easing him back from the stove. He dug in the drawer, pulled out a whisk, and then said, "Get me a skillet and the butter out of the fridge."

Magnus pointed to the skillet on the stove, then grabbed the butter sticks out of the refrigerator. When he returned, he saw Trey pulling a measuring cup out of the cabinet.

"I assume she likes these," Trey said softly as he began churning the batter like a professional.

Magnus hopped up on the counter beside the stove. "She did when she was ten."

Trey's eyes slid over his face. "You get to spend a lot of birthdays with her?"

Magnus shook his head. "That was the only one I really recall. I remember all of Tabby's. My parents usually did it up in high fashion. Big parties and shit. But I don't remember any for Ava."

"Except this one?"

He nodded. "She spent the night with Tabby the night before because Renee had been having one of her episodes. Or that's what I heard my parents talking about. From what my mom said, Renee was insisting that Ava didn't deserve to be weighed down by a mother who was so messed up. It wasn't the first time, nor was it the last, but for whatever reason, it hit me that Ava had been spending a lot of time at our house."

When Trey lifted an eyebrow, encouraging him to continue, Magnus did.

"At the time, I was too self-centered to care. I mean, shit. I was twelve. I didn't care about my kid sister's friend. Still, that morning, when I watched my mother deliver chocolate chip pancakes, complete with a single candle poked right in the middle, to Tabby's bedroom, I witnessed something I'd never seen before. Ava's face lit up in a way that didn't make sense to me at the time. One look at the candle and her little chin began to wobble, and tears started to stream from her eyes, but that smile … it never vanished."

It'd been Ava's birthday, and her mother had sent her somewhere else. But leave it to Magnus's mother not to forget something so important.

Every year on her birthday, although Magnus didn't get to see her, he would text Ava. At least since she'd started to drive, and he saw her a few times. Sometimes she would respond, sometimes not. But this year, he finally had the chance to do for her the one thing that had put a blinding smile on her face all those years ago.

"She's never mentioned her birthday," Trey noted.

"No. And she won't. I'm not even sure she celebrates it anymore."

Trey smiled. "But you're gonna make sure she does."

"I'd like to, yeah. Too bad I suck in the kitchen."

Trey's smirk turned devious. "You suck in a lotta other rooms, too. You'll never hear me complainin'."

Magnus nearly barked a laugh but managed to hold it in. It would ruin the surprise if he woke Ava now.

He watched Trey work at the stove, looking as at home there as he did anywhere else. It wasn't the first time he'd noticed how domesticated Trey was. He'd done a lot of the housework while they'd been taking care of Ava when she first got out of the hospital. He pretended it was no big deal, but to Magnus, it had been everything.

"Mama used to make us muffins on our birthdays," Trey acknowledged, flipping the first pancake with ease. "Blueberry was my favorite. It was also Tori's and Bryn's, so they always gave me shit that it wasn't really for me. The girls are older, so they tried to convince us they were the favorites."

Magnus smiled, warmth filling his insides because Trey was opening up.

"She would get up early"—he waved the spatula—"kinda like this. She'd go into the kitchen and start cookin'. As we got older, we started wakin' up before her so we could help her." He smiled, staring into the pan. "For whatever reason, they tasted better when we did."

The man amazed him with his talents and his stories, so many of which Magnus hadn't had an opportunity to hear because Trey had kept himself closed off for so long. Having him here … it made Magnus's throat tighten, the emotion threatening to strangle him. He loved this man and had for so long he hardly recognized what was going on anymore. He'd convinced himself that he would only ever have what little parts of Trey he would unknowingly share, and he would be grateful.

"I hope you got a candle," Trey said as he piled the last five pancakes on a plate.

"I didn't," Magnus said softly, praying Trey wasn't going to ask him the reason why.

Trey looked up, his forehead was creased with concern, but then his eyes cleared. Magnus didn't have to tell him, the man already knew.

"I know it's fucked up," Magnus muttered. "It just… The fire. It…"

"Terrifies you?"

Magnus met his eyes, surprised by the words. "Yes."

"It's not fucked up," Trey noted, stepping in front of him. He leaned in and kissed his lips lightly. "But it does allow you to make a new tradition of your own."

"What're you talkin' about?"

Trey smiled. "She's always messin' with those damn dandelions. Pickin' 'em and blowin' all the seeds off."

Magnus chuckled as he hopped to his feet. "My dad used to tell her and Tabby that if you could blow all the seeds off in one breath, the person you love would love you back."

He heard Trey chuckle as Magnus slipped out the back door and around to the side of the house, where there was a huge patch of them. He grabbed the fluffiest one he could find and gently carried it into the house, blocking it with his hand.

Trey was waiting, holding up the plate of pancakes.

Magnus poked the stem delicately into the pancakes, doing his best not to damage the fragile flower, or weed, or whatever the hell these things were.

"Perfect," Trey said. "Now take 'em to her." He leaned in and kissed Magnus again. "I'm gonna make a few more and take 'em to Billy since I know you traded shifts with him."

Magnus swallowed around the tightness in his throat. "Thanks."

This time when Trey smiled, Magnus was almost certain he saw Trey's heart in his eyes.

AVA WAS ROUSED FROM A GOOD DREAM by a delicious smell. She wasn't sure what it was, but it was definitely food.

She rolled from her stomach to her back, sniffing the air as she opened her eyes and brought the room into focus. It was dark, with the exception of the lamp on Magnus's nightstand. It was dimmed, but she could see enough to make out his form sitting on the edge of the mattress.

"Mornin'," he greeted softly.

She smiled. "Mornin'. What time is it?"

"Five."

Ava grumbled, closing her eyes and covering them with her arm. "But I don't hafta get up till six."

"Today you do."

"Why? Are you plannin' to ravish me again?" She peeked out from under her arm. "Because I certainly wouldn't say no to that."

"I'll be more than happy to, but first, I made you breakfast."

Too curious not to look, she dropped her arm and opened her eyes. "Magnus Storme, you don't know your way around a microwave. How'd—"

Magnus produced a plate of chocolate chip pancakes with a dandelion sticking out of the top. The moment she saw them, she grinned so wide, her eyes darting to his face as her belly did a somersault.

"Happy birthday, Ava."

Her throat constricted, and tears formed, but she couldn't stop smiling. She knew she looked like an idiot, but these were her favorites. The last time she'd had them had been... It had been so long ago.

"It was your tenth birthday," Magnus said softly. "You stayed over, and my mom made these for you."

"An all-you-can-eat pancake breakfast," Ava noted.

"I didn't realize the significance of them until I watched her give them to you. You fought the urge to cry even though your smile was so bright it nearly blinded me."

"You remember that?"

"Every detail."

Ava propped up on her elbow and plucked the dandelion from the center. "And the significance of this?"

"Trey's idea. I didn't..." His gaze lowered. "I don't have any candles."

She put a hand on his arm. "This is even better."

Ava knew Magnus didn't have candles, not for birthday cakes and not for home decor. There wasn't even a lighter in the house, nor were there any matches or anything else that would produce a flame or require it. Even the stove was electric, as were the water heater and the heat pump. She understood why, although Magnus had never said.

"It's perfect." She drew it closer but resisted the urge to blow on it since the seeds would go everywhere. "Your dad was right when he told us if we could blow them all off in one breath, the person we loved would love us back."

Magnus set the plate of pancakes on the nightstand, took the dandelion from her fingers, and set it aside before pulling the blankets off her and crawling into bed. His warmth was more than enough to keep the chill at bay.

"Where's Trey? He still makin' pancakes?"

"He's takin' Billy some. A thank you for lettin' me be here with you."

As he moved over her, she curled her arms around his neck. "I knew you didn't make them."

"At least this way, they're edible," he whispered, placing a kiss on her lips.

Ava took advantage, holding his head to her so she could keep him where she wanted him. Magnus didn't resist, but he did try to roll over. She knew what he was doing—and why—but she refused to let him go.

"Make love to me, Magnus," she breathed against his lips. "Just like this."

He lifted his head so he could look at her. "You sure?"

"I've never been more sure of anything in my life."

Trusting that he wouldn't try to flip their positions, she released his neck so she could shove his shorts down. His mouth descended on hers, and somehow they managed to rid him of the shorts without him ever moving off of her.

Ava sighed as he entered her slowly, his head lifting again so he could watch her as he did. She held his gaze, wanting him to see that this was exactly as it should be. Together—the three of them in any combination—was as it should be. She wasn't scared of them.

"God," she gasped, dropping her head back as he thrust his hips forward, burying his cock deep inside her. "Magnus."

He continued to watch her, pumping his hips as he made love to her slowly. It was just as intense as all the other times, but maybe a little sweeter. She let the waves of pleasure roll through her, building her up slowly.

"I could stay like this forever," he whispered, burying his face in her neck.

Ava cupped the back of his head, rolling her hips to meet each thrust. Movement out of the corner of her eye caught her attention. When she looked over, she saw Trey standing in the doorway. He had one shoulder propped on the doorjamb, his hooded gaze locked on them. She held out a hand to him, but he shook his head. She didn't see worry or concern, only approval.

It was more than she'd ever expected, so she gave herself over to the moment, to Magnus.

She held on as he continued to drive her to the point of ecstasy, his big body covering her in a way that made her feel safe.

She could see Trey still standing at the door, so she ensured her voice was loud enough to carry to him, although she spoke to Magnus. "I've been blowing on those dandelions since I was a girl. And even more lately."

Magnus sank into her and paused, lifting his head to meet her gaze.

"Since it worked so well with you … I had to amend my wish to include Trey." She smiled up at him. "For both of us."

He dropped his face to her neck again and groaned against her skin, his hips bucking harder. "Oh, Jesus, Ava."

His pace increased, driving her right to the precipice. And when she came, she pressed her lips to his ear and whispered, "I love you, Magnus."

AFTER TREY HAD DELIVERED PANCAKES TO BILLY, he should've stayed to help him with morning chores. It was what he'd intended to do, but only because he'd wanted to give Ava and Magnus some privacy. Having heard Magnus's story about her tenth birthday, Trey realized how deeply the love between them was rooted, and he wanted them to express that to one another.

But something had lured him back to the house. And when he'd realized the bedroom door was open, he ventured that way. He hadn't planned to watch them, but now that he was, he couldn't regret it. Although he wasn't on the bed with them, he was as much in this moment as they were. Trey couldn't deny they were beautiful to watch. He never would've considered himself a voyeur, but now that he'd seen them, he was certain it wouldn't be the last time.

Something changed in him the moment Ava looked over. He'd seen the invitation in her eyes and in the way she gestured him to join. He had resisted because he'd wanted them to have this moment.

Trey had realized then that those precious moments were what was in store for them if he would stop being so damn stubborn. They could share more times like this. Not only between Ava and Magnus but between him and Magnus and him and Ava. He wasn't sharing Magnus's body with Ava the way he'd convinced himself he would have to. They were sharing so much more between all three of them.

As Magnus and Ava climaxed together, Trey slipped down the hall and out of the house. He headed for the main office, Ava's words echoing in his head.

I've been blowing on those dandelions since I was a girl. And even more lately. Since it worked so well with you … I had to amend my wish to include Trey. For both of us.

He wasn't sure what it was about that statement or the sentiment behind it, but a switch had been flipped. As though someone had turned the light on, and he finally understood what it all meant.

Chapter Eighteen

Thursday, August 11, 2022

AVA PURPOSELY WAITED UNTIL MAGNUS LEFT TO lead one of his SAR training classes and Trey was busy helping to rearrange the equipment shed before she snuck up to the front office to use the computer. Considering how Magnus was reacting to her requests to go back to her house, she didn't think he'd be too happy with her if he learned she was doing research into Harrison's past.

Granted, it wasn't so much research as it was reviewing everything JJ had unearthed since she'd first started digging up dirt on the man back when the Off the Books Task Force began searching for her. At Ava's request—which she'd done via text message after she acquired JJ's number by snooping in Trey's phone—JJ had sent Ava a link that allowed her to access all the files.

Now, whenever she got the chance, Ava read through those notes. And while it turned her stomach to learn the heinous truth about the man she had married, it somehow helped her to get closure. Well, maybe not closure, but it helped her to realize the man she'd married wasn't who she'd thought he was.

Ava didn't like that someone else—another woman who'd been even younger than JJ when the bastard seduced her—had fallen victim to Harrison, but for some warped and twisted reason, knowing it eased her mind. Ava had always blamed herself for being stupid, for falling for his lies. Now she realized he'd set out to seduce her because he was a predator, and she'd been an easy target.

But the worst part was Ava wasn't sure Harrison hadn't come by his deceit naturally. Based on JJ's notes, it looked like his father was as much a predator as his son.

She skimmed the first page of JJ's notes again, looking for one specific thing.

- Born Franklin Joseph Harris.

- Harris = Harrison (was that why he chose?)

- Rivers lived in Colorado until 2011, when he relocated to Texas, publicly stating he was pursuing a senate seat in Texas.

- Lived in various places from Dallas to Houston, then landed in Austin in 2015.

- Criminal record: nothing public, but cited several times for drunk and disorderly from the time he was 18. (Those were buried deep)

- Arrested for inappropriate actions with a minor when he was 22. The girl (Shayla Andrews) was 16. (Info also buried deep)

- Charges dropped, applied for marriage license, license never filed.

- His mother (Maria Delgado) was a maid employed by Rivers's father.

- Adopted by the Rivers family when he was 3.

- Father's wife took him in, pretended he was hers.

- Birth mother deported in 1993. (Supposedly—missing since 1996, Rivers would've been 6 at the time)

Ava sat back, staring at the last two lines. If Harrison's birth mother had been missing, there was a good chance Harrison's father had a hand in that disappearance. But what intrigued Ava was the fact Harrison's birth certificate listed his last name as Harris. If Maria was deported to Mexico, that meant she hadn't been legally in the US, right? But where did that last name come from? Was she married? If so, wouldn't that make her a citizen? And to whom?

Technically, Ava didn't know the first thing about immigration laws, so she wasn't sure marriage was even a way to remain in the country. However, it was a trope they used on television, so perhaps there was some truth to it. But why would his mother give him someone else's last name?

She pulled out the keyboard drawer and began typing those questions into the notes section, then she texted JJ to see if she had that information. The response was quick: *Nice catch. Let me check, and I'll get back to you.*

Ava was sending a thank you when the front door opened, and Trey walked in. She immediately clicked the screen to hide the window as she got to her feet.

"Hey," she greeted, hating that she felt guilty for what she was doing. More so that she probably *looked* guilty, too.

"Hey, yourself." Trey glanced around. "Magnus get back yet?"

"Nope. Need something?"

Ava felt her insides warm when he smiled this time. She was beginning to learn Trey's grins. He had one for every mood, and the one currently planted on his beautiful lips said he was feeling mischievous.

"Hey, Ava! You think you could come help me for a minute?" Gia shouted from one of the back rooms.

"Put that on ice, handsome," Ava told Trey, matching his smirk. "Duty calls."

Trey winked, and the move was so damn sexy she all but ran out of the room. Otherwise, Gia would've been SOL because Ava would be climbing that man like a tree.

TREY WATCHED AVA HURRY OUT OF THE room, and he couldn't help but laugh. She looked like a scared rabbit, but he knew better. More than likely, Ava was trying to keep from acting on her impulses. She'd made no attempts to hide her desire for him or Magnus, nor did she pretend she wasn't horny more often than not.

He damn sure wasn't complaining. Not about anything at the moment.

When she disappeared down the hall, Trey made his way behind the counter and pulled out the keyboard drawer. He needed to update one of the client files to reflect his medication had run out and, according to the prescription on the bottle, there would be no more refills.

He clicked the mouse to open another application, but when he did, a screen popped up. He quickly scanned the information until he realized what it was.

Son of a bitch.

Trey peered down the hall Ava had snuck out, then back to the computer screen. The notes were all about Harrison Rivers, and based on the familiar shorthand, these had come from JJ.

He exhaled heavily and opened the application to update the medical file before he forgot to do it. Once that was done, he hid Ava's notes once more, retrieved his phone from his back pocket, and headed outside for privacy.

"Hey. What's up?" JJ asked, a smile in her voice.

"Why are you havin' Ava look at your notes on Rivers?"

"First of all, Sherlock, I'm not *havin'* her do anything. She called me. Said you gave her my number."

He certainly had not, but he didn't bother to tell JJ that.

"And secondly, why does it matter?"

Trey could think of a thousand reasons, most notably the fact that Magnus would go apeshit when he learned about this.

"She's a grown woman, Trey," JJ stated firmly. "She doesn't need anyone's permission."

He paused for a moment, wondering if he'd spoken out loud.

"Plus, she's rather intuitive. She noticed that Harrison's birth name doesn't match his biological mother or father and wants to know why."

"How's that intuitive?"

"Because I didn't even catch it. She's right to ask because if there was another man in Maria Delgado's life, he could very well be a lead. Perhaps he knows why she's been missing since Rivers was six. And get this—"

"Stop," Trey interrupted. "Don't tell me this shit. I don't wanna know."

JJ was quiet.

"If Ava's lookin' into it, that's between the two of you. If she wants my help, she'll come to me."

Not that Trey expected that to happen since Ava was keeping this on the DL. But if Magnus learned that Trey was complicit, he didn't want to think about the hell that would rain down on them. Ava had a right to look because it was her life, but Trey wasn't going to do this backward. He had no intentions of keeping secrets from anyone. Especially not now that things were finally on the right track for him and Magnus.

"Okay, then. I'll give her a call and let her know what I found."

"JJ?"

"Yes?"

"I don't mean to be an asshole."

"No. I get it. You don't wanna overstep."

"It's not that," he corrected. "It's… Tell me one thing. Do you think there's any chance you'll find somethin' that's worth puttin' her through this again?"

JJ sighed, and her voice was kind when she said, "I think there's somethin' to find. I know Rivers is at fault for what happened to her, but I believe he's also at fault for Shayla Andrews."

"He's dead, JJ. It's not like he can be prosecuted for the crime."

"No. But his father can be."

"His father?"

"If that asshole was complicit in coverin' this up—which I truly believe he was—he needs to be held accountable."

Trey didn't have a rebuttal for that. She was absolutely right.

Question was: was it worth putting Ava in the line of fire? God only knows the lengths the Rivers family would go to to keep this shit buried.

Chapter Nineteen

One week later…
Friday, August 19, 2022

"Whatcha workin' on?" Trey asked when he found Ava coming down the hallway from the kennels.

It had been a week since Trey had talked to JJ and decided to ignore what he'd learned. Since then, Ava hadn't approached him, nor had she filled Magnus in on what she was doing, so he figured it was safe to say she didn't want them to know. He wasn't keen on what she was doing, but he trusted JJ to protect her at all costs, something he'd reiterated twice since that phone call. And if that meant letting the bastard's father slide on his previous crimes, so be it. It didn't exactly sit well with Trey, but as far as he was concerned, Ava's safety was all that mattered.

"Arbuckle hurt his paw," she told him, her expression sad. "He'll be fine, and I don't think he's in pain, but I'm gonna call his owner and see if she'll mind if I have the vet come out."

Trey stared at her, and for the first time since he'd met this woman, he noticed something. Something that surprised the ever-loving shit out of him. Not once in his entire life had Trey considered having kids. At least not since the brief time he'd entertained the idea when he and Paul were together. Since then, Trey hadn't gotten his hopes up. Adoption or a surrogate was his only option, and since he'd sworn off relationships—until Magnus flipped his world upside down—he'd figured it wasn't worth thinking about.

However, now that he'd fallen in love with a woman…

The acknowledgment nearly had him tripping over his own feet, but he hid it well, coming to an abrupt stop in front of Ava. He couldn't explain his overwhelming urge to kiss her, but he acted on it anyway. Reaching for her when she approached, Trey pulled her to him and leaned down to meld his mouth with hers. Ava hummed softly, her fingers sliding into his hair.

"What was that for?" she whispered breathlessly when they finally parted.

"Couldn't help myself."

"Maybe you could do it again?"

He gladly obliged her, but this time he went a step further. Trey gripped her ass and lifted her off her feet. She wound her legs around his hips as though it was the most natural thing to do. He moved two steps so he could press her against the wall and kiss her deeper. Her fingers twined in his hair as her tongue danced with his.

He didn't mean to take it that far, but Trey found he couldn't help himself. It didn't help that she was grinding against him, rocking her hips, seeking whatever friction she could get from where they were touching.

"Trey…"

"Tell me, girl," he rasped against her mouth. "Tell me what you need."

She whimpered, her mouth crushing to his again. Trey gave her the reprieve because he already knew. He braced his hands once again and carried her the few steps to the laundry room, kicking the door closed behind him.

When he set her on the washing machine, Ava immediately tried to yank his shirt off over his head.

"Not right now," he growled softly. "You're the one who's gonna come first."

Her blue eyes flashed with fire, and she spread her legs wider when he slipped his hand through the loose leg of her shorts. He tugged her panties aside and caressed her clit lightly.

"God, yes." Ava's hands shifted behind her to prop herself up as she humped his hand. "Trey…" She hissed softly, her eyes closing. "Don't stop doin' that."

Trey couldn't resist watching her glistening sex as he alternated between sliding one finger inside, then coating her clit with her own juices. He fucking loved how soft and silky she was, how that delicate tissue parted as he sank his finger in deeper.

"Damn, that's pretty," he whispered. "I wanna make this pussy come."

Those were words he'd never imagined himself ever saying, but they felt right to him. *She* felt right to him.

"Please, Trey…" Ava grabbed her shorts and pulled them out of the way, allowing him to use both hands. He circled his thumb over her clit and fucked her with two fingers.

"Oh, God … oh, God … oh, God…"

He watched her beautiful face, the way she bit her bottom lip and tilted her head back. Her chest rose and fell rapidly, her sweet moans echoing in the small room. And when she came, he loved how she sucked her bottom lip into her mouth in an attempt to be quiet.

"Fuck, that was hot." He licked his fingers clean, then stepped up and pressed his mouth to hers. "You taste so fuckin' good."

Ava kissed him back hungrily, but he put the brakes on when she tried to pull his shirt off again.

Trey stepped back and smiled. "That one was for you, girl." He leaned in and pressed his mouth to her ear. "I intend to take mine from Magnus."

"When?"

His dick kicked against his zipper, and he knew if he didn't walk away now, there was a good chance he was going to come inside her in under three minutes.

"I think you'll know," he told her, softly kissing her mouth before helping her down from the washing machine.

She peered up at him with wide, curious eyes. "How?"

"Because I don't intend to let him come."

Her lips quirked. "And he'll have to, so he'll come find me."

"That's the plan."

"I'll be ready and waiting."

He smacked her lightly on the ass, watching as she bounced out of the room, her sadness from earlier replaced with a wide, satisfied grin on her face.

Trey didn't waste time going in search of Magnus, but not before he found the bottle of lubricant he knew Magnus kept in the top drawer of his desk. He concealed it in his hand and headed back through the front office, nodding at Gia as he passed. She was being nicer to him now that he was back. Trey didn't have the heart to tell her he wasn't sure if it was permanent or not. He hadn't yet had that conversation with Magnus. They would, soon enough. But now was not the time.

He found Magnus in the supply closet, where they kept the clean towels and various other supplies. He was counting items on a shelf when Trey walked in and pulled the door closed. Since there was no lock, they would have to be quiet or risk someone coming in. Trey was so fucking hard, he didn't care if someone stumbled upon them, but he figured Magnus might since it would be one of his employees.

"What are you—"

Trey shut him up with a kiss, backing him against the wall. "Can you taste her?"

"Oh, fuck … did you…?"

"I just made Ava come on my fingers," he admitted, bringing his fingers to Magnus's mouth. "Then I licked them clean, but I bet you can still taste her."

Magnus sucked his two fingers into his mouth, holding Trey's stare.

"Where?" Magnus asked when he released him.

"In the laundry room." Trey reached for the button on Magnus's shorts, tugging it free. "I set her on the washer and pulled those little shorts aside"—he lowered the zipper—"then buried my fingers inside"—he fisted Magnus's cock, gently squeezing to punctuate his next words—"her tight … wet … pussy."

Magnus's hips bucked forward.

"You like that I can't get enough of her, don't you?"

Magnus nodded.

"I can't get enough of you, either," he warned, stepping back so he could turn Magnus around. "Put your hands on the wall, and don't move 'em."

Magnus did, and Trey dragged his shorts and boxers down. They were baggy enough that Magnus freed one foot, which allowed him to spread his legs wide.

While he assumed the position, Trey freed his cock from his jeans and coated himself with lube.

"This might hurt," he warned, not taking the time to grease Magnus's hole. He couldn't wait.

Magnus thrust his hips back, opening himself to Trey. Trey stepped up to him, guiding his cock to the tight hole he loved so fucking much. He positioned Magnus how he needed him, then pushed in slow and deep. He thrust into him several times, easing the way with the lubricant on his cock. Once Magnus began to hum softly, Trey fucked him.

Hard.

He didn't let up, using Magnus the way he'd done all those months before. The way Magnus had always begged him to do. Trey curled his fingers over Magnus's shoulder and held him tightly while he rammed in deep, letting the blistering heat drive him right to the pinnacle. He didn't hold back, not even pretending this was for Magnus's benefit. It wasn't. He would get his later. Right now, Trey wanted the man to feel every inch of him, to remember that Trey's hunger knew no bounds.

Trey growled low in his throat, trying to swallow the sound so they didn't alert anyone to what they were doing. He clamped his jaw shut and let the pleasure overwhelm him. He came with a grunt, driving into Magnus's ass as deep as he could.

MAGNUS WAS PROBABLY WALKING FUNNY WHEN HE managed to turn around and face Trey. It could've been due to the soreness from Trey's incredible fucking or because his dick was so damn hard. He would be dealing with the former for a while, but he intended to take care of the latter as soon as he could find some privacy.

When Trey was finished cleaning up with the wipes Magnus had been doing inventory on, he pulled up his jeans and walked out, smirking as Magnus attempted to redress. He left him with a parting shot. "You should find Ava. She's waitin' for you."

Magnus couldn't believe this was the same Trey Walker who'd been putting distance between them for months. The man had done a complete one-eighty, showing signs of the same horny man Magnus had fallen in love with. Only now, he was playful.

He had no fucking clue what to make of that, but Magnus was not about to take it for granted. He liked this side of Trey. A fucking lot.

After he pulled up his shorts, he slipped out of the closet and made a pit stop in the bathroom to clean himself up. Once he was satisfied, he went in search of Ava. He started his hunt in the front office but found Gia on the phone. He looked in his private office but came up empty. He trekked back through the building, looking in the small kennel area, then the indoor training room, before venturing outside. One of the part-timers mentioned seeing her heading into the storage barn, where they kept lawn equipment, cold-weather gear, and extra cages.

Magnus couldn't imagine what she was doing in there.

He stepped inside, closing the sliding door behind him.

"Ava?"

"Over here."

"Are you lookin' for somethin'? And if so, wh— Oh, fuck me," he hissed when he stepped around one of the partitions to find Ava perched on a wooden box crate, a blanket beneath her. She had her legs spread wide, her hand tucked into her shorts. He couldn't see what she was doing, but it was pretty fucking obvious.

When she started to pull her hand out of her shorts, he shook his head and moved toward her. He kneeled on the floor at the edge of the crate.

"Let me watch," he urged, tugging her shorts aside so he could see her little fingers teasing her clit.

"Trey made me come like this," she whispered.

"With his fingers?"

She nodded.

"Not his mouth?"

Ava shook her head.

"Then that's *my* treat."

When he leaned in, Ava moved her fingers away, and Magnus licked her like an ice cream cone twice before focusing on her clit.

He teased her as he spoke. "One of these days, I'm gonna lick Trey's cum out of your pussy."

"That's ... hot," she moaned, reclining back and spreading her legs wider. "Did Trey find you?"

Her voice trembled only slightly as he feasted on her.

"He did."

"What did he do?"

"Fucked my ass in the storage room."

She inhaled sharply. "I love watching him fuck you. It makes me wet."

"So does my tongue," he said as he speared her pussy.

"Have you ... ever ... fucked him?"

"I have."

"I want to watch..."

The thought of Ava watching him fuck Trey was more than he could take. He pushed to his feet and began unbuttoning his shorts.

"Take off your shorts," he instructed.

Ava lifted her hips, shucking her shorts and panties quickly before lying back and spreading her legs again. She planted her little white tennis shoes on the edge of the crate, offering herself up to him.

He'd never seen anything quite so exquisite.

"Oh, fuck, baby," he growled. "I need that pussy."

She giggled. "Then you better take it."

Magnus gripped her behind her knees and pulled her toward the edge.

"Put your legs over my shoulders," he said, pushing her knees toward her chest.

Ava draped her legs over his shoulders and gripped the blanket beneath her.

"Don't let me hurt you, Ava. I want you so fuckin' bad right now," he warned as he leaned forward and planted one hand beside her head. He guided his cock into her sweet cunt with the other, groaning as her heat enveloped him.

He sank to the hilt and planted his hand on the other side of her head, holding himself up with his arms. He retreated slowly, then drove his hips down, filling every inch of her. Her eyes glittered in the shadows as she held his stare. Magnus couldn't look away as he claimed the one woman he'd wanted for so long, he couldn't remember anyone else.

Sensation took over. Magnus fucked her hard, impaling her with rough thrusts of his hips. Ava moaned and sighed as his hips bumped up and down, his cock sinking in deep before retreating.

"Don't let me hurt you," he repeated.

"You're not, Magnus. Fuck. Me. Harder."

Ah, hell. Those words from that innocent mouth… It did him in. He couldn't stop himself, hammering away at her tight pussy until he felt the electrical storm brewing in his spine. His balls drew up close to his body as he fought for one more delicious thrust, and then another and another until he was panting, sweat trickling down his neck and back.

"I'm gonna come, baby," he barked gruffly. "I'm gonna fill this beautiful pussy."

Ava cried out, and there was no way it wasn't heard from outside, but Magnus didn't give a shit. He followed her right over, spurting deep inside her until he was replete, both body and mind.

"Fuck, I love you," he whispered as he leaned forward and pressed his lips to hers.

She kissed him back. "I love you, too."

He lifted his head, his cock still buried deep inside her. "Do you?"

"I do, Magnus. With all that I am." Ava smiled, and it was the most beautiful smile he'd ever seen.

Despite the fact Ava had to tend to an injured animal, which broke her heart, she felt as though she was walking on a cloud for the rest of the day.

She still couldn't believe that Trey had fingered her in the laundry room, then made a game out of it by telling her what he intended to do to Magnus. He'd warned her that Magnus would come searching for her, and she'd been banking on that when she slipped into the equipment shed only to have him blow her mind.

She'd never felt quite this ... free. That seemed like the right word. Trey and Magnus gave her something she'd never had before. They made her feel beautiful and sexy and wanted.

Now, as she waited with Arbuckle, a five-year-old golden retriever who, according to his records, had been coming to the camp for nearly two years, she let those memories fill her with warmth while she cuddled and petted the sweet dog. Arbuckle was one of their most rambunctious clients, hopping around, playing in the water every chance he got. That's why Ava had noticed that something was wrong this morning when she found him curled up against the wall while all the other dogs chased each other around the yard.

His owner was on the way, and Ava wanted to be there when she came in. Mrs. Arbuckle—that's what Ava was calling her since she kept forgetting her name—hadn't been all that worried when Ava called her, but she did finally give her approval for Ava to call the vet. Granted, that was only after Ava had told her they would pay for it.

"Don't worry, sweet boy," Ava crooned softly. "The vet said you'd be good as new in a day or two. I just wish I knew how you hurt yourself."

The vet said it was only a slight strain and nothing that wouldn't heal if he stayed off it for a few days. He gave Ava some pain medication, along with a sheet of paper detailing how to treat a strain, and told her to follow the directions. He said the pain medication was more to keep him calm since golden retrievers were known to be rambunctious. He'd then administered one of the pills, and since then, Arbuckle had been sprawled out with a little doggy smile on his face.

Or at least, that was what Ava was hoping.

But what she loved the most was that Sarge and Aurora had remained with Arbuckle for most of the afternoon, hovering nearby as though protecting him. They were currently lying on the other side of the room, their attention shifting from Ava to Arbuckle and back to the door as they heard noises coming from the front office.

It was a few minutes before closing when Mrs. Arbuckle—Ava was pretty sure her name was Kelly or maybe Shelley; she didn't know for sure—arrived. Gia brought her back and motioned toward Ava, sitting with him.

Ava got to her feet. "He's completely fine," she said quickly, not wanting the woman to panic. "Dr. Stryker said it was only a sprain, and he'll be good as new in a couple of days, but he'll need to stay calm and not move around as much as possible."

The woman put her hands on her hips and stared down at the dog. She didn't move closer or even acknowledge him at all, and Ava's heart broke for him.

"Is something wrong?" Ava asked.

Mrs. Arbuckle glanced over and shook her head. "This dog's always getting into trouble. It's all I can do to keep him in his kennel at the apartment."

Ava stopped herself from asking why she kept him in a kennel at home. Golden retrievers were social animals and made excellent house pets, provided they were given lots of love and attention, not to mention exercise.

"The vet prescribed some pain medication. He said it should help keep him calm, which will help him heal faster."

"How many can I give him?" she asked.

"What?"

"If I give him a couple, will he sleep for a while?"

"Uh..." Ava didn't know how to respond to that.

"And will he poop or pee while he's medicated?"

"Of course," she said.

"Oh." Mrs. Arbuckle looked disappointed by that.

Before Ava could think better of it, she said, "Would it be easier if we kept him here for a few days? I'll make sure someone stays with him at all times."

"I'm sure that'd be great for you," she snapped. "All the money you'd get to milk out of me."

"It's no charge," Ava said quickly.

"Really?"

Ava nodded.

Mrs. Arbuckle sighed. "God, I just wish my ex-husband would've taken him. It was his dog in the first place. It's been two months, and he's driving me crazy."

Ava wondered if she was talking about Arbuckle or the ex-husband. Or both.

Ava frowned, looking down at Arbuckle. His tongue was lolling out of the side of his mouth, but his eyes were open as he peered up. His tail, which had been wagging earlier, was motionless.

"I told Chad I was gonna sell him. He told me to go ahead. I listed him on Craigslist, but no one's willing to pay me what I'm asking."

She knew she shouldn't, but Ava asked, "How much are you asking?"

"Eighteen hundred. It doesn't even come close to covering all his expenses over the years. I should really be asking five grand."

This woman was willing to sell her dog? How could...?

That thought triggered another, causing Ava to pause. It occurred to her that perhaps that was what happened to Harrison's birth mother. After Ava had asked JJ about the hyphenated name, JJ dug deeper. Turned out Maria Delgado-Harris's husband was still employed by Harrison's father. In fact, he was the man's campaign manager. Had Harrison's father paid off his mother?

"I'm just stuck with him. Eventually, someone'll take him, I'm sure. That or—"

"I'll give you two grand," Ava blurted, shoving the other thoughts aside.

Mrs. Arbuckle looked her way. "Really?"

Ava nodded emphatically but kept her tone cool as she laid it out. "Two grand in cash right now. You'll have to sign him over." She motioned toward the front. "We've got a form you can fill out."

"Two grand cash?"

"Yes, ma'am."

"And what about his daycare for this week?"

"It's covered. You'll owe us nothing."

Her eyes shifted back to the dog. Not once did she lean down to pet him or attempt to soothe him with words. She looked on like he was a hiccup in her day that she didn't want to deal with.

Ava was about to offer twenty-five hundred, but thankfully, the mean lady formerly known as Mrs. Arbuckle agreed.

Half an hour later, the woman was gone, Arbuckle officially belonged to Camp K-9, and Ava was calling Magnus on his cell phone.

"Hey, you headed in soon?"

"I kinda need your help," she told him as she sat beside Arbuckle again, gently stroking along his side. His tail had resumed its steady thump against the bed he was resting on.

"What's up?" Magnus sounded worried.

"Nothin' major. But you should come back to the office. I'm in the playroom."

"Okay. Be there in a sec."

Magnus and Trey arrived five minutes later, both of them walking in with matching expressions of confusion.

Ava gestured toward the dog. "Meet Arbuckle."

"We've met," Magnus said, strolling closer and squatting down so he could scratch him on the head. "What's up, little dude?" Magnus looked at her. "I saw Dr. Stryker in the parkin' lot. He said his paw's gonna be fine."

"I know. It's not that. I … uh…" Ava took a deep breath. "I kinda bought him from his former human." She lowered her voice as though Arbuckle wouldn't hear her. "She's a mean bitch and doesn't deserve him."

Trey chuckled.

Magnus's eyebrows slowly lifted. "You *bought* him?"

She nodded. "I took two grand out of the petty cash box—I'll pay you back, I swear."

"Did you get her to sign a waiver?" Trey asked as he came forward.

"I did. She counted out the money before she left. Gia helped me with it all."

Magnus's gaze swung to Sarge and Aurora, who were still sitting nearby, keeping guard.

"I don't wanna leave him over here tonight," Ava finally said, which was the real reason she'd asked Magnus to come over. "The vet gave him pain medicine... I don't think he should be alone."

"He wouldn't be alone," Trey acknowledged, although Ava got the impression he wasn't disagreeing, merely stating a fact.

"I know, but I think he needs more personal attention."

"You're sayin' you want him to come in the house?"

"That's what I'm sayin'." She glanced at Sarge and Aurora. "And I think his bodyguards wanna come too. I mean, they used to live in your house. I don't really know why—"

"Okay," Magnus said, standing tall.

"—don't have—Okay? Really?"

"Of course. He's your dog now."

"Well, technically, he belongs to Camp K-9," she admitted, staring up at him from her spot on the floor.

"Like I said, he's *your* dog now."

"Really?" Ava had never had a pet of her own, but she certainly liked the idea. "Okay then." She took a deep breath. "Can you help me get him to the house?"

"I'll carry him," Trey offered. "Y'all can open the doors for us."

And just like that, Ava fell deeper in love with both of them.

And Arbuckle, too, of course.

Chapter Twenty

Two weeks later…
Friday, September 2, 2022

TREY HAD SPENT THE PAST TWO WEEKS with Magnus and Ava. Most of it, anyway.

He didn't spend every night there, claiming he needed to take care of shit at his house. The truth was, he'd only done it so they could get some alone time. They'd never requested it, but Trey was still feeling his way around this whole threesome thing. It didn't feel as awkward as he'd expected, but he worried he didn't understand the rules. Each time he mentioned going home, Ava would ask him to stay, but Magnus never did. Whether that was because he was giving Trey space or simply guarding himself, Trey wasn't sure.

However, he stopped overthinking everything, figuring it would work itself out if it were meant to. Since the first time he'd watched Magnus make love to Ava, he'd started to see things in an entirely different light.

He was partly satisfied when Magnus finally broached the subject of Trey returning to work in an official capacity. It had been an easy conversation, resulting in Trey agreeing but not until he'd insisted Magnus blow him to prove how much he wanted him there. It had been a joke, but the resulting orgasm had been appreciated. Of course, he'd returned the favor, letting Magnus know that the feeling was mutual.

Did he mention Ava had watched? Yes. Yes, she had.

Not only was Trey a voyeur, turned out, he was also an exhibitionist.

Who knew?

Of course, coming back full-time required him to commit fully to the job, which included overnight shifts. He'd reluctantly agreed, admitting to Magnus his fear that something would go wrong. Magnus had assured him that he was only a phone call away—plus it would take him less than a minute to get there—so Trey had conceded.

Now, as he settled in at the camp, taking his first official overnight shift, he tried to relax. Magnus was convinced he would do fine. At least someone was. There wasn't much he had to do except be there in the event one of the dogs needed him or in case of another emergency. Trey wasn't sure whether all kennels were like this, but he appreciated the fact Magnus cared enough to ensure all the animals were taken care of.

"All right, y'all," Trey said as he made his way through the kennel one last time. "It's time for some shut-eye. Lights out in one."

He stopped at each cage—they had seven in residence—looking in to ensure each dog was doing well. Monster, a two-year-old terrier mix, was the only one not curled up already.

"You need to rest, little guy," Trey told him, wagging his fingers through the bars.

Monster backed up at first, then finally stepped forward to sniff Trey's fingers.

"It'll be mornin' before you know it, and we'll—" He caught himself before he said *play*, which was a trigger word for some of the others. "We'll have a good ol' time. And I'll leave the door cracked, just in case."

He went to the door and flipped off the main light. There were two nightlights plugged in. They offered enough to see clearly into the room but not disturb the dogs. Then again, he'd seen these dogs sleep in the middle of the room, in broad daylight, with others trampling around them. He didn't think falling asleep would be a problem.

At least not for them.

He was a different story altogether.

Trey wandered around the office for a bit, checking that doors and windows were shut and locked. By the time he made his way to the bunk room, he was thinking about what Magnus and Ava were doing in the house. Used to be, thinking about them gave him a sense of trepidation. These days, arousal was the only thing that plagued him. Granted, he was surprised his dick wasn't broken at this point, considering all the sex they'd been having as of late. Trey wanted to blame it on Magnus, but Ava was actually the culprit. That sassy little woman had a libido that rivaled a teenage boy's. Didn't matter how many times a day they sated her, she was always angling for more.

He smiled into the dark as he reclined on the bed, letting that thought settle him. It wasn't long before he drifted off, fantasies of what the two of them were doing inside the house playing in his head.

A couple of hours later, Trey was startled awake by a sound. He didn't move, waiting to hear it again.

"Shh. You'll wake him up," Ava whispered.

One of the dogs barked. Another yipped. In a minute, they'd have a chorus because Ava somehow thought they were being quiet.

Trey smiled in the dark. Were they seriously trying to sneak up on him like a couple of kids?

It took everything in him not to laugh out loud as they fumbled their way into the room, finally getting the door closed. It was pitch-black, so he understood their lack of finesse, but it didn't sound like they'd planned this out well.

Instead of alerting them to the fact he was awake, Trey remained where he was, closing his eyes.

"You know, strippin' his clothes off while he's asleep is just weird," Magnus whispered to Ava.

"To you, maybe. He might like it. You don't know."

Trey drew his lips into his mouth to keep from laughing even as he felt a hand sliding up his leg.

"I found him," Ava said.

This time, he couldn't hold back. A chuckle escaped.

"Are you awake?" she demanded.

Her voice came from right beside him, but with not even a sliver of light, it was a bit disorienting.

"The moment y'all came in the front door," he told her.

"Well, that's no fun."

He didn't have to see her to know the expression on her face. It would've been a mix of disappointment and amusement. She sported that one anytime she didn't get her way.

"What're y'all doin' here?" he asked, keeping his voice low so they didn't wake all the dogs in the back room.

"Thought you might like company," Ava said.

"No, she thought you might like a blow job."

Trey grunted, his cock jerking to attention.

"I felt that," Ava said.

"No, you didn't," Trey countered. "Your hand's on my knee."

"Your cock is really loud when he wants somethin'."

"You said you *felt* it," Magnus corrected her from somewhere near Trey's head. "Not that you *heard* it."

"Shush," she told him as she fumbled for the button on Trey's jeans.

"I am all for whatever it is you want," Trey told them. "But you're gonna have to turn on a light."

"No lights," Ava hissed. "This is supposed to be a surprise."

"So surprise us, Trey. Take off your damn clothes," Magnus grumbled.

Laughing, Trey did as they asked.

"I'm naked. Now what?"

He prayed like hell they weren't going to flip on the lights and yell surprise or some shit. He was trusting them, something he rarely did with anyone.

Ava's small hand began moving over his leg again. It was obvious she was attempting to figure out how he was positioned. Since he was flat on his back and every light graze of her fingers made his cock swell, it didn't take her long to map out her destination.

"Mmm," she murmured, her fingers curling around him.

She stroked him a few times, even as she crawled onto the cot with him.

"You know this thing won't hold all our weight," Trey warned when she lay out beside him, her fingers drifting up over his stomach, higher until she was cupping his face.

"I'm the only one gettin' on here," she said softly. "Magnus can bend over and suck your cock."

Trey's dick jumped. He wasn't sure if it was due to the promise or the fact Ava had said it. Either way, he was eagerly awaiting their follow-through.

A moment later, he felt the flutter of Magnus's fingers over him, followed by the warmth of his breath.

When Magnus took him in his mouth, Trey grunted, his hand gripping Ava's ass and jerking her closer.

"Jesus, that feels good."

"It's better in the dark, huh?"

He couldn't speak, his brain obliterated by the pleasure that shot from his dick to his balls.

"You realize I'm gonna pay you back for this, right?" Trey muttered, dragging air in on a groan.

"First, you're gonna enjoy," Ava whispered, her mouth close to his ear.

That was all he could do as Magnus proceeded to blow his mind with his wicked fucking mouth.

And when he was done, when Trey had come down his throat, they slipped out the same way they'd come in. Ridiculously loud for two people trying to be quiet.

Magnus spent his entire Saturday catching up on paperwork while manning the main office. He'd given Billy the day off and traded with Gia so she could handle the SAR training when it would've been his turn. He knew how much she enjoyed doing it, and since she'd filled in at the camp more times than he could count, he figured she was due.

Unfortunately, his day was long from over since it was his turn for an overnight shift. Since Trey had taken it last night, it had left them all with a little breathing room. Enough that Magnus wondered whether he should promote someone else to full-time so they would all be required to fill in less each week. Used to be he didn't mind spending nights out here. It was no different than being in the house alone, so he had taken most of them on himself. These days he wanted to spend more time with Ava and Trey, which meant work was suddenly getting in the way of life.

He honestly hadn't ever expected that would happen. Now that it had, he wondered if it were time to make those changes he'd set in motion all those months ago. With Trey around more and more and their relationship progressing, he could see it all laid out before him so clearly. The phone call he'd received a month ago would've set the ball rolling, except Trey had left, and Magnus had been in limbo. With things taking a turn for the better, maybe he could make that move after all.

Of course, that meant having a conversation with Trey. Since they'd yet to truly define what this was between the three of them, he wasn't sure they were quite ready for … something more permanent.

Or were they?

He would have to think on that.

Good thing, too, since it would give him something to do other than sit out here and wonder what Trey and Ava were doing alone in that house.

"I'm gonna take a bath," Ava told Trey when the show they were watching ended.

"Not yet," he muttered, tightening his arm around her. "I'm comfortable."

They'd been camped out on the couch since Magnus returned to the main office after dinner. It was his night on duty, which meant Ava would've had to spend the night alone if Trey hadn't agreed to stay. To her surprise, he hadn't batted an eye when she made the request.

Granted, based on the way he was laid out behind her, she was starting to think he was just too tired to drive home.

"What's goin' on in that pretty little head of yours?" he asked, his breath fanning the back of her neck.

"I was wondering if you were too tired."

"Too tired for what?"

She smiled, although he couldn't see her face. "To make love to me."

His body stiffened behind her.

"I didn't mean it like—"

He pressed his face to her neck, nibbled softly. "I'm never too tired for that, girl."

She really did love when he called her that. It had something to do with the gruff rasp of his voice as he said it. And the hungry gleam he'd get in his eyes.

Ava covered his arm with her hand, where it rested over her stomach. "You sure?"

"Positive."

"Because if—" Her words were cut off as she squealed, surprised when Trey launched himself up off the couch.

Nope, he's definitely not too tired, she thought when she found herself draped over his shoulder, fumbling for something to hold on to as he carried her down the hall. She laughed, both stunned and thrilled by this turn of events. And when he dropped her onto the bed, she erupted into more giggles.

"I've never carried a lover like that before," he admitted, crawling over her.

"Because you never had me before," she told him.

"No," he agreed. "Never did." His eyes met hers. "Didn't have the first clue what I was missin'."

"You mean bein' with a woman?"

Trey shook his head. "No. I mean bein' with *you*. I don't want just any woman, Ava. That'll never change."

She could hear the sincerity in his tone, and she couldn't deny it made her feel incredibly lucky. For the first week or so after this became their new norm, Ava had wondered if Trey would wake up one day and realize he wasn't truly attracted to her or that he didn't want to be intimate with her anymore. Her stomach had knotted with the fear those possibilities induced.

However, with each passing day, they'd been growing closer. Not only physically but emotionally as well. It wasn't all about sex, even though she wouldn't deny she was angling for as much as she could get. Seriously. Two smoking-hot guys at her disposal? What straight woman wouldn't take advantage of that?

Ava cupped his jaw, sliding her fingers over his silky beard. He'd yet to shave it off, so it was filling in more. She wasn't sure how he could stand it during a Texas summer, but it looked like he was keeping it for the duration. She liked the beard, if she was being honest. And she really liked the way it tickled the insides of her thighs when his mouth was down there.

She shivered from the memory.

"That usually means you're havin' a dirty thought, girl," he growled softly, turning his head and planting a kiss on her palm.

"I was thinkin' how I like the way your beard tickles me when you've got your tongue on my pussy."

His eyes widened, his jaw falling open.

Ava knew she'd shocked him. She'd done it a few times to both of them. It had actually become the highlight of her day. She was trying to come up with more and more ways to do it because it was a surefire way to get one of them to give her an orgasm.

"You better strip off those little shorts then. 'Cause now I'm ready for dessert."

Ava giggled when he tickled her, then hurried to strip off her shorts and panties. She didn't stop there, getting rid of her shirt and bra, too.

"Your turn," she teased, staring up at him as his heated gaze moved over her.

His eyes shifted to her face for a moment before he began taking his clothes off. She admired every glorious inch of him as it was revealed and was lost deep in thought when he gripped her ankles and pulled her to the edge of the bed.

Trey went to his knees on the floor and pressed a kiss to the back of her thigh as he kept her legs raised in the air. She could only imagine what she looked like from his vantage point, and she'd be damned if that didn't turn her on more.

She heard the rumbles in his chest as he pressed the lightest of kisses along her legs, then her butt, before returning to where she wanted him most. She couldn't see what he was doing, so when he dragged his tongue along her slick pussy, she gritted her teeth and moaned. The pleasure was intense, more so as she felt his beard brushing over her skin. She knew he was doing it on purpose, ensuring she got what she wanted. But it wasn't long before he stopped focusing on that and put all his efforts into licking and sucking. When he drew her clit between his lips and flicked it with his tongue, she launched right over the edge of the cliff, free-falling into the ether.

When she got her wits about her, Trey was repositioning her on the bed so he could join her. He went slow, moving over her. She knew he was doing it so he didn't scare her. It didn't matter how many times she told them she wasn't, they still worried enough to take the time. It made her love them both even more.

"I want you inside me," she whispered as he kissed his way over her chest.

"Then put me there," he growled low in his throat, moving so that his cock was nestled between her thighs.

Ava didn't hesitate, reaching between them and pressing the head of his cock to her entrance. She watched his face, saw the way the lines around his mouth tightened when he pushed his hips forward. As he slipped inside, she reached for him, bringing his head down to hers.

"Jesus Christ," he whispered gruffly. "You feel…"

"Good? Amazing? Perfect?" she teased.

He looked in pain when he said, "All of the above. Fuck."

She was serious when she'd said she wanted him to make love to her. While they'd had a few encounters where it was just the two of them, they had usually been in the shower or once on the couch.

This was different.

This felt like more.

And the one thing she wanted from Trey was more.

"I'm tryin' to go slow," he said against her lips. "I don't usually do slow."

"But you can with me." She slid her arms around his neck. "I've got you, Trey."

She felt him shudder as he sank in to the hilt, his hips pressed to hers. Her muscles clenched around him, making him groan.

"Love me, Trey," she whispered against his ear. "And let me love you back."

He did. Trey made love to her for what felt like hours. He brought her to the brink numerous times, pulling back before she could career over. And when he finally did let her come, he joined her, the two of them free-falling together.

Half an hour later, as they cuddled in Magnus's darkened room, Ava's head on Trey's chest, her finger drawing circles over his stomach, she broached the subject she'd been putting off for a while, a topic she'd promised Dr. Briggs she would bring up with Trey.

"I know you were the one who led the task force during the search for me," she said softly.

He didn't answer right away, but she waited. When he finally spoke, his words were deep and low.

"It was a joint effort."

"Yeah, but you pushed because you cared about Magnus."

Trey didn't respond.

"You've never asked me what happened. How it all played out."

He still didn't say anything.

"Do you want to know?"

"No." Trey's arm tightened around her back, pulling her closer. "Not unless you feel the need to tell me."

Ava wasn't sure what to make of that.

Trey shifted, his lips brushing her forehead. "Sometimes, when I close my eyes, I still see you as we found you at Gloria's. Have you ever heard someone say they were so angry they saw red?"

"Yes."

"It's a real thing, and I experienced it that day." He exhaled. "As soon as I saw you, a red haze clouded my vision. It took everything in me not to hunt that bastard down and kill him. The only reason I didn't is because of Magnus. He needed me to take care of him so he could take care of you."

Ava's hand stilled on his stomach. She waited patiently for him to say more.

"Plus, I knew my brother was gonna do everything in his power to ensure Rivers could never do that to anyone else again."

"My mother beat him to it."

Trey hugged her closer. "She did."

"I like to think of it as her way of slaying the monster for me," she whispered.

"I don't think you're wrong in thinkin' that." He pressed another kiss to her forehead.

They were quiet for a moment, and Ava was convinced he'd fallen asleep when his gruff voice broke through the silence.

"I know what you've been workin' on with JJ."

She flinched. "You do?"

Trey exhaled heavily. "Ava, I know you want justice for that woman—"

"She deserves it," she countered before he could finish that sentence.

"She does. However…"

It took everything in her not to pull away, but she waited patiently for him to speak his piece.

"I need you to let the task force handle it."

"Why?"

Trey shifted back, and Ava could feel the heat of his stare. She forced her gaze to meet his.

"Because we wouldn't survive if somethin' happened to you."

Ava wanted to counter that nothing would, but she'd already given that some thought. After JJ had dug deeper into Harrison's father, Ava learned just how powerful the man—the whole family—really was. If she and JJ were right, he was powerful enough to make people disappear. Not only that, but he had the connections to ensure they were never found or looked for.

So rather than argue, Ava conceded. "If I promise I won't speak up or draw attention to myself, can I still relay information to JJ so she can look into it?"

Trey relaxed, pulling her closer again. "You've got to tell Magnus."

Ava clamped her teeth together. She'd been battling that dilemma for the past couple of weeks. She hated keeping secrets from him, but she knew if she told him what she'd been doing, he'd lose his mind. Ava told herself she'd kept it a secret for his benefit.

"I'll be right there with you," Trey assured her, kissing her forehead again.

"Okay." Ava wrapped her arm over his stomach and hugged him close. "Trey?"

"Hmm?"

"I love you."

She felt more than heard the hitch in his breath and waited patiently for his reaction. She'd wanted to tell him how she felt, but she'd been scared it would send him running. She knew Magnus was still keeping some distance between them for that very reason. And while she respected his need for self-preservation, Ava didn't have that much restraint.

"I just wanted you to know," she whispered when he didn't respond.

"I love you, too, girl," he said just as softly.

Tears formed, and her heart swelled, but she held the emotion in. She knew it hadn't been easy for him to admit that, and the last thing she wanted was to send him into a panic.

Chapter Twenty-One

Sunday, September 4, 2022

MAGNUS WALKED INTO THE HOUSE THE FOLLOWING morning to the scent of bacon and eggs filling the kitchen. He'd intended to run in and take a shower before heading back to camp to help get the day underway, but there was no way he was going to pass up on breakfast. Certainly not if Ava had made it.

"Hey," she greeted, casting him a quick smile over her shoulder. "I just finished cooking, it's—"

Before she could finish that sentence, Magnus grabbed her around the waist and dragged her over to the only counter that wasn't covered in dishes and food.

"What are—"

Ava squealed when he spun her around and lifted her, settling her on the countertop.

"I recall a very specific fantasy you laid out for me," he said, sliding his hand behind her neck as he leaned in and brushed his lips to hers.

She giggled. "I remember."

He took a quick peek at the stove.

"It's all done," she said, cupping his cheek and redirecting his gaze back to her. "It probably needs a minute to cool."

"A minute, huh?"

She smiled and nodded.

Magnus tugged her shirt up—or should he say *his* shirt—to reveal that she was naked beneath.

He leaned in and inhaled the sweet scent of her skin, pressing a light kiss to each of her nipples. "I'll admit, I don't mind overnight shifts when the mornin' starts like this."

Ava helped him along, lifting the shirt higher.

"Take it off," he growled, taking her pretty pink nipple between his teeth.

She faltered for a moment but then managed to get the shirt off, tossing it to the floor at Magnus's feet.

"Damn, that's pretty," he whispered, unable to hide the reverence in his tone.

This woman undid him no matter what she did, but naked in the kitchen … this was a new high for him.

Magnus slid one finger through her slick folds as he dragged his mouth back to hers. He nibbled on her bottom lip. "I'm gonna eat this pussy before breakfast."

"I'm gonna let you," she said with a chuckle.

"Minx," he muttered, pushing his finger inside her.

Ava whimpered, leaning back against the wall that separated the living room from the kitchen, her legs spreading invitingly.

He held her gaze as he eased down on one knee, bringing him eye level with her delectable pussy. He continued to finger her, loving the way her pussy contracted.

"Oh, Jesus," he moaned. She smelled like sex, which could only mean one thing. "Did Trey fuck you last night?"

"And this morning."

Magnus's cock swelled even more at the thought of them together. He wished he'd been here to see it, but the idea of licking her pussy after Trey had come inside her… His day just kept getting better.

He'd just begun to feast when he heard footsteps coming down the hall. He caught sight of Trey out of the corner of his eye, but he didn't stop what he was doing.

"Fuck, you taste good," he groaned before pushing his tongue inside her.

Ava gripped his hair, pulling him toward her as he continued to torment her with gentle licks and light flicks against her clit.

"You're a tease," she whimpered.

"Maybe he needs a little incentive," Trey mentioned, stepping around behind him.

When he did, Ava released his hair, propping herself up with her hands behind her.

Magnus maintained his focus, lapping at her sweetness, even when Trey went to his knees behind him. He didn't falter when Trey's arms came around him, his fingers deftly releasing the button and lowering the zipper on his shorts. But the moment Trey's hand curled around his cock, Magnus's resolve dissolved completely.

"Oh, fuck."

He could feel Trey's breath on his ear when he said, "Make her come, and I'll make you come."

"If you keep doin' that..."

"I'm not stoppin'," Trey noted. "But don't you dare come first."

That was a tall order considering Trey wasn't pulling his punches, stroking him with a firm grip.

Magnus peered up to see Ava biting her lower lip.

He drove two fingers inside her as he drew her clit between his lips and flicked it with his tongue. He matched the pace of Trey's strokes as he fingered her. Her soft moans were the only thing he could hear as the pleasure intensified. He closed his eyes, unable to focus as he worked to get her off before Trey made him explode.

"Magnus ... oh ... right there..."

He lashed her clit with his tongue, fingering her faster. The moment he added a third finger, she cried out, her pussy spasming. He let her ride it out as he sucked in air, trying to hold off long enough to bring her back down. As soon as she relaxed, Magnus fell back against Trey, gripping his free hand as he pumped his hips, meeting Trey's strokes until he couldn't take it anymore.

"Come for us," Ava demanded.

That was all she wrote.

Magnus came in Trey's fist, roaring as the release barreled through him.

Half an hour later, after he'd showered, dressed, and finished their reheated breakfast, Magnus started for the door, ready to get back to work.

"Magnus, wait," Ava called. "I ... uh ... need to tell you something."

Her tone made him wary, but he turned around, noticing that they were both trying to avert their gazes. A chill danced down his spine, and he wondered if this was the other shoe getting ready to drop. He'd battled a foreign sense of foreboding for a few weeks now, never quite allowing himself to get too comfortable with how things were going.

"Tell me what?" he prompted when Ava began wiping the condensation off her juice glass.

Her gaze lifted slowly. "It's nothing bad, I promise."

Trey cleared his throat.

Ava huffed. "Fine." She met Magnus's gaze. "A few weeks ago, when Trey took me to one of my appointments, we ran into JJ. The woman he—"

"I know who JJ is," Magnus stated, still on edge.

"Anyway, she mentioned that during her research when y'all were looking for me ... she found out Harrison had ... well, she *suspected* ... and she's right."

"Ava," he said through gritted teeth.

"Okay, I've been working with JJ to see if we can figure out whether or not Harrison's father covered up the disappearance of the first girl he ... you know."

Magnus stopped breathing. At least, that was what it felt like as he stared at Ava. "You *what?*"

"I was only looking at JJ's notes. I asked her a few questions. She found the answers. The more we dig, the more we uncover." Her next words came rapidly. "I think Harrison killed a woman, and his father covered it up."

He glanced at Trey, saw that he was watching him closely. "Did you know about this?"

"I found the notes she"—he nodded toward Ava—"was lookin' at. She left 'em on the computer at the office. I recognized them as JJ's, so I called JJ to confirm."

Ava spoke up. "I didn't tell you because I knew you'd make me stop."

Magnus continued to stare. He wasn't sure what he was supposed to say.

"Don't be mad," Ava added. "Last night, Trey made me promise that I'd be careful. I will," she reiterated. "I'll make sure no one knows I'm the one looking."

"JJ's the best at coverin' her tracks," Trey mentioned. "I told her that Ava's safety is paramount. I don't want her lookin' into it any more than you do."

"Technically," Ava continued, "I'm a grown-ass woman, and I can do what I want."

As he continued to watch them, Magnus realized Ava was already getting defensive, and he hadn't said anything yet.

"Say something," Ava demanded.

"I'm not sure what to say," he admitted. "I'm not sure if I wanna paddle your ass or wrap you in cotton so nothin' and no one can ever hurt you again."

"If it's all the same to you, I'd like to select door number one."

Magnus's cock twitched, but he mentally told the damn thing to heel.

"Are you mad?" Ava asked, sounding like a kid who just got caught playing with her toys when she was grounded.

"I'm not mad," he said, and it was the truth. He met her gaze. "I'm hurt."

Her eyes widened.

Magnus took a deep breath. "I'm hurt you felt you had to keep it from me." He glanced at Trey. "That you both did."

With that, Magnus turned and walked out of the house. He needed some air.

"STAY HERE," TREY COMMANDED WHEN AVA SHOT up out of her chair, ready to go after Magnus.

"I need to talk to him."

"Let me," he said firmly, gently grabbing her wrist.

"But—"

Trey pulled her toward him, then pressed a kiss to her forehead. "I think this runs deeper than you not tellin' him about this."

Ava frowned, her eyes skimming his face.

"Trust me."

She nodded, then sat back down.

Trey went to the main office, found it empty. He'd expected as much. Although Magnus had remained calm during that discussion, Trey had noticed the tension in his shoulders. It doubled when Trey admitted that he'd known what Ava was up to, which was why he suspected this was more than simply Ava not telling Magnus.

He found Magnus in the weight room, which was just a fancy term for a small storage space that held a handful of weights and a bench.

Trey closed the door behind him, then leaned against it, watching as Magnus stood with his hands on his hips, his gaze directed at the floor.

"Are you jealous that I knew?" Trey prompted, figuring he might as well get to the heart of the matter.

"Of that, no."

"About what, then?"

Magnus didn't respond, didn't move from his spot.

Trey sighed. "I don't know how this is supposed to work, Magnus. I've never been in a relationship with two people before. Hell, I haven't been in a relationship with *one* in a damn long time."

Magnus slowly turned, his head lifting, eyes blazing as they pinned Trey in place. "You've been in a relationship for the past year and a half, Trey. You were just too fuckin' stubborn to admit it."

He had a fair point, and that comment confirmed Trey's suspicions. This wasn't about Ava keeping a secret. It was about the distance that still remained between him and Magnus. Trey understood because he felt it, too. They might be fucking like rabbits, but they'd yet to address the big issue. The one that involved three words and a few dozen apologies.

Trey took a step forward. "You're right. I was too fuckin' stubborn to admit it."

Magnus's eyes narrowed.

Trey continued toward him. "Not only that, I was a chickenshit." He stopped when he was a foot away. "I was scared," he admitted. "Scared that I'd lost the best fuckin' thing that's ever happened to me. When I saw you with Ava at the hospital ... the way you looked at her ... fuck, Magnus. It shredded me because not only did I love you, I fuckin' needed you. And there you were, givin' every ounce of your attention to her."

Trey held up a hand to stop Magnus from speaking.

"She needed you a helluva lot more than I did," he clarified. "But acknowledgin' that didn't change the fact that I was gutted." He waved toward the door. "You think I worked here to help you out? Hell no. That's an excuse. An altruistic reason, and we both know that's not me. I *really* worked here because I wanted to be in your life. I didn't care how, I just needed ... I fuckin' needed *you*, Magnus."

Trey swallowed past the lump forming in his throat. "It wasn't easy to watch you and Ava fall in love with each other more and more every single day, but I did it. And it ate at me and ate at me." He shook his head. "Don't get me wrong. I've seen it from day one. The reason you love her. She's easy to love. So fuckin' easy. That girl's got a will of steel and a heart of pure gold. Which is probably why I fell so fuckin' hard even though it didn't make a damn bit of sense."

Magnus's eyes shone with tears, but Trey pushed on, taking another step forward so he could touch Magnus. He put his hand on Magnus's throat, his thumb under his chin. He didn't use force because it wasn't about aggression. It was about ensuring this man understood him.

His words came out raspy when he said, "I fell in love with you so long ago ... I don't even remember a time without you. But I've been down that road before. I've been told exactly where I'm lackin'."

"You're not lackin' a goddamn thing," Magnus bellowed, grabbing Trey's wrist. "The idiots who claimed you were—"

"I fall fast, Magnus. It's what I do. I don't know why." He held his stare. "But it was different with you ... it *felt* different. I didn't just fall fast; I fell hard. And ever since the mornin' I woke up in the hotel room in Dallas with you in my bed..."

He swallowed, needing to get this next part out without breaking.

"You came to me. No one's ever fuckin' come *to me*, Magnus. No one." Trey swallowed hard, couldn't hide the emotion burning his throat. "I've always been the one chasin', tryin' to hold on to something. Hell, *anything*. Then there you were. I knew that mornin' that you were what I'd been lookin' for all my goddamn life."

Trey took a few deep breaths, forged ahead. "I never told you how I felt, and when I wanted to, everything was changin'. You. Ava. So I stayed because I was too fuckin' selfish to go. And durin' those months when we were takin' care of Ava, I didn't realize that somethin' else was changin'. *Me*. I changed. I don't know when she did it or how, but Ava burrowed under my skin. I didn't know it until recently, but I'd been fallin' in love with her all along." He tightened his grip on Magnus's throat and leaned in. "I was fallin' for her because I'd already fallen for you."

He pressed his lips to Magnus's, choking back the tears that threatened. "I love you. I should've told you that a long fuckin' time ago, Magnus, but I'm tellin' you now. I don't wanna be anywhere else but here with you and her."

Magnus pulled back, met his gaze. "You had me at *I was too fuckin' stubborn…*"

Trey barked a laugh and rubbed his fingers in his eyes. "Did you just misquote *Jerry McGuire*?"

"Ava's favorite movie," Magnus noted.

"Oh, I know. I've had to sit through it three times since she came home from the hospital." Trey took another deep breath and slid his hand behind Magnus's neck, pulling him close, resting his forehead on Magnus's. "I love you. I wanted to tell you what Ava was doin', but it wasn't my place. She's resilient as hell and twice as stubborn. But I trust her. And I trust everyone on the task force. They'll watch over her. And because I love you and know how important she is … to both of us … I've kept an eye on her. I swear to you, I won't let anything happen to her. Or you."

"I…"

"Tell me you love me, Magnus. Tell me now."

A soft chuckle sounded before Magnus tilted his head back. "I've loved you from the first day I met you."

"Had to top me, didn't you?" he teased.

"Just wait till later. I'll top you the right way."

Trey chuckled. "We'll just have to see about that."

"And I love you both!" Ava shouted, racing into the room.

Trey grinned. "Did you know she was there?"

Magnus shook his head, stepping back when Ava shoved her way between them. "No, but I suspected."

Yeah, Trey did, too.

Later that night, after they'd gotten the camp closed down, with Gia taking the overnight shift, Trey made his way to the house. They'd had an early dinner, so it didn't surprise him to find the kitchen dark. He ventured toward the living room, fully expecting to find Ava and Magnus curled up watching a movie, but the room was empty. He detoured down the hall to the bedroom, opening the door slowly.

"Damn, that feels good," Magnus moaned softly.

"What do y'all think you're doin'?" Trey asked, realizing *why* they weren't watching a movie. Hell, this was far more entertaining.

Magnus's hooded gaze slid over, and a smile pulled at his mouth.

The blanket moved back as Ava lifted her head, releasing Magnus's cock from her mouth. "I think the better question is … why aren't *you* doin' it with us?"

Oh, she was something else. The girl had come into her own over the past few months, but she'd come out of her shell completely these past couple of weeks. Now that Trey was spending every night here, she seemed happier. And most definitely hornier. A fucking blessing as far as he was concerned because he was right there with her, fucking both of them as often as he could and still not getting enough to sate the desperate ache that consumed him constantly.

Ava cast him a sassy smirk before she ducked beneath the blanket and turned her attention back to Magnus's cock.

Trey considered giving them a few minutes to themselves but decided against it. He lived for these moments as much as they did.

He moved to the end of the bed, grabbed the blanket, and dragged it off her, letting it fall to the floor. Eager to take advantage of her cute little ass—all naked and inviting—lifted in the air, Trey made quick work of stripping off his shorts, admiring the way she spread her legs, purposely giving him a better view of the goods between.

He placed his palms on her ass. They easily covered each rounded globe, and not for the first time, he appreciated the sheer difference in their sizes. Admittedly, that was one of the things he liked so much about Magnus. The man was several inches shorter, which gave Trey both a height and weight advantage. However, Magnus could hold his own with Trey while Ava ... well, she was feisty in her own right, but Trey didn't want to manhandle her. He settled for loving her the best way he could.

As he kneaded her ass cheeks, Ava hummed softly around Magnus's cock, causing him to grunt, even as his eyes trailed every move Trey made. He met Magnus's gaze, wanting him to see his intentions. It was time they introduced their woman to what it meant to be claimed by them both at the same time. They'd been teasing her these past couple of weeks, fingering her ass more and more so she'd get used to the sensation.

Trey leaned in, brushing his beard over her skin before he licked along the crack of her ass.

Ava's head lifted and her back arched. "God, yes. Keep doin' that, Trey."

That was another thing he loved about this woman. She wasn't afraid to ask for what she wanted. In fact, she sometimes demanded it, and that was fucking hot. And she *definitely* liked having her little hole rimmed.

"You think you're ready for us, baby?" Magnus asked, shifting off the bed to get the lubricant out of the drawer.

"Oh, yeah," she moaned as Trey pressed his tongue against her anus.

She whimpered, pushing her hips back, trying to get him to go deeper.

Magnus came around, doing the honors of slicking his fingers so he could work her little ass open, preparing her for Trey's cock. While Trey watched him intimately stretch her virgin hole, he greased his cock generously, stroking until he was so fucking hard it hurt.

"You sure you don't want the maiden voyage?" Trey asked Magnus.

Magnus laughed. "Nah. I'll let you have the honors."

Ava raised a hand in the air, her head hanging down. "Girl over here who needs to get fucked. Less talkin', more doin'."

Trey barked a laugh and swatted her ass. "Yes, ma'am."

When Trey was ready, he took over for Magnus, crawling on the bed behind her. He pushed two fingers deep into her ass, scissoring them gently.

"Trey … I need more," Ava pleaded.

"We're gonna give you more, girl. I promise."

She tried to fuck herself on his hand, but Magnus stilled her movements as he positioned himself on the bed once more. When he was laid out on his back, Magnus urged Ava to crawl over him, the shift causing Trey's fingers to dislodge. He wiped his hands on the shorts he'd discarded, then tossed them away and got into position behind her.

Sitting back on his haunches, he stroked his cock while he watched Magnus's impressive cock split her pussy wide as she sank down on him, taking him to the hilt. Trey fucking loved this part … watching the two of them … it had become one of his favorite pastimes. But while he didn't mind entertaining his inner voyeur, he much preferred being an active participant.

Ava began rocking faster on Magnus's cock, so Trey lightly spanked her ass again, reminding her he was there. She giggled as she stilled her hips, allowing him to guide his cock to her back entrance.

"Relax, baby," Magnus crooned. "Let it feel good."

Ava leaned down to kiss him, her asshole stretching wide as Trey pushed in slowly, curling his fingers around her hips and inching her back on him. As he gained ground, Magnus's cock slid out, but that was the goal. Trey didn't want to overwhelm her yet. They alternated, each pushing in a little more before retreating until Magnus's cock moved against his deep inside her.

Ava whimpered as she pushed against him, urging him inside her.

"Yes ... God, yes..."

Since she seemed to know what felt good, Trey let her fuck herself onto his dick. She gently rocked, her smooth passage stroking him so sweetly as she took him inch by inch.

When he was balls deep, Trey stilled. He'd never felt anything like this before, and he wanted to savor it. Her hole was so tight and so goddamn hot, he wasn't sure he would survive more than a minute. He gripped her hips and held her still, waiting as Magnus pushed inside her, filling her pussy and stroking Trey's cock through the thin barrier that separated them.

It was Trey's turn to whimper, and he couldn't even find it in him to be embarrassed. Nothing had ever felt this fucking good before.

"Please," Ava cried. "Fuck me."

Trey swallowed, digging his fingers into her hips as he slowly inched out, her asshole gripping him tightly as though fighting to keep him inside.

After a few minutes, the overwhelming desire to come faded somewhat, allowing him to fuck her properly. He maintained a slow pace, alternating thrusts with Magnus as they fucked her thoroughly. Ava peered back at him over her shoulder, gifting him with a sexy grin.

"Feel good, girl?"

"Better than good. But I know that's not all you've got."

Oh, that cheeky little minx.

"You asked for it," he said with a smirk, picking up his pace.

Her head snapped back around, her shoulders tensing as Trey began fucking her harder. Deeper. Faster. He gave her all she asked for, stealing some pleasure for himself in the process. Ava dropped her hips slightly, the move allowing Trey to provide the momentum for her to fuck herself on Magnus's cock while Trey drilled into her ass.

Ava's soft moans grew louder, her voice guttural as she begged them to make her come.

Trey kept a steady, rapid pace, pounding into her ass as Magnus's hand disappeared between their bodies, presumably to give her little clit some attention.

"Yes!" Ava squealed. "Yes! Yes! God, yes!"

Her body locked down on his cock, and Trey had to grit his teeth, but even that didn't help.

"Ah, fuck," he growled roughly. "Ah, hell ... Magnus ... I'm gonna come."

Magnus's leg muscles tightened beneath him, and he knew the man was letting himself go.

Trey slammed into Ava's ass one final time and let the ecstasy consume him.

Chapter Twenty-Two

"YOU SURE THIS IS WHAT YOU WANNA do?" Trey asked Ava as he steered his truck into the driveway of Ava's old house.

It'd been three days since Trey had declared his love to Magnus and Ava had promised not to keep secrets from anyone. Of course, once she said that, she'd proceeded to tell them all the shit she got into in high school. Enough that Trey was wondering whether some secrets were better left untold.

"I am," she said from the backseat, her tone full of conviction.

Trey glanced at Magnus in the passenger seat. "You good?"

Magnus's jerky nod didn't inspire a lot of confidence, but Trey knew he was still on the fence. Ava had discussed this little field trip during her session with Dr. Briggs yesterday, and according to Ava, Piper had agreed that it could be a step forward for her, but she warned her to take things slow. This morning, Ava woke up and informed them that today was the day.

Evidently, *slow* was not in Ava's vocabulary because here they were.

The house was as impressive as one would've expected it to be, considering Harrison Rivers had come from money. It wasn't something Trey considered homey, but it was nice for those who liked cookie-cutter subdivisions with HOA restrictions that kept the lawns glowing green and the flowers blooming regardless of the season. You wouldn't find trash cans at the curb when it wasn't trash day, nor would you see a beat-up junker in the driveway, needing to be worked on. This was the sort of neighborhood Trey's ex-husband had dreamed of living in. Not because it was a good place to raise kids or start a family but because it signified status and would mean he'd made it in life.

Trey preferred small-town living. He liked that Tommy Barnes, his neighbor across the street, called him over to help him get his old truck started so he could move it into the garage and begin the restorations because *this '65 princess ain't gonna fix herself.* And he preferred that Mrs. Sheridan, the widow who lived next door, would ask him if he would mow her lawn when he mowed his that week. Not because she was worried she'd get a notice and potentially have to pay a fine but to let him know she was visiting her daughter in Georgia because her fourth grandbaby was due any day.

Hell, he doubted the people in this neighborhood even knew their neighbors.

Trey helped Ava out of the truck, then they met Magnus at the front of it. Neither of them looked thrilled to be here, but Trey hadn't expected this to be an outing to write home about. He wanted to get Ava through this and then back home where she belonged, and if that meant spending an hour or more—God forbid—walking down memory lane in a house that could've been right out of *The Amityville Horror* for more reasons than one, then he would do it with a smile on.

Well, maybe not with a smile, but he would do it.

But if he heard anyone whisper, *Get out,* he was gonna throw Ava over his shoulder and make a run for it.

Trey dug the key out of his pocket when they reached the front porch. Because he'd come over here before, he wasn't unfamiliar with the process of getting inside, which involved unlocking the door and then decoding the alarm on the panel just to the left. He did so without getting in Ava's way, then stepped back as she walked into the foyer. Trey noticed how she shivered, but it wasn't because of the temperature. The house was set at seventy-four—which would've been ridiculous if he'd been living here—and only because they'd reduced it this morning using the app Magnus had on his phone, lowering it from the balmy eighty it remained on since the place was vacant.

"I never liked this house," Ava mentioned as she looked up the stairs toward the second floor. "It always felt too pretentious."

Trey could see that. The furniture and decor looked as though they'd been pasted in right from a magazine. It was as though Harrison Rivers preferred people *didn't* want to come over and visit. In all fairness, how could he? After all, he'd been beating his wife, and anyone who would've been here for more than a minute would've seen her bruises and recognized the skeletons hanging in the bastard's many closets.

Ava glanced down the short hallway to the left that led to the master suite. She stood there for a moment, then turned to the stairs again. She went up slowly, Trey following her when Magnus got his feet moving. They followed her across the expansive upper floor, complete with an open living area and several bedrooms. She continued to the room that was the farthest from everything else. The door was pulled closed but not latched, so she pushed it open with the tip of her finger.

Trey knew this had been Renee's room. He'd come in here before, wanting to get anything that might've been important to Ava. He'd found nothing. There were no pictures or albums, no trinkets or knickknacks, only more gaudy decor and ugly furnishings. The room was about as inviting as a dentist's chair when you were anticipating a root canal.

"She hated it here," Ava muttered, sliding her hand across the floral-patterned bedspread. "But she hated it everywhere. The only place I ever recall her being happy was the house I grew up in, but even then, those memories are few and far between."

Magnus stepped up behind Ava and put his hands on her shoulders. She leaned into him.

"I bought her a few things over the years, but Harrison destroyed everything personal. It was how he tried to keep her in line."

And he had put Renee in a hospital in order to keep Ava in line, Trey knew.

"We can get rid of it all," Ava mused, taking a deep breath.

She stepped away from Magnus and moved toward the door. They followed her back into the hall and then to one of the guest rooms. It was fully furnished just like all the other rooms, as though someone came to visit often, but he doubted the bed had ever been slept in.

Ava didn't linger; she moved with purpose, walking through the room and into the adjoining bathroom. Trey could've told her he'd checked everything. The only things he'd found were toiletries and linens in any of the rooms, so he was surprised when she returned a minute later with a long, rectangular wooden box. It looked like something a chess set or backgammon game would be stored in for safekeeping.

"I never saw that," he told her. "I'm sorry."

"I kept it in the false bottom of the vanity," she said as she set it on the bed and lifted the lid. "I didn't want Harrison to find it."

Inside were stray pictures and a few other things that looked like they might be sentimental. A tassel likely from her high school graduation, a silver locket with an ivory heart on the front, a small piano-shaped jewelry box that was only big enough to hold a ring or something equally small. When she flipped it open, he saw it was empty, but Ava seemed more intrigued by it than what would've been inside.

She turned to Magnus, holding it.

"This was Tabby's," she said, her voice trembling. "She gave it to me on my tenth birthday, right after your mom brought us pancakes. She wanted me to have it since my mom didn't get me a gift, said it was her most prized possession because—"

"I gave it to her," Magnus choked out.

Ava looked at him with tears in her eyes. "Yes."

Trey felt the tightness in his chest when Magnus took the small trinket in his hand.

"She said that one day I could keep my wedding ring in it when I went to bed." Ava released a watery chuckle. "She said it seemed only right since I was gonna marry her brother."

Ah, damn.

Now Trey had tears in his eyes. He turned away from them but not because he felt he was intruding. He didn't want either of them to see him all choked up.

Magnus laughed. "She was a smart girl, my sister."

Trey managed to get his emotions under control, turning back to find they were both looking at him.

"What? I got dust in my eye," he said as he wiped the corner of his eye at the same time he batted the air. "Damn dust motes."

They both laughed, and for some reason, that broke through the somberness of the mood.

"This is the only thing I wanted to come back for," Ava explained, gesturing toward the box. "I hid it the day I moved in here. I had packed it with my mother's things because, at the time, I was worried Harrison would be bothered by my wanting to keep something that reminded me of my first love. I was glad I did because he would've burned it if he knew about it."

Ava looked up at Trey, then over to Magnus. "I'd like to go home now."

"There's nothin' else you want?" Trey didn't bother telling her that Harrison's father had sent a representative down to get his personal items, of which there hadn't been many. Trey had been here for that. It'd felt like an FBI hunt for incriminating evidence. They'd combed through the place from top to bottom. Clearly, they weren't all that thorough since they'd missed the false bottom of that vanity. He was glad they had.

Ava shook her head and reached for the box, but Magnus got there first. "Nope," she answered. "I'd like to donate it all to charity: a battered woman's shelter or something. And you can sell the house. I'm not sure how much we'll get for it since there was a murder-suicide here."

Trey didn't bother mentioning that she'd be surprised by the crazies willing to buy up real estate like this. Whether they wanted it for its fifteen minutes of fame, for potential paranormal activity, or because they intended to gut it and turn it into their own McMansion, someone would snatch it up.

As quickly as they'd walked in, they walked back out. Trey set the alarm, locked the door, and left the house right where it belonged.

Behind them.

"BEFORE WE HEAD BACK TO THE HOUSE, you mind makin' a detour?" Magnus proposed as Trey was pulling out of the neighborhood.

"Not at all." Trey cut his eyes to him briefly. "Where to?"

"Coyote Ridge."

Trey did a double take, his eyebrows dropping low. "Really?"

Magnus nodded, then sat back and watched the road in front of them. It was evident Trey was looking for an explanation, but Magnus wasn't ready for that yet. He'd take the next half hour to figure out exactly what he wanted to say. And if his stomach stopped threatening to launch into his throat, perhaps he'd get the words out.

They rode in silence; the only sound was the random flip of that jewelry box as Ava clutched it in her hand. He'd been so stunned to see it he'd nearly hit the floor. It had been a gift he'd given Tabby when she was seven or eight, he couldn't remember. At the time, she had some little tin ring their parents had gotten her, and she thought it was the most precious thing in the world. Magnus had found the little jewelry box at a yard sale he'd gone to with his dad. They'd had a shit ton of yard tools and a bunch of other random crap. The second he'd seen the jewelry box, he'd thought of her. It wasn't fancy, the silver having turned mostly black from neglect. It'd cost him two bucks, but the way Tabby's face had lit up, you would've thought it had come from Tiffany's.

"Which way?" Trey asked when they reached the exit for Coyote Ridge.

"It's across the street from Brantley's."

Trey looked confused. "Jesse Mercer's place?"

Magnus nodded, swallowing hard.

Even as he steered the truck in that direction, Trey lifted an eyebrow, a silent request for Magnus to fill him in.

"From the first time I went to Brantley and Reese's to meet Tesha, I felt some strange connection to the area."

"Tesha's their dog, right?" Ava asked.

"Yeah." Magnus kept his eyes on the road in front of them as he spoke. "I couldn't explain it, nor could I ignore it, so one day, I made a detour to Jesse's house on my way out. I didn't know his name at the time, but I knocked on the door, introduced myself." He glanced at Trey. "Nice guy, if not a bit surly."

Trey chuckled. "He's about as nice as a rattlesnake."

"Not once you get to know him."

"I've gone to church with him my whole life," Trey countered. "Not sure how much more I could get to know him."

Magnus continued. "I told him who I was and what I did, and that's when he recognized my last name." He could sense both of them listening intently. "Turns out he knew my dad. Jesse was one of the hands at Dead Heat Ranch. Retired about ten years ago," Magnus explained. "His son Cody works there now. Mechanic and whatnot."

"Small world," Trey mumbled, pulling down the road leading to their destination.

"Jesse told me they met when some of DHR's cattle got loose and came on our property. My dad helped them wrangle 'em up and get 'em home. After that, they'd talk from time to time. Not great friends, but…" Magnus swallowed. "The night of the fire, he said they could smell the smoke and went to check it out. By the time they got there … they tried to help Edgar, but their fire extinguishers were no match for the inferno."

Magnus put his hand on Ava's when she reached forward and gently squeezed his shoulder.

"Anyway. Jesse was tellin' me about his land. Said he'd bought it up years ago in hopes of one day buildin' a spread like Dead Heat Ranch. It never happened, and now all the land was just sittin' there, unused. I mentioned that if he ever decided he might wanna sell, to give me a call first."

"Why're you lookin' to buy more land?" Trey asked, pulling the truck to a stop at the end of Jesse's driveway.

"I never planned to stay in Embers Ridge," he admitted. "It's got too many bad memories. Yeah, I've got the house, but it's not the same. It doesn't *feel* the same. It's too small, but it's crammed in between all the other buildings, so it doesn't make sense to add on. And I can't move the kennels since most of the land's in a flood plain, for good reason. There's a stream not too far away that DHR dammed up years ago to try to help those downstream…"

He exhaled heavily, realizing he was straying from the point.

"Why Coyote Ridge?" Trey asked.

Magnus noticed he wasn't looking at him, so he touched his arm to get his attention.

When Trey met his gaze, Magnus said, "Because whenever you talk about your hometown, there's this light in your eyes. You once told me you couldn't imagine livin' anywhere else. I thought…"

Ava finished the sentence for him. "You thought if things worked out between you, you could give him this."

Magnus nodded, still looking at Trey. "Yeah." He managed to look away. "Jesse called me a few weeks back, said he'd been thinkin' about my proposal. Decided he wanted to sell off some of the land. Said he'd let me have first claim to whatever I wanted."

"A few weeks ago?" Trey asked.

"I told him I needed a few days." Magnus hadn't been ready to concede the end of his relationship, although he'd fully anticipated never seeing Trey again. "I knew I couldn't move the camp here if—"

Trey cut him off. "How much land's he sellin'?"

"He's got a hundred acres total. Wants to keep five around his house. He mentioned diggin' out a road to separate a few sections if I didn't want the whole thing."

"Do you want all of it?" Ava asked.

Magnus turned and peered back at her. "I wanted to see what y'all think." He glanced at Trey. "If it's even somethin' you'd be willin' to consider."

He waited patiently for some sort of response, but Trey remained silent, his eyes fixed on the horizon.

"I'm not tryin' to be presumptuous," Magnus said softly. "If it's not the right thing for us…"

He let his sentence fade, staring at the man he loved with his whole heart while said heart was lodged painfully in his throat.

AVA WATCHED THE TWO OF THEM IN the front seat, the pivotal moment settling over them like a wet blanket. She held her breath, not moving, not wanting to make a sound. She could see the tension in Trey's shoulders, but she couldn't begin to know what he was thinking. This was a huge step for both of them. Ava had all but said she was all in, so she didn't think her opinion mattered. Not nearly as much as Trey's did.

"I want all of it," Trey finally said, his voice gruff.

"All the land?" Magnus asked.

Trey shook his head as he turned to look at Magnus. "I'm not talkin' about the land."

Ava's chest constricted, and her belly twisted. If he wasn't referring to the land, there was only one thing he could be alluding to. She wanted to hear him say it. But she knew Magnus *needed* to hear him say it.

The silence was so loud it was deafening.

"I want *this*," Trey said, his words low and guttural. His gaze shifted to her. "I want what we've got right now."

Ava nodded her head so he would know she wanted that, too. But she didn't say a word. Couldn't.

"The three of us," Trey clarified. "But I don't wanna half-ass it. If I'm gonna do this, it's all or nothin'."

Magnus's voice was trembling when he said, "Meanin'?"

Trey was silent for a moment, his gaze skimming over them both before he took a deep breath. "I wanna get married. I wanna have kids. I want the three of us to sleep under the same roof every night. In the same bed. I don't even know if we're on the same page there yet."

Ava did move then. She reached for Trey, curling her hand under his arm and gently squeezing. "I am," she admitted. "Wherever you two are, I'm right there with you."

Trey's eyes moved over her face, and she could see the fear lingering. Ever since he'd mentioned that he'd been married before, she'd wondered what had happened. And though she didn't know the story, she got the feeling it had ended badly for Trey. It explained why he kept himself closed off, why he had pretended that what he had with Magnus was only temporary. He was scared to get his heart broken again.

"Then marry me, Trey," Magnus said gruffly.

The hair on the back of Ava's neck stood on end as excitement danced down her spine.

"I've been married before," Trey blurted. "It didn't work out so well for me."

"I'm not Paul," Magnus declared.

So that was his ex-husband's name.

"You're not." Trey shook his head. "But you haven't seen the side of me he said he hated."

"What side is that?" Ava questioned.

"He called me clingy, said I expected too much because I didn't want to live separate lives."

"That doesn't make you clingy," Ava informed him, wishing she could punch that man in the mouth. How could he take Trey's heart and throw it back at him like that? "It's what the rest of the world calls love, Trey."

His blue-gray eyes swirled with emotion as he stared between them.

"She's right," Magnus said tightly. "And Paul was a fuckin' fool."

Ava added, "Anyone who'd willingly let you walk away's a fool, don't you know that?"

Her teasing lightened the mood for a moment, then Magnus spoke again.

"I want this, too, Trey. Whatever that looks like for us, it's what I want. It's all I've ever wanted. As long as I've got the two of you…"

Ava squeezed his arm, fighting the tears that filled her eyes.

When she'd woken up this morning, she'd never imagined this was how it would go. They'd reached a good place, the three of them, and the only thing she'd anticipated was moving forward. She was willing to go as slow or as fast as they wanted. These days, the only plans she made were to live. And maybe to smile more. Years of trudging through each minute, hating everything about her life, had changed her.

And she'd long ago accepted she loved Magnus and Trey. She figured as long as her future had them in it, she would be fine. Better than fine, really. She was happy for the first time in her life, and that was more than enough.

"Marry me, Trey," Magnus repeated.

Another chill tickled her skin as she waited for Trey to answer.

"Are you askin'? Or are you tellin'?" Trey grumbled, a smile pulling at the corners of his mouth.

"Either," Magnus answered easily, his expression softening.

"Both," Ava added.

"How the fuck did we go from lookin' at land to plannin' a weddin'?" Trey mumbled, his smile growing wider.

"And the land?" Ava asked since he had a point. This was why they were here.

"All of it," Trey stated. "But I'll need five of it for somethin' else."

"What?" Magnus asked.

"An ag barn for the school," he said simply.

"Y'all have an FFA program?" Magnus inquired.

"Yeah. But they've got this little shit hole they call a barn. It sits on less than an acre. Not big enough to hold goats."

"You wanna build an ag barn for the school?" Ava asked, grinning. "To help the future farmers of America?"

"We'll get the kids to help build it," Trey informed them. "That way, they can make it their own."

Ava glanced at Magnus, saw his eyes were shiny.

"You never cease to amaze me," he whispered.

"It's why you love me."

Magnus's shoulders squared, and he leaned forward. "I do love you, Trey."

"I know."

"Now you're quotin' *Star Wars*?"

Ava smiled even as she held her breath.

When neither man moved, merely stared into each other's eyes, Ava cleared her throat. "What about me? A girl likes to hear it, too, you know."

Trey looked at her first, his eyes softening. "Yeah, girl. I love you, too."

"I know," she said, using their words.

"Y'all know you'll have to meet my parents," Trey noted. "And my brothers." He chuckled. "And my sisters."

"Tell me the time and place, and we're there," Magnus said, his voice sturdier than before.

"It'll have to be before Brantley and Reese's weddin'. Otherwise, that'll just be weird."

"And when is that?"

"A couple of weeks from now." Trey glanced at her in the rearview mirror. "You've got time to get a dress."

Ava grinned. "I *knew* blowin' on those dandelions would work."

Epilogue

Ten days later…
Friday, September 16, 2022

TREY WOKE ON FRIDAY MORNING BEFORE AVA or Magnus. They'd had a very eventful evening, so he expected they'd sleep in since it was their day off. And if they didn't, more than likely, they'd get some exercise of the horizontal variety while they had the chance.

As he'd done the last couple of weeks, Trey slipped out of the room without making a sound. He made a pit stop in the guest bathroom before venturing to the living room to find Sarge, Aurora, and Arbuckle waiting patiently for someone to appear.

Well, to be fair, Sarge and Aurora were patient. Arbuckle was an entirely different story. According to Ava, his owner had kept him in a kennel in an apartment for most of the day and night, so he was taking advantage of being *out* of a kennel. Thankfully, he was only wandering around and sniffing everything and anything he could reach. He was officially enrolled in their new puppy training class—despite him being five years old—but it was slow going. To keep him preoccupied, they'd brought some toys in for him to play with, but his favorite pastime seemed to be trying to get Aurora to play keep-away. He'd start by wagging a toy in her face to pique her interest. When that didn't work, he would lie down in front of her and bark incessantly in her face while she ignored him. Or pretended to, anyway.

The little paw injury he'd suffered was ancient history; those few days of sleep had energized him for the month. He rarely sat still. Like now, as he bounded over and sat in front of Trey, staring up with those big brown eyes and the goofy grin on his face.

"You wanna go out?"

The dog was so expressive Trey couldn't help but find him adorable.

"All right. Come on."

They went outside into the gated side yard, and Trey let them wander around until they did their business. Once they were finished, he got them back in the house and dished up their food. Since Sarge and Aurora were on a fresh food diet—something Magnus swore by—they were slowly shifting Arbuckle over, too. He didn't seem to care what he ate—he scarfed it down regardless.

Trey had spent the better part of the past two weeks with Magnus and Ava, dealing with the legalities of buying land.

It wasn't as simple as it sounded, but the three of them put their heads together, as well as their money, and they'd come up with a plan. It would take about a year to do all they wanted to do—build a house, relocate the business, etc.—and it would require a few concessions, including Trey selling his house and Ava selling hers, but it worked on paper, giving them a mortgage payment they could afford. They would take the money from the sale of the houses and put it into their future, building a dream for the three of them. A place big enough to raise kids, a business they could all be a part of, and enough money set aside to do the things they wanted to do.

While it was a huge step, it felt right to him. More so since he'd introduced Magnus and Ava to his family—the immediate ones, anyway—and as he'd predicted, they'd fallen in love with them both as fast as Trey had. His mother was thrilled their family tree was growing.

The only reason Trey hadn't yet revealed the news of the house and the move to anyone, including his family, was the fact everyone was so focused on Brantley and Reese's upcoming wedding. He didn't want to rain on his brother's parade, so he convinced Ava and Magnus to keep it to themselves until that was out of the way. It was just a good thing that the wedding was tomorrow. Otherwise, Trey was pretty sure Ava would explode.

In the meantime, it was business as usual. Trey was working at the camp alongside Magnus, Ava, Gia, Billy, and the recently promoted Brock McGee—the twenty-two-year-old kid who worshipped Magnus like he was the sun, moon, and all the stars— like he had never left. Only now, Trey wasn't pretending it was a temporary gig. He was inserting himself in everything, learning the ropes with the intention of being able to carry his weight like everyone else.

"Now it's time for y'all to go to camp," Trey told the dogs when they were lounging around, their bellies full. "You get to hang with Billy today."

Sarge's ears perked up at the man's name. Sarge wasn't loyal to any one human, he happened to like most of them. Which worked out well because Magnus used Sarge and Aurora to help train other dogs, including the puppy classes and whatnot.

It didn't take long for Trey to get them over to the camp and into capable hands. He promised Billy that he'd be back shortly, once he dragged Ava and Magnus out of bed.

"And don't forget, the three of us will be outta pocket tomorrow. My brother's gettin' married."

"If I don't remember later, tell those boys congrats for me," Billy said. "And to live long and prosper."

"I'll be sure to tell 'em, Captain Spock," he assured the older man before heading back to the house.

MAGNUS SPENT THE ENTIRE DAY WALKING AROUND in a fog. The encounter that morning had left him with his head in the cloud, a smile firmly planted on his face. Waking up to Ava was always an adventure. This morning, he'd let her have her wicked way with him, something she was getting really, *really* good at.

Of course, the encounter was magnified tenfold when Trey returned and joined them. At that point, Magnus had been at their mercy, fucked by them both at the same time. For the record, *between them* was his new favorite position.

Some might think that it was simply the sex that put him in a good mood, but that hadn't been *sex*. That word didn't even begin to describe the intensity of their joining. Hell, for a minute there, he'd thought he had died and gone to heaven. What they'd shared … that was a sinful cornucopia of pleasure.

And yes, he knew he was waxing poetic about it, but damn if he could help himself. He couldn't remember a time in his life when he was this happy.

That's the thought he carried with him throughout the day and still as he made his way to the house after they'd closed things down for the evening. Brock was taking the overnight shift and would be helping Gia and Billy tomorrow so Ava and Magnus could accompany Trey to his brother's wedding. He'd received an invitation of his own, but Trey had insisted on updating his original response to let his mom and JJ know that he would be bringing a plus-two. Magnus knew it was a gesture on Trey's part, and he appreciated it more than the man would ever know.

"What smells so good?" Magnus asked when he stepped into the house.

He found Trey standing at the stove, his back muscles shifting beneath his T-shirt as he worked.

"Chicken fried steak."

Magnus squeezed in to wash his hands at the kitchen sink. "You're tellin' me you can make chicken fried steak?"

"Not tellin'," Trey countered. "Did. Get Ava, and y'all take a seat. It'll be ready in a second."

"I'm here," Ava announced as she strolled into the room with a beaming grin on her face.

Magnus dried his hands on a towel, pressing a kiss to her lips when she offered. He tossed the hand towel aside and followed Ava to the table, wanting to get out of Trey's way. The kitchen was barely big enough for one person, let alone three. That wouldn't be the case in their new house. Now that he knew Trey could cook, he intended to give them a gourmet kitchen so they could do so together. Well, so Ava and Trey could cook while Magnus sat back and admired them.

"What's this?" Ava asked. "Oh, my God. Did you…?"

Magnus stopped at the chair on the opposite side of the table. Ava was holding something in her hand. It took a second for it to register that the gleaming silver was actually the little piano jewelry box that Ava had gone back to that house to get.

"You had it cleaned?" Ava asked, looking at Magnus.

"Not me," he admitted.

"I cleaned it," Trey said, bringing a plate of chicken fried steak over, setting it in the center along with the cream gravy, green beans, and cornbread he'd already brought over. "It's real silver. Just needed to be polished."

"It's beautiful," Ava whispered.

Magnus looked at Trey. Sometimes he thought his heart would explode for the sheer amount of joy this man gave him.

Ava's shocked squeal had Magnus's gaze snapping over. "What?"

Her hand was trembling as she held the piano out, the lid lifted. Tears filled her eyes as she looked at Trey.

"I wanted to make it official," Trey said gruffly, as though speaking around a lump in his throat.

Magnus's head snapped over again when Trey went down to one knee right there in their tiny kitchen.

"Will you both marry me?"

Magnus felt like his head was on a swivel, turning his attention back to the piano. That's when he noticed two rings inside—a sparkling diamond engagement ring set in platinum and another platinum band, only larger and lacking diamonds.

Ava set the piano down, her hands shaking. Then she launched herself at Trey. He tumbled to the floor, grinning like a fool, and Magnus couldn't help but do the same as he stared down at them.

"I'm hopin' that's a yes, girl," Trey crooned.

"Absolutely, yes!"

Trey's eyes shifted to him, and Magnus recognized the hint of fear in them.

It took a second for Magnus to get his voice to work, but he finally did. "What she said."

As if there could ever be any other answer than that.

"Do I have to keep this a secret, too?" Ava grumped.

Trey laughed. "Nah. Just don't show off the ring until Brantley says I do. After that, who cares."

"Deal," she said, planting a big, wet kiss on his face.

Magnus took a deep breath and held it in.

This.

This was so much more than he could've ever dreamed of.

He sent a silent thank you heavenward, hoping his mom, dad, and sister knew how grateful he was. After all, he fully suspected they'd played a hand in this.

ACKNOWLEDGMENTS

Many readers have asked me over the years who my favorite character is. I can honestly tell you, I don't have a favorite. With that said, there are many who stand out, some I think about day in and day out. From the first moment I wrote Trey's POV, I knew he was going to stick with me for a long time. That has definitely been the case, and as I wrote this book, I grew to love him more and more. Deep down, Trey's got insecurities like the rest of us. He wants to love and be loved, but he's been hurt before. Because of that, he shrugged off love, settling for less. Or at least, he tried to. It took a man as strong and persistent as Magnus to bring him around, but I truly believe that Ava is the glue that will continue to hold them together. She is and likely will be one of my favorite female characters from here on out. I want to thank all the readers who sent emails and messages insisting that I write Trey's story. I hope you enjoyed it as much as I enjoyed writing it.

Of course, I have to thank my wonderfully patient husband, who puts up with me every single day. While I was writing this book, we had some unexpected personal hits - some that threw us both for a loop. Steven, if it weren't for your strength and courage, I'm not sure where I'd be today. Your belief that I can do this is what keeps me going, and your unwavering support keeps me grounded. You have been my backbone, my rock, and the very reason I continue to believe in myself. I love you for that, babe.

I also want to thank Wander Aguiar. I'm not sure how you do it, but you're notorious for bringing my muse to life. This time was no different.

Chancy and Jenna ... the two of you put up with a lot from me. I know it irks you that I never answer the phone, but know that it still means everything that you take the time to call. I value your friendship even if I've got a shitty way of expressing it.

I also have to thank my street team. I'm not sure what I've done to deserve your unwavering support, but it means so much to me.

I can't forget my copyeditor, Amy, at Blue Otter Editing. It's been great working with you these past eight or nine years. I appreciate everything you've done for me.

Nicole Nation 2.0, for your constant support and love. You've been there for me from almost the beginning, and I have grown to depend on you to lift me up when I'm down and make me smile when I didn't realize I needed to. Your encouragement makes this journey so fulfilling.

And, of course, YOU, the reader. Your emails, messages, posts, comments, tweets… they mean more to me than you can imagine. I thrive on hearing from you, knowing that my characters and my stories have touched you in some way keeps me going. I've been known to shed a tear or two when reading an email because you simply bring so much joy to my life with your support. I thank you for that.

About Nicole Edwards

New York Times and *USA Today* bestselling author Nicole Edwards lives in the suburbs of Austin, Texas, with her husband, their three fur babies, and the youngest of their three children, who has threatened never to leave home. When Nicole is not writing about sexy alpha males and sassy, independent women, she can often be found with a book in hand or attempting to keep the dogs happy. You can find her hanging out on social media and interacting with her readers - even when she's supposed to be writing.

Connect with Nicole

I hope you're as eager to get the information as I am to give it. Any of these things is worth signing up for or feel free to sign up for all. I promise to keep each one unique and interesting.

Nic News: If you haven't signed up for my newsletter and want notifications regarding preorders, new releases, giveaways, sales, etc., then you'll want to sign up. I promise not to spam your email, just get you the most important updates.

Ramblings of a Writer Blog: My blog is used for writer ramblings, which I am known to do from time to time.

Nicole Nation: Visit my website to get exclusive content you won't find anywhere else, including sneak peeks, A Day in the Life character stories, exclusive giveaways, cards from Nicole, or join Nicole's review team.

NICOLE NATION ON FACEBOOK: Join my reader group to interact with other readers, ask me questions, play fun weekly games, celebrate during release week, and enter exclusive giveaways!

INSTAGRAM: Basically, Instagram is where I post pictures of my dogs, so if you want to see epic cuteness, you should follow me.

TEXT: Want a simple, fast way to get updates on new releases? Sign up for text messaging. If you are in the U.S., simply text NICOLE to 64600. I promise not to spam your phone. This is just my way of letting you know what's happening because I know you're busy, but if you're anything like me, you always have your phone on you.

NAUGHTY & NICE SHOP: Not only does the shop have signed books, but there's fun merchandise, too—plenty of naughty and nice options to go around. Find the shop on my website.

Website:	NicoleEdwards.me
Facebook:	/Author.Nicole.Edwards
Instagram:	NicoleEdwardsAuthor
BookBub:	/NicoleEdwardsAuthor

By Nicole Edwards

THE WALKERS

ALLURING INDULGENCE
Kaleb
Zane
Travis
Holidays with The Walker Brothers
Ethan
Braydon
Sawyer
Brendon

THE WALKERS OF COYOTE RIDGE
Curtis
Jared (a crossover novel)
Hard to Hold
Hard to Handle
Beau
Rex
A Coyote Ridge Christmas
Mack
Kaden & Keegan
Alibi (a crossover novel)
Trey

BRANTLEY WALKER: OFF THE BOOKS
All In
Without A Trace
Hide & Seek
Deadly Coincidence
Alibi (a crossover novel)
Secrets
Confessions
Bounty

AUSTIN ARROWS
Rush
Kaufman

CLUB DESTINY
Conviction
Temptation
Addicted
Seduction
Infatuation
Captivated
Devotion
Perception
Entrusted
Adored
Distraction
Forevermore

DEAD HEAT RANCH
Boots Optional
Betting on Grace
Overnight Love
Jared (a crossover novel)

DEVIL'S BEND
Chasing Dreams
Vanishing Dreams

MISPLACED HALOS
Protected in Darkness
Salvation in Darkness
Bound in Darkness

OFFICE INTRIGUE
Office Intrigue
Intrigued Out of The Office
Their Rebellious Submissive
Their Famous Dominant
Their Ruthless Sadist
Their Naughty Student

Their Fairy Princess
Owned

PIER 70
Reckless
Fearless
Speechless
Harmless
Clueless

SNIPER 1 SECURITY
Wait for Morning
Never Say Never
Tomorrow's Too Late

SOUTHERN BOY MAFIA/DEVIL'S PLAYGROUND
Beautifully Brutal
Without Regret
Beautifully Loyal
Without Restraint

STANDALONE NOVELS
Unhinged Trilogy
A Million Tiny Pieces
Inked on Paper
Bad Reputation
Bad Business
Filthy Hot Billionaire

NAUGHTY HOLIDAY EDITIONS
2015
2016
2021